ENIGMA

DETECTIVE CARLA MCBRIDE CHRONICLES
BOOK 5

NICK LEWIS

ROUGH
EDGES
PRESS

Enigma
Paperback Edition
Copyright © 2023 Nick Lewis

Rough Edges Press
An Imprint of Wolfpack Publishing
9850 S. Maryland Parkway, Suite A-5 #323
Las Vegas, Nevada 89183

roughedgespress.com

Paperback ISBN 978-1-68549-245-8
eBook ISBN 978-1-68549-244-1
LCCN 2023931502

For Frank and Mary Stopski
I know they would be proud of me.
Sending much love to them in Heaven.
May they continue to rest in peace.

ENIGMA

CHAPTER 1

Zoe Elizabeth Pendergast, an innocent young child, prepared for school like any other day. At ten years old, her world was simple and carefree. Her mom, Judy, lost her husband several years ago to pancreatic cancer. As a single mother, working and raising Zoe had taken its toll on her. Every morning, Zoe tested her mother's patience. She liked to sleep as long as possible before finally making it to the kitchen for a quick breakfast. Her favorite Eggo waffles, smothered with Log Cabin syrup, awaited her while a glass of cold milk would wash them down. As she savored the yummy waffles, her mother's scowl created a curious expression across her face.

"What, mommy?"

"Honey, hurry up. I can't be late for work again, okay?"

"Yeah, mommy. Why are we always in a hurry?"

"Because you like to sleep late. Now, take that last bite, gather your bookbag, and let's go, okay?"

"Uh-huh."

With Zoe buckled up in the back seat, Judy started the car and pulled away from the curb. Her route took her by Oakmont Memorial Gardens, the city's main cemetery. With the entrance a block away, the traffic was light on this peaceful morning. Suddenly, sirens blared, breaking the morning's serenity. After glancing in the rearview mirror, she moved to the side, allowing the emergency vehicles safe passage. An ambulance, several police cruisers, and a coroner's van passed then turned into the cemetery. Judy glanced at the rearview mirror, where inquisitive eyes grabbed her attention.

"Sweetie, what is it?"

"What's going on, mommy? Did somebody die at the cemetery?"

"Honey, after people die, that's where they are buried. You know that, right?"

"Uh-huh. Daddy's buried there, right?" Watching her mom nodding, she continued, "What's the other van? Coron...?"

"Coroner. They're called when somebody dies."

"So, mommy, did somebody die there?"

"Umm, sweetie, I don't know."

As Judy pulled away, Zoe continued to stare at the coroner's van, wondering what was happening. In the distance, more flashing lights approached them. As those vehicles passed, Zoe couldn't help noticing a black man driving one of the police cruisers.

Finally arriving at her school, Zoe unbuckled herself and hurried out of the back seat, waiting for her mother to send her off. After a hug and a kiss on the forehead, she entered the school. Rushing into her classroom, she quickly took her seat, waiting for the day to start. Usually, spelling began each school day. However, today was quite different. It was career day. Two young ladies stood talking with her teacher, Diane Finley. As Zoe stared at them, she wondered what they did.

"Alright, class, please settle down. You remember, today is career day. Carla McBride and Shelley Ashby are college students at the university. They're roommates and sorority sisters, as well as friends of mine. Miss McBride is studying for a career in law enforcement, maybe a police officer or a detective. Miss Ashby is studying to be a lawyer, and perhaps, a judge. I want you to give them your full attention, okay?"

As innocent nodding filled the room, Zoe's mind drifted back to the situation at the cemetery. The image of the black policeman flashed in her mind. As she listened to Carla McBride, her interest in law enforcement was born. Although her mother wanted to shield her from the world's craziness, she was a brilliant child and knew something terrible had occurred at the cemetery.

When Sergeant Bernie Kowalski entered the cemetery, a flurry of activity in the distance jolted his soul. Kowalski, the only African American on the police force, was up for a promotion to detective. If promoted, it would also be a first in the Oakmont Police Department. After continuing down the main road, he stopped behind several cruisers and unmarked cars. Once out of the car, he noticed Detective Charlie "Ace" Hutchinson near the coroner, George Cox. Approaching Ace, the sight of a white sheet covering a body answered the many questions floating in his mind.

"Ace, what have we got here?"

"Kowalski, what the hell are you doing here? It's not your beat."

"Right, but I was near and thought I could help."

"Well, you can't. We have a Jane Doe, pretty bad. I can't say I've seen anything like this before. No identification, really nothing that could tell us who she is or her age. Do you want to take a look?"

Kowalski nodded, and Ace motioned the coroner to pull back the sheet.

"Bad, huh?"

After acknowledging him, he looked away and walked to his cruiser, with Ace following. His stomach cramped up, and he took deep breaths to relax the emotions erupting in his soul.

"So, I told you it was bad."

"Yeah, you did. What happened to her hands and fingers?"

"Looks like acid burns to me."

"Who would do something like that?

"I don't know. We live in a whacky world, you know that. Regarding the acid burns, I guess someone didn't want her identified."

"Yeah, but that's creepy and sick. That young lady didn't deserve that."

"No, she didn't. Anyway, as I said earlier, I haven't seen anything this bad before, and I hope I never experience it again."

"Yeah, me neither."

"I hope we don't have the beginnings of a serial killer on our hands in our quaint and quiet town."

"Do you really think that?"

"Who knows? Anything is possible these days. I have a feeling the victim is not from around here. She was killed somewhere else and then dumped here. The only thing we have to go on is the jean jacket she is wearing. I asked Officer Dannie Spencer if she'd ever heard of the Angel Hardesty clothing line, and she hadn't. She said it might be some regional brand. I assigned her to check it out. We'll see what she comes up with and then proceed with our investigation."

"Umm, that might make this case hard to solve, right?"

"Yeah."

"Well, for what it's worth, if I can help, let me know, okay?"

"I appreciate the offer, but we got it. Dannie and Joe are the best. We'll give it our best shot. Maybe we'll get lucky with the jean jacket. Besides, you need to concentrate on that promotion you want if you're going to move up in the department. If *I* can help *you*, just let me know."

After nodding, Kowalski entered his cruiser and closed his eyes, trying to erase the disturbing image of Jane Doe. He left the cemetery, hoping never to encounter such a thing again.

CHAPTER 2

ABOUT TWENTY YEARS LATER

With their last case behind them, Detectives Carla McBride and Bernie Kowalski turned their attention to Beth Pendergast's cold case. Beth, the police department's forensic psychologist and profiler, had quickly become a valuable member of the McBride-Kowalski crime-solving juggernaut. About a year and a half ago, she joined the force to work on cold cases and assist McBride and Kowalski with their ongoing cases. Her first cold case assignment was personal to her. The fifteen-year-old case involved her childhood friend, Penny Miracle. She quickly delved into it and was instrumental in breaking the case wide open. Beth's out-of-the-box philosophy was also instrumental in their most recent case.

Now, the Angel Hardesty cold case was testing her experience and resolve. Everyone who worked on the case was no longer with the police force, making getting useful information more difficult. Charlie "Ace" Hutchinson had been the lead detective. He was comfortably retired and living on Lake Jackson. The only thing he cared about these days was whether the fish were biting and the beer was cold. That was his life now, and he made it known to everyone he wanted to be left alone.

At the time of the crime, Beth, or Zoe had been in elementary school. McBride was in college, pursuing her dream and law enforcement aspirations. On the other hand, Kowalski had been a veteran police officer up for promotion. Police Chief Brock Evans didn't even live in Oakmont when the case went cold. The only thing she had to start with was the physical evidence and Ace's interview transcripts and notes. If Ace chose to be involved, his fading memory would be her best bet on where to begin.

The Daily Reporter's coverage of the Jane Doe yielded very few tips or leads. All of the employees, including the publisher, had since left for greener pastures. The current publisher, Walt Blevins, was only an acquaintance of hers. Although he had a law enforcement background and had helped Carla and Bernie with The Gold Fedora and The Black Rose cases, she wasn't sure how much help he could be.

As she examined the evidence, she envisioned that day in her mind. On that cold, raw winter morning, the cemetery's caretaker found the body of a petite female. The body, fully clothed, was submerged in about eight inches of cold and muddy water in a ditch at the back of the cemetery. While studying the picture, Beth noticed how her short brunette hair complemented her slender face. Her innocent eyes gave her undeniably admirable qualities. Beth could see that she was once a pretty Caucasian woman with her whole life ahead of her. However, some sick bastard squashed it. Beth wondered why and was determined to tell her story.

After reviewing the information, nothing found on the body identified her: no driver's license, wallet or purse, or credit cards. However, Jane Doe was wearing a jean jacket. The label on the collar read Angel Hardesty, and with nothing else to go on, Ace named the case after the label. There were a lot of Jane Does in the world, and they didn't want to add another one to that list.

Transcripts of the interviews in the file yielded very little. After *The Daily Reporter*'s story hit the streets, the young woman's death shattered the community. However, after a photo of her failed to generate any leads, the public's interest in the case quickly faded. With no reports of missing persons in the region, male or female, the case slowly became another one put on the back burner. It had remained there until Beth Pendergast arrived on the scene. After reviewing all of this information, it became vividly clear that solving this case would test her ability and resolve.

She sat in the conference room with every bit of physical evidence and information scattered on the table. Cataloging everything on a legal pad, she noticed the absence of an autopsy report. She pondered where it might be and ran her hands through her long hair. The more she thought about it, she left the room, heading to forensics. Hopefully, Sherry Caudill, the department manager, could shed some light on the missing report.

Arriving at her office, the door was partially open. Knocking, she met Beth's questionable gaze.

"Do you have a minute, Sherry?"

"Of course. What do you need?"

"I'm reviewing the Angel Hardesty cold case files, and everything seems to be there except the autopsy report. Do you know where it is?"

"If the coroner ordered one, it would be there."

"Then, where is it?"

"Maybe one wasn't done. Not all deaths require one."

"Yeah, I know. But given the circumstances, wouldn't the coroner have ordered one?"

"Primarily, autopsies are done to determine the cause of death."

"Yeah, I know."

"I didn't work here at the time, but what was the cause of death?"

"With that many stab wounds inflicted, she bled out."

"Maybe that's the reason the coroner didn't order one. He didn't feel it was necessary. Umm, you could have asked George Cox, the coroner back then. However, he passed away about five years ago. Maybe Ace can tell you more. Sorry I couldn't be of any help."

Beth nodded and returned to the conference room with more questions than answers. Frustration controlled her soul as she reviewed the toxicology report and the DNA analysis. A pair of jeans, a button-up black blouse, and a jean jacket were all she had to work with.

As she reviewed Ace's notes, Beth could see he thought it was a waste of time to continue his investigation. Missing person requests sent out to other law enforcement agencies yielded nothing. After her photo ran in the newspaper, no one came forward to identify her. Ace's team determined Angel Hardesty was a nobody and wasn't worth the resources to continue their investigation.

However, in Beth's mind, she was a daughter, and she was someone's friend. But most of all, she was a human being, which mattered to her more than anything. Angel Hardesty didn't deserve to be put on the back burner. Now, Beth would try her best to unravel the mystery, giving those who loved her some measure of closure.

CHAPTER 3

Beth, mentally exhausted, left the conference room. Upon reaching the team's workstation, she saw Carla and Bernie were engrossed in their usual love-hate bantering. She had come to love that between them. However, seeing in-your-face birds flying around or Carla calling Bernie a big dickhead was a bit much today.

"I can't believe you two are still at it while I have been busting my ass on this cold case. Really, can't you find something more useful to do with your time?"

"Sorry, Beth. We have been arguing over what he will wear at my wedding."

"Yeah, Carla wants me to walk her down the aisle in a penguin suit. I told her I ain't no penguin. A nice black suit will do fine. What do you think, Beth?"

"Guys, I'm not getting in the middle of this, but if you want my opinion, Bernie, you'll look very dashing and handsome in a penguin suit. Besides, it's her special day. Do it for her."

"See, Bernie? Us ladies know what's best. So, get

your ass measured for a tux and all the accessories. Chris picked out a style you'll like, and you will look marvelous walking me down the aisle."

"I agree. So how are the wedding plans going otherwise?"

"Well, Beth, will you be my bridesmaid? That's my final piece of the puzzle."

"Umm, no way. Wasn't your sorority sister, Shelley, going to be your bridesmaid? The wedding is just weeks away."

"Right."

"What happened?"

"After profusely apologizing, she said it's work-related. Her big case finally went to trial. She's a prosecuting attorney in Pinellas County, Florida. Plus, her husband unexpectedly had to travel out of the country for business. Anyway, to make up for it, she invited us to visit them after our cruise, and I accepted. I'm disappointed she canceled, however, spending an extra week of our honeymoon on the white sandy beaches with ocean breezes and margaritas…it was easy to forgive her."

"Wow, that sounds great. I don't blame you."

"Yeah, her condo is right on the beach in Redington Shores. It should be fun. I can't wait to reconnect with her. So, are you in?"

"Are you kidding me? Hell, yeah. It will be a first for me as a bridesmaid. Wow, thank you."

"Cool. How's the case going?"

"Well, Carla, all I can say is that it's going, and solving it won't be easy. I feel like getting in a time travel machine, hoping it takes me back to that day. It would be so much easier."

"Whoa, now. That's not the Beth I know. Think outside the box, sister. You'll find the right path."

"Thanks, Bernie. I guess you're right. There's not much to go on. Those that worked on the case are few and far between. It also appears that those individuals didn't give the case, you know, the due diligence it deserved. She was considered a nobody and a loner to them. The case went cold way too early. Charlie 'Ace' Hutchinson is my best option on where to start. I called his number, and his voicemail picked up. It said something about going fishing. I didn't leave a message. I didn't want to spook him."

"Maybe you'll have to go fishing with him."

"Seriously, Bernie, I've never fished in my life."

"Always a first time, right, Carla?"

"Yeah, you must do everything to solve this case. If that means fishing for catfish, get your gear ready."

"I guess so. I'll try him later this evening and see where that goes. Now, what about those wedding plans?"

"Well, now that you are stepping in for Shelley, everything is in place. A small ceremony under the gazebo at the country club, a reception under the big tent with music by Exile, and lots of bubbly stuff. It will be a fun night, just as I imagined growing up."

"Great. What else?"

"You have to be fitted for a bridesmaid dress at Maggie Oliver's. Ironically, you and Shelley are about the same height and weight, so maybe just some minor alterations should do it. Her place is just down the block from McGruder's. We can walk there after lunch, okay?"

"Sounds great. Is Bernie going to go along with us?"

"No, he's doing lunch with Chris, Walt, and Jeff at the country club. Bernie calls it male bonding. However,

I call it a free lunch and a beer. Then he'll get fitted for the penguin suit at Amsbury's Fine Clothing."

"Who's Jeff?"

"Oh, Jeff Clark. You're walking down the aisle with him. One of Chris's frat brothers. Nice guy."

"Okay, lunch at McGruder's, then to Maggie Oliver's."

"Great, now back to the case before we go to lunch, right, Bernie?"

Silence met Beth and Carla. Still sulking over wearing the penguin suit, Bernie continued to ignore them. As glaring daggers flew at him, his phone rang. After answering it, his sulking quickly turned into a concerned scowl. With his eyes moving in every direction, his worried look told Carla lunch was off.

"Carla, we got a body at the cemetery, a young female."

"That's not good, Bernie."

"No, it's not. Beth, you need to go with us.

"Why do I have to go?"

"Trust me. You'll see once we get there."

"I don't like the sound of that."

As Beth's complexion quickly soured, her respiration and pulse began to race. Carla met her frightful gaze, and sent Beth a reassuring smile.

"Listen, Beth, it may be nothing. Just take a few deep breaths to calm down, and let's go."

Oakmont Memorial Gardens was just a ten-minute drive. As Bernie pulled through the main entrance, pulses began to race, especially Beth's. Ever since Bernie said she needed to go, angry butterflies erupted in her soul. Off in the distance, the coroner's van sent her pulse into turbo overdrive. Pulling alongside the coroner's van,

Bernie cut the engine, and everyone exited the car. The outline of the young female grabbed Beth's heartstrings. As they approached DJ Franklin, the county coroner, similarities to Beth's cold case flashed in her mind. She thought that a young, deceased female lying in a drainage ditch at the back of the cemetery wasn't a coincidence. As she scanned the scattered grave markers on her left, one immediately froze her soul.

CHAPTER 4

After regaining her composure, Beth focused on the body. Staring at the victim's face, tears clouded her vision. The reality of this heinous crime sucker-punched her soul once more. The young female's blank stare glared back from the ditch. Again, her cold case flooded her mind. The photos flashed before her eyes. Carla and Bernie's stoic expressions met her gaze as she surveyed the victim's clothing.

Chills moved up and down her spine as she studied the victim. The jean jacket was eerily similar. A button-down black blouse looked familiar, while her jeans weren't much different from those in the evidence box of the cold case. No shoes, no socks—all too familiar. Beth wondered, could this be happening all over again? The victim's hollow eyes spoke to her with sadness. A pretty face surrounded by dark brown hair, accented with auburn highlights, would have ordinarily made her a striking young lady, but not today.

After the pain and sadness in her soul subsided, Beth inquired, "DJ, manner of death?" As he opened up the woman's blouse, Beth looked away for a moment before glancing at the body again. "Close it, please. I don't need to see it again."

"Again? What do you mean?"

"My cold case. You weren't coroner back then, right?" DJ shook his head. "Then you wouldn't know. The cuts and the damage are the same. Acid burns on the hands and fingers are familiar. Discovering the body here can't be a coincidence, guys. It's hard to believe this is happening again. Any ID?"

"Nothing."

"I'm not surprised. Time of death?"

"Hard to tell at this point, but one thing I do know is this isn't the original crime scene. There is no blood, no tissue, nothing. She was dumped here."

"Sound familiar, guys?" Carla and Bernie nodded as they stood staring at another Jane Doe. "DJ, without disturbing anything, can you see what label is on the collar."

Nodding and carefully tilting her body, he pulled the collar back. "Looks like, umm, Ang—"

"Angel Hardesty, right?"

"Yeah, how the—"

"My current cold case."

Beth, Carla, and Bernie were at a loss for words. They had another Jane Doe on their hands, and the only clue was an Angel Hardesty jean jacket. The bright, cheery day quickly turned into a gray shitty one.

"Guys, if there aren't any more questions, I need to get her off to Frankfort for an autopsy, okay?"

"So, you *are* going to order one?"

"Why wouldn't I?"

"I don't know. One wasn't done in my cold case."

"I don't know about that, Beth, but unless Carla doesn't want one, I'll find out how she died and why. Carla, is there any—"

"Order it, DJ. We know forensics won't find any evidence here. They didn't years ago, and they won't with this one, either. Let us know as soon as possible what the autopsy reveals, okay?"

"You got it, Carla. Good luck."

What they just saw killed any appetite they had this morning. Carla and Beth's visit to Maggie Oliver's was on hold, while Bernie's bonding with the boys got derailed. This year's version of Jane Doe took precedence over everything. On the way back to the police station, a somber silence surrounded them with sorrow. Until today, Beth had little to go on. Although, as bitter-sweet as it was, she got what she wanted. Instead of going back in time, the past came to her. Were these seemingly identical deaths connected? Did they have a serial killer on their hands? No one knew. Complicating matters, the second victim found near the first one's final resting place was disturbing and creepy.

Arriving back at the police station, they grabbed their copy of the cold case files and convened in the conference room. Before beginning their discussion, Carla left to inform Chief Brock Evans of this disturbing new death investigation. Carla rejoined them, ready to discuss what had upset the apple cart. With Carla's wedding just two weeks away, things began to unravel. First, her brides-maid canceled unexpectedly, and now, Jane Doe, aka Angel Hardesty number two, came to be. While silence grabbed the room, Beth opened her laptop and searched for the Angel Hardesty clothing brand. It took quite a while for the information to load. The results were disappointing.

"What did you find out about the jacket?"

"Not much, Carla. It isn't a major brand sold in the big national retail stores like JC Penney, Sears, Belk, Macy's—you get the picture. I'd never seen or heard of it until I opened the evidence box from the cold case."

"If not at the national retailers, then where?"

"That's the million-dollar question. There is very little information, and it's from about twenty-two years ago. The jean jacket was a small entrepreneurial start-up by Janice Hardesty in Williamstown, West Virginia. Says it was sold in small local boutiques in Ohio and West Virginia. When I clicked on the 'where to buy link,' a list loaded. From it, the shops are in small towns along the Ohio River. It's not a long list. I'll start by calling each one and see where that leads me. Given the impact of the Great Recession several years ago, who knows how many are still in business. That could be the reason there isn't much information."

"That's it?"

"Yeah, Bernie, that's it. It doesn't mention that it went out of business. There just isn't any other information on it. Like it just disappeared from the face of the earth."

"Carla, I guess this isn't what you wanted so close to your wedding, huh?"

"Yeah, Beth. What's next?"

"Well, my cold case just became your current case. We're all in this together. I'll start by calling the number in Williamstown and see what happens. Based on what I find out, I'll create a list of boutiques to contact. We can divide it up and get on the phones. Let's reconvene later this afternoon and go from there, okay?"

"Yeah, sounds great."

"You know, ladies, at first, I'd lost my appetite after returning from the crime scene. However, my tummy is growling. Let's get lunch at McGruder's, and then I'll meet Chris at Amsbury's to get measured."

"My tummy is growling, too. What do you say, Carla? Lunch, and we'll go to Maggie Oliver's. We need to get that out of the way today. Then we'll focus on our cases."

CHAPTER 5

McGruder's was unusually busy for a Monday. After entering, a glance at their favorite booth brought a smile across Carla's face. Quickly walking over to the booth, Carla took her usual side, and Beth slid in beside her. Bernie sat across from them and began his ritual of getting comfortable. Although that bugged the hell out of Carla, she ignored him today. As he wiggled his toosh side to side, disgust met his eyes. In his peripheral vision, breaking news flashed across the television, grabbing his attention. Motioning toward the TV, Carla and Beth locked eyes with Kiersten St. Clair, who was waiting to begin her report.

Bernie quickly retrieved the TV remote on the bar and ramped up the volume. Upon returning to the booth, Bernie glared as Kiersten St. Clair began. Suddenly, Police Chief Brock Evans appeared on the screen. As the camera backed off a little, St. Clair held a microphone toward him.

"This morning, a cemetery maintenance worker

discovered a body at the very back of the cemetery. My sources indicate it was a young female in her late teens or early twenties. Would you like to comment on that, Chief Evans?"

"I will confirm a caretaker found a deceased female near the back of the cemetery. Her identity is unknown at this time. The manner of death is also unknown until the state medical examiner completes the autopsy. That's all I have to say at this time."

"Chief, my sources indicate that this death might be connected to a cold case recently re-opened. Would you care to comment on that?"

"No further questions, please. We'll send out a press release as soon as we have more details. That's all for now."

As Chief Evans walked toward the police station, Kiersten St. Clair rambled on, and the broadcast quickly returned to regular programming. Bernie hit the mute button, and silence grabbed the booth until Sam arrived.

"Welcome, guys. What will it be today?"

"The usual for everybody, right, ladies?"

"So that's two Reubens with chips and iced tea for you ladies. Fish and chips for you, sir, correct?"

"Isn't that what I said?"

"Got it, Bernie. What was that all about, you know, the breaking news flash?"

"You heard it—a dead female found at the cemetery. Now, would you place our orders, Sam? I'm hungry."

"Wow, aren't you a real charmer today, Bernie?"

"Don't mind him. It's not been a good start to the week. Besides, he's getting measured for his penguin suit after lunch, which is not something he is thrilled about. You know he's walking me down the aisle, don't you?"

"Yeah, he'll look dashing and debonair. I'll place your orders right away."

As Sam left, darts of disgust penetrated Bernie's soul. He knew Sam didn't deserve his disrespectful abruptness. However, hearing Kiersten St. Clair's report struck an angry chord in his soul. Hearing her mention that a possible connection existed between the victim found today and the cold case hit him the wrong way. He often wondered who her sources were; maybe he'd find out one day. At the moment, there weren't many in the department that knew much about either case. He knew putting that information out in the public's eye might cause panic. However, as much as he hated that, maybe this was one of those times it couldn't hurt.

While Bernie sat with his elbows on the table he massaged his temples. Sam arrived and set three glasses of iced tea in front of them. He met her cheery smile.

"Sam, I'm sorry I bit your head off. Please forgive me, okay?"

"Yeah, of course. We all have bad days. Honestly, I've never liked Kiersten. She's such a snobbish bitch, and I don't trust her. Anyway, lunch should be out shortly."

He nodded and sampled his iced tea. Beth and Carla observed Bernie's distant demeanor, wondering where his mind was, or maybe if he was having a bad day when he awoke this morning. As a sincere smile and rolling eyes met his tired eyes, he whispered, "Now what."

Before Carla could respond, Sam placed their lunch orders in front of them. Bernie quickly dug into his fish and chips, not making eye contact with anyone.

"Hey, guys, I'll bring more tea in a moment. Is there anything else I can get you?"

"Nah, I think we're fine for now, right, ladies?"

After nodding, Sam left. A reserved silence continued between them as they enjoyed their lunches. The muted chatter in the background grew louder and louder, drowning out any meaningful conversation between them. With their lunches consumed, the background noise began to fade away. Sam returned with the iced tea, filling each glass up to the brim, and then left.

"So, Bernie, why are you so upset, or are you just being an asshole today?"

"Carla, that Kiersten bitch…we didn't need that out in the community just yet. We don't even know if there's a connection or not. The jean jacket is the only link, right, Beth?"

"Well, yeah, but what I saw this morning is almost identical to the pictures in the cold case. Then, what you guys didn't see, was the grave marker near the victim."

"Grave marker…it's a cemetery. They're everywhere."

"Yeah, Bernie, I know, but…"

"But what?"

"The grave marker of the victim in the cold case was across from the body. The inscription read, Jane Doe, aka Angel Hardesty, RIP. Coincidence? No way. We've got a real problem on our hands."

CHAPTER 6

News traveled fast in Oakmont, and the recent discovery of a young lady found in the cemetery ran roughshod throughout the community. Authorities could no longer deny Kiersten St. Clair's inference regarding a connection between the two cases. Although the police released very little information to the general public about either case, unfounded rumors were rampant.

The Daily Reporter's coverage was almost identical to the cold case years ago. The first story was about the discovery of the body in the cemetery. A follow-up story the next day contained a headshot of the victim, which generated a lot of interest and sales, but no leads. As the newspaper's coverage faded with the cold case, Beth didn't want that to happen with this one. Although risky, she welcomed Kiersten St. Clair's inference no matter who her sources were.

As Carla's big day drew closer, she began to distance herself from the case. Her priority was making sure the wedding went off without a hiccup. The responsibility of moving this case forward fell completely on Beth and Bernie's shoulders. Over the past several weeks, they had investigated numerous Angel Hardesty connections. That began with Beth's initial phone call to locate Janice Hardesty of Williamstown who created the jean jacket brand.

Beth knew that calling the number listed on the Angel Hardesty web page was likely a waste of time. However, as a lady answered, a smile crossed Beth's face. In her mid-forties, Janice Hardesty had created the designer casual clothing brand named after her first child, Angel. Janice was a Home Economics teacher in the Wood County School System. She informed Beth the clothing brand began as a hobby that filled her summers away from teaching.

In the beginning, she marketed her clothing brand to small boutiques in the Mid-Ohio Valley and sold it at flea markets. However, as her brand grew, small towns along the Ohio River became her primary market as far as Point Pleasant, West Virginia, and Gallipolis, Ohio. The brand caught on and continued to grow until The Great Recession exploded. Sales dried up as small boutiques failed. Near the end of 2009, she decided her hobby wasn't worth the effort any longer. She had two daughters involved in everything imaginable and had no time available for her hobby anymore. After notifying every boutique carrying the Angel Hardesty brand, her cousin's boutique in Point Pleasant bought her remaining inventory and the brand itself. Janice was happy that the Angel Hardesty brand would be kept in the family.

Gabriela's Boutique was now the owner of the Angel Hardesty brand. The boutique was one of the first outlets to carry it. The owner, Gabby Marcinco, wanted to develop the brand further. To do that, she purchased the current inventory at every boutique. This strategy gave her time to develop the brand and be ready to market the new items after The Great Recession ended.

As Beth and Bernie were ready to wrap up the discussion of their findings, Carla entered the conference room to check in with them. She had been absent throughout much of their investigation efforts. However, she still wanted to be kept up to speed on how the case was progressing. Furthermore, she could jump right in if the case was still open when she returned from her honeymoon. After bringing Carla up to date on their findings, the conversation moved to Carla's most pressing issue— her wedding.

"Okay, guys, it sounds like you're making progress. The jean jacket is our best lead, and we have to run with it. What's next?"

"Well, we'll take a road trip to Point Pleasant, and visit Gabriela's Boutique. Maybe the victims bought their jean jackets there, and perhaps we'll get a break. After talking with Janice Hardesty, I don't believe she could tell us anything to help us. So, we'll start with Gabriela's and go from there. I have a gut feeling the victims are from that area.

"Bernie, don't you agree?"

"Yeah, I struck out everywhere I called, so, what Beth found out, we'll run with it. Never been to Point Pleasant before. Should be interesting."

"I bet it will. Are you ready to give me away?"

"Ready as I'll ever be."

"Okay, you both remember the rehearsal is tomorrow evening, right?"

"Of course, we do. Bernie and I have got everything down pat."

"Great."

"What about you, Carla? Is everything in order, including your honeymoon plans and your visit with Shelley?"

"Of course. Shelley is interesting. She's from Point Pleasant. I'm pretty sure her husband is from that same area, too."

"Why's that interesting?"

"I don't know. It just popped in my head, Bernie. Shelley and Paul were high school sweethearts. She received a golf scholarship at the university here, while Paul received one in a baseball. Shelley and I ended up in the same sorority. She was a good golfer but a better sorority sister. Guess it all worked out for them. I hope it works out for Chris and me as it did for them."

"It will, right, Bernie?"

"Of course. I've given Chris several pointers already, so you're good to go. Trust me, it will all work out."

"Right, dickhead."

"Okay, Carla I think we are way past you calling me that. It's getting really old, okay?"

"Sorry, I thought you liked me calling you that."

"I did, but not anymore. Let's move on."

"What else are you guys thinking about?"

"Well, Carla, after we get back from our road trip, we hope the DNA analysis we requested is ready. Maybe we get a hit on our first victim since the DNA process is much more sophisticated now."

"Yeah, let's hope so, dickhead. Oops, sorry."

"And if we do, maybe it will help lead us to the

second victim's identity. Maybe the victims could even be related, right, Beth?"

"Umm, seriously? That's a pretty bold statement, Bernie. But hey, you never know these days. We know to expect the unexpected, so it's possible."

"That we do. Well, guys, I need to tie up any loose ends. See you both tomorrow at 6:00 PM sharp. The rehearsal dinner is at the country club. It should be a fun evening. Don't be late."

CHAPTER 7

As Bernie stood with Carla, waiting for the wedding march to start, heartstrings began to rock his soul. It had always been his dream to give his daughter away on her wedding day. However, he never got that chance, that honor. His daughter, Macy, died of a rare childhood disease at seven years old. That was over twenty-seven years ago, and the heartbreak still lingered in his soul.

When Carla asked him to give her away, he did it to honor Macy. He wanted to experience the excitement and joy that every father wants. As the wedding march blared from the Memorial Gazebo, his weathered cheeks experienced the emotional roller coaster rising in his heart. After wiping away tears of joy, Carla's arm around his arm sent his pulse racing all the more. It was showtime; that's what Carla called the significant events in her life. Up to now, many of those big events usually put her in dangerous situations. However, today, the happiest day of her life was the biggest event of her life.

As they watched Laura and Walt proceed to the gazebo's steps, Bernie's moment of truth was near. With Laura and Walt in place, Beth and Jeff proceeded down the walkway, taking their respective positions beside Laura and Walt. It was now showtime for Carla and Bernie. While glancing at him, his eyes glistened with happiness and bittersweet memories. After feeling a nudge on his arm, he smiled at Carla. Her face beamed with joy.

"You ready for this?"

"Of course. Why are you crying?"

"I'm not."

"Yes, you are. Is everything okay?"

"Yeah. There's our cue. Someday, I'll tell you the story. Let's do this, okay?"

"Amen, papa bear. Thank you for everything. I love you, partner."

Bernie nodded. As a genuine and caring smile met her eyes, her heartstrings silently exploded in her soul. After she wiped a tear away, her friends and colleagues stood in anticipation. Taking the first step and then another, they maneuvered the ceremonial walkway to this momentous event. Their respiration and pulse began to quicken as they approached the gazebo, where Chris stood waiting for the love of his life. After reaching him, Bernie unexpectedly raised Carla's veil and planted a kiss on her cheek.

After lowering it, he nodded at Father Tim and then sat beside his wife. While sitting there, his thoughts drifted to his daughter, Macy. He knew she would be proud of him for giving Carla away. Before Bernie knew it, Father Tim announced Carla and Chris as husband and wife. After the ceremonial kiss, applause rang out. After walking up the walkway to cheers, they proceeded to the historic house to receive their guests. After an evening of champagne bottles popping and the music of Exile, showtime was over. Most guests were gone, leaving Carla and Chris time with their wedding party.

Carla and Chris flew to Tampa, Florida, for their honeymoon cruise the following day. After returning from the cruise, she and Chris would extend their honeymoon by staying with Carla's college sorority sister and husband.

The stark reality of solving crimes returned for Beth and Bernie. A road trip to Point Pleasant was on their calendar for Tuesday. It was going to be a long day for them. The round-trip drive would consume at least six hours of their day. However, they were looking forward to it because the murder of two Jane Does, aka Angel Hardesty, almost twenty years apart, needed solving, and those who loved them needed closure wherever they may be.

With Carla and Chris somewhere in the southern Caribbean enjoying the sun, ocean breezes, and margaritas, Beth and Bernie crossed into West Virginia on Tuesday morning. After cruising east on Interstate 64, they exited on Merritt's Creek Road. After turning left, they headed west towards the Ohio River, where State Route 2 would take them towards Point Pleasant. While this road trip was their first together, awkward silence took second fiddle to the radio and Bernie's car karaoke version of Tim McGraw's *Live Like You Were Dying*.

Since Bernie was up to trying new things, he had done some internet recon for the different lunch options along the way. He somehow stumbled on an obscure eatery on Route 2. The name captured his curiosity. After he'd researched Hillbilly Hotdogs and read their menu, he wouldn't leave the state without trying one of their dogs. It was right up his alley, and he didn't care what Beth thought. He was going to have a "Hillbilly Hotdog Experience" on the banks of the Ohio River before going to Point Pleasant. With Beth in her world and not paying attention to him, he turned right onto the gravel driveway to Hillbilly Hotdogs. The sight of an old school bus brought Beth back to the real world. She looked at him and shook her head.

"What are we doing here?"

"This is lunch today, and it's a culinary experience like no other. This place is famous. I read their hotdogs are to die for. It was even on *Diners, Drive-Ins and Dives* years ago."

"Okay, and…"

"Just imagine yourself sitting at one of those picnic tables enjoying a gourmet hotdog. Watching the Ohio River flow by on this sunny spring day. You'll thank me later, just wait and see."

With their Hillbilly Hotdogs Experience complete, they headed north to Point Pleasant for their rendezvous with Gabriela Marcinco, owner of Gabriela's Boutique. Thirty minutes later, they parked in front of the boutique just outside of the historic downtown area. As Beth thought about the questions she wanted to ask, Bernie interrupted her mental regimen.

"So, Hillbilly Hotdogs didn't disappoint you, did it?"

"I have to admit, you were right. The gourmet dog I had would give the Reuben at McGruder's a run for the money. Thank you for the experience."

"See, I told you so."

"Don't gloat. Get your game face on. It's showtime, baby."

CHAPTER 8

U pon entering Gabriela's Boutique, a lady, probably early to mid-forties with long dark hair, was at the check-out counter helping a customer. They assumed it was Gabriela Marcinco. While waiting for her to finish, they wandered around the boutique together until Beth spotted a display of jean apparel. A placard above the collection identified it as the Angel Hardesty brand.

While Beth examined the jean apparel, Bernie continued to roam the store until they could speak with Gabriela. Within a few minutes, she walked toward Bernie, who was looking around in the grown-up section. He was always on the lookout for something for his wife. As she approached him, he immediately flashed his identification badge. Beth had been watching this unfold and quickly joined him and took over.

"Miss Marcinco, I'm Beth Pendergast."

"Just call me Gabby."

"Yeah, of course. Thank you for seeing us today. We'll try not to take up too much of your time."

"That's okay. Sally and Iris can handle the store for a while. What's this about?"

"Do you have an office where we can have more privacy?"

"Yes, of course. Follow me."

Entering through a door at the far end of the check-out area, her small but adequate office had two chairs facing an old army-gray metal desk. It was neat, just like the store. Gabriela's pride in her store was present everywhere. As they sat in front of her desk, she nestled in her chair. A picture of two young ladies in basketball uniforms caught Beth's attention.

"Okay, now, what brings two detectives from Oakmont, Kentucky, to my store."

"Well, first of all, he's the detective. I'm just a profiler and forensic psychologist. Anyway, we have a few questions about your Angel Hardesty collection. However, before I get to that, is that you in the picture on the wall behind you?"

"Oh, yeah. That's my cousin and me from our high school days. Shelley was a great golfer, earned a golf scholarship to…umm, you're from Oakmont, right?"

"Yeah."

"That's where she went to school. Have you ever heard of Shelley Ashby-Montgomery? That's her married name. She lives in Florida now."

"Yeah, we have. It's quite interesting, how we heard of her."

"How so?"

Bernie interjected, "She was supposed to be in my partner's wedding, but she backed out at the last moment. Small world, right?"

"That's not like her. Too bad. What else may I help you with, Miss Pendergast?"

"Sorry to sidetrack you. We know all about the history of the Angel Hardesty brand from Janice Hardesty, so we'll cut to the chase. The same brand jean jacket was found on two deceased young ladies in our fine city, both murdered."

"That's horrible. What a shame, but what does that have to do with me?"

"Most likely nothing, but we have to check out every tip or lead, and the only lead we have is the jean jacket."

"Okay, what do you want to know?"

"Before we ask you any questions, you need to understand the two murders are about twenty years apart."

"Wow, I didn't expect that."

"Yeah, neither did we."

"Well, I started carrying the jean jacket when it first came out, about twenty-two years ago. I bought the brand from my cousin, Janice, right after the Great Recession."

"We know that. Please continue."

"Yeah, of course. She still makes a few specialty pieces for me, one-of-a-kind, special orders. Anyway, how may I help you?"

"I have pictures of the victims. Would you see if you recognize either of them?"

"Sure. What makes you think the victims are from around here?"

"Just a hunch of mine, and we have to start somewhere. Here's the picture of the first victim. She was found in a ditch in the city's cemetery. She was probably eighteen or nineteen back then." Gabby took the photo and studied it intently before giving it back. "Does she look familiar?"

"No, but the jean jacket does. Wow, that's one of the first ones. I didn't have many at that time. What else?"

Bernie asked, "Since there weren't many, do you have any sales records or receipts from back then?"

"Lordy, no. Destroyed them a long time ago."

"Here's the other victim. Please take a close look." As Gabby studied it closely, she glanced at them, then returned her glassy eyes to the photo for a moment before handing the phone back to her. Gabby's eyes moved around the room, deflecting Bernie's curious gaze. "Gabby, do you know her, or have you seen her before?"

"Miss Pendergast, she does look familiar, but that's all I know. She could have bought a jacket here, or maybe I've seen her around town. I just don't know for sure."

"Are you aware of any missing person reports?"

"No, our local news comes from Huntington or Charleston. I don't recall anything on the news."

"That's okay. We'll check with the local police and sheriff. That should do it. Thank you, you have been a big help. Here's my card. Please call me if you think of anything else that might be pertinent."

Gabby took Beth's card and walked with them to the door. As she opened the door, Beth asked, "Gabby, do you know where the young people hang out?"

"My daughter says the Pixey Stix Café is the in place. Try it. She's a bartender there."

"Is she working today?"

"Yeah, ask for Courtney. And good luck, Miss Pendergast."

Beth and Bernie made their rounds with local law

enforcement and struck out on missing person inquiries. Their last stop before heading back to Oakmont was the Pixey Stix Café. After Beth pulled it up on Google Maps, she clicked on directions, and they loaded. It wasn't far from them, just walking distance from the police station.

After about a fifteen-minute walk, they entered the café. The young lady behind the bar was the spitting image of her mother. With it being early afternoon, the lunch crowd had left, and only a couple of people remained at the bar. They sat at a table away from the bar for privacy. Courtney noticed them come in and take a table by the window. Carrying two glasses of water, she approached them.

"What may I get you?"

"Courtney, right?"

"Yes, do you know me?"

"Nah, we met with your mom a few minutes ago. I'm Beth Pendergast, and he's Bernie Kowalski. We're with the police department in Oakmont, Kentucky."

Not wanting to waste any time, Beth brought up a picture of Jane Doe number two on her iPhone and handed it to Courtney.

"Do you recognize this young woman?"

CHAPTER 9

After Courtney took Beth's phone, she studied the photo for about thirty seconds. Her eyes turned glassy as she sat down. While continuing to hold the phone, her heartstrings exploded in her soul. Returning the phone, she wiped a tear from the corner of her right eye. Although the sight of Jane Doe number two's morbid complexion was enough to upset anyone, knowing that person sucker-punched her in the gut.

"So, you know this person, right?"

"Uh…well…sort of."

Being the gruff person he was sometimes, Bernie interjected, "Either you do, or don't. Which is it?"

"Bernie, have some compassion, will you?" A look of daggers met his wandering eyes. After apologizing, he continued, "So, Courtney, what does 'sort of' mean?"

"I've seen her around town on the streets, and in here a few times when she needed to get out of the cold."

"So, she's homeless, is that what you are saying?"

"Yeah, I guess, but I'm not sure. I think she's been in foster homes a lot while growing up. She knows that her birth mother didn't want her and gave her away, at least that's what she told me last winter. She was here most days during the cold spell we had."

"Okay, do you know her name?"

"Not really. She called herself Zioneé."

"Interesting name. Do you know why she called herself that?"

"She said it meant Heavenly One. Not sure who told her that. Maybe she made it up."

"Okay, when did you see her last?"

"Probably about a month, or maybe two months ago. She stopped in one day. I felt sorry for her and gave her water and a bowl of soup. She didn't have any money at all."

"Do you recognize the jean jacket in the photo?"

"Yeah, of course. My mom designs and sells them."

"Right. Did you ever see her wearing it?"

"Yeah, every time she stopped in she had it on. I believe that along with jeans and a black blouse might be all the clothing she owned."

"Could we get a glass of iced tea with lemon?"

After nodding, Courtney left and returned with three glasses of iced tea with lemon. After handing Beth and Bernie theirs, she sat down. Silence moved around the table as each enjoyed a sip of the fresh iced tea before continuing.

Now understanding Courtney's empathy toward Zioneé, Bernie asked, "What else can you tell us about her? Take your time. We don't have to be anywhere, okay?"

"Thank you. As I mentioned before, she told me she'd been in many foster homes, even ran away a few times to get out of, you know, bad situations."

Beth took back over the conversation and asked, "So, she grew up here?"

"Yeah, like I said, she was in a lot of foster homes. Once she was eighteen, she left the foster care program for good. Don't know if everything she told me was the truth."

"I see. We stopped by the police and sheriff to see if there were any missing person reports. They said they were not aware of any."

"Well, you know, it's hard to be missed when no one loves you, or no one wants you."

"Yeah...I understand. Anything else you can tell us, no matter how trivial it may seem? Did she ever come in with anyone before?"

"She was always alone. Even when I would see her on the street, she was never with anyone. Sorry I can't be of more help."

"Hey, you've been a big help. Maybe it's time for us to head home. Do you have any other questions, Bernie?"

"Nah. Thank you, Courtney. What do we owe you for the iced tea?"

"Nothing, it's on the house."

As Courtney cleaned up the table and left, Beth and Bernie watched her go behind the counter and disappear through the door leading to the kitchen area. After walking over to the bar, Bernie pulled out a twenty-dollar bill and laid it on the counter.

They enjoyed the sun's warmth while walking back to Bernie's car. After reaching his vehicle, they got in, and silence surrounded them as they pondered what Courtney had told them about Zioneé. Suddenly, Beth got out of the car, startling Bernie. He watched her enter the police station. After a couple of minutes, she returned with a piece of paper in her hand. After getting back in the car, Beth handed him the note. Ten minutes later, they pulled in front of the Mason County Social Services.

Once inside, Beth introduced themselves and asked for Natalie Shepperd. A receptionist told them she was currently in a meeting and wasn't to be disturbed. Disappointed, they knew they might as well get on the road and thanked the receptionist. After walking toward the door, Beth turned around, seeing a lady at the receptionist's desk. She read the woman's badge and immediately approached the receptionist's desk with Bernie following.

"Miss Shepperd, I'm…Beth."

"Natalie, I told them to set up an appointment."

"It's okay. My meeting is over."

"How may I help you, Beth…?"

"Beth Pendergast, from Oakmont, Kentucky. He's Detective Bernie Kowalski. May we have a few words with you? We'll be quick, and then we'll be on our way, okay?"

"What's this about?"

"May we go somewhere more private?"

"Of course. Follow me."

They followed her through double doors and entered the first room on the right. Once inside the room, she closed the door and joined them at the table. Beth pulled up Jane Doe number two and showed it to her. She took the phone, studied the picture intently, and returned it to Beth.

"Do you know her?"

"Ashlee Roberts, she called herself Zi—"

"Yeah, we know, Zioneé, the Heavenly One."

"Right. To be honest with you, I'm not sure Ashlee is her real name."

"What do you mean?"

"Detective Kowalski, when we found her at our front door about twenty years ago, the t-shirt she was wearing had the name Ashlee embroidered on it. Until we placed her in a home, that's what we called her. We placed her with her first foster parents, the Roberts, thus Ashlee Roberts was born. Unfortunately, they moved out of state, and social services placed her in the home of George and Mary Carson until a horrible auto accident took their lives. So, you can see, she had many foster homes and a traumatic life."

eth and Bernie felt like they had struck gold. Miss Shepperd gave them a real name, but they also knew they couldn't be that lucky. They knew this case was not over by any means. Jane Doe number two was no longer a nobody; Ashlee Roberts had loved ones somewhere. They hoped those loved ones were still living in the Point Pleasant area, and perhaps they would catch another break. As Beth focused on Miss Shepperd's stoic expressions and less-than-caring attitude, she surmised that she had experienced this discussion many times before. Silence smothered the room. The photo of a deceased human being always did that. While watching her wipe a tear from her cheek, her lips quivered slightly.

Bernie had had enough of the emptiness in the room and asked, "So, what else can you tell us about her?"

"In and out of foster homes. Over the years, Ashlee just wasn't what people wanted in a daughter. She never quite made it to the adoption altar. That poor soul, may she rest in peace. How did she die?"

"We're not at liberty to talk about that as it may be connected to another death investigation."

"I understand."

Since Bernie let the cat out of the bag about the cold case, Beth pulled out her iPhone and brought up a photo of Jane Doe number one. She figured she had nothing to lose.

"How long have you worked here?"

"Over forty years, why?"

"This is an off-the-wall question, but take a look at our other victim he mentioned a few minutes ago." After taking Beth's phone, she studied the picture for about twenty seconds and handed it back. "I know it's a crazy question, but do you recognize her? Maybe she was from here as well, maybe in the foster system."

"Sorry. The two young women look similar. However, the photo doesn't ring a bell with me. How did she die?"

Bernie interjected, "We're not at liberty to discuss that. What was the last known address for Ashlee?"

"That's private. I hope you understand."

"Ma'am, Bernie and I are trying to get as much information as possible on her. We believe both cases are connected, we just don't know how or why. Maybe her last foster parents can help us bring closure to their loved ones. Anything will help, okay?"

As Beth smiled at her, looks of compassion moved back and forth between them. Miss Shepperd suddenly turned around and pulled out the bottom drawer of her file cabinet. Removing a file, she closed the drawer. She placed the file on her desk and opened it. While studying its contents for a moment, she searched her soul for compassion.

Suddenly, she stood, smiled at Beth, and excused herself. While caught off guard, neither was sure what to do. Was it the break they needed? After about thirty seconds, Bernie stood and walked around the desk. Glaring up at him was Ashlee's last known address. After memorizing it, he quickly returned to his chair. As they waited for something else to happen, Miss Shepperd returned to the room, took the file, and put it back in the drawer.

"Sorry for the interruption. Is there anything else I may help you with?"

"No, we want to thank you for your assistance."

"Of course, and good luck, Miss Pendergast. Oh, and by the way, let me know how this turns out. You know, whether the two cases are connected."

"Why?" Bernie asked.

"Just curious, that's all, detective."

"Yeah, we can do that, right, Bernie?"

Bernie nodded, and she walked them to the lobby area. Beth and Bernie left and arrived at Harold and Ramona Montgomery's home fifteen minutes later. While sitting in the car, they observed the neighborhood. An old-established part of town that had seen its day. Compared to other homes on either side, they had taken good care of theirs. It made a good impression on abandoned or abused kids that this was a safe home, and they would be loved. After exiting the car, they walked up onto the inviting porch. Bernie did the honors and rang the doorbell. Melodic chimes rang out as footsteps on the hardwood floor pleased their ears. Within seconds, Ramona Montgomery, they assumed, stood behind the storm door facing them. Her smile was genuine, caring, and welcoming.

Beth smiled. "Ramona Montgomery?"

"Yes." While flashing their badges, Beth introduced themselves. "How may I help you?"

"We'd like to ask you a few questions about Ashlee Roberts. May we come in?"

"What's this about? I haven't seen her since she left our home about two years ago."

Instead of responding, Beth took out her phone and pulled up a photo of Ashlee. After holding it close to the storm door, Ramona's sincere smile morphed into tears of quiet sadness. Wiping the tears away, she opened the door, welcoming them into her home. After showing them into the living room, she motioned them to sit on the sofa. Ramona sat across from them in one of the chairs, fronting a rectangular coffee table. While silence flowed between them, Beth's eyes moved around the room, looking for pictures of Ashlee. There were none.

As composure found Ramona's face, she broke the silence. "How did she die, Detective Kowalski?"

"Before I comment, we're sorry for your loss. Because of certain circumstances with a cold case, we cannot discuss the cause of death. Over a week ago, a caretaker at the city cemetery found her body in a ditch. She was wearing an Angel Hardesty jean jacket. That led us to Gabriela's Boutique. After asking around, talking with law enforcement, and social services, it wasn't hard to find you."

CHAPTER 11

As Beth and Bernie anxiously waited for Ramona to compose herself, a respectful silence captured the room. Ramona grabbed a Kleenex and dabbed the corner of her eyes. After a minute of silence, she rose from her chair and walked to the kitchen. Several minutes passed as they anxiously waited for her to return. From the kitchen, they could hear ice tumbling to the bottom of tall glasses. The commotion from the kitchen fell silent as footsteps on the hardwood floor moved closer and closer. She entered carrying a tray with three tall glasses of fresh iced tea complemented with a lemon slice. A smile crossed her face, and she placed the tray on the coffee table and returned to her chair.

"Please, it's fresh."

After nodding, they each grabbed a glass and squeezed the lemon on top of the tea. The lightly sweetened tea soothed their dry mouth. After grabbing her drink, Ramona took a sip and smiled again.

"Detective Kowalski, tell me more about what

happened to Ashlee. Did she live in Oakmont, you know, things like that?"

"Mrs. Montgomery, thank you for the tea. It's delicious. Like I said earlier, we can't discuss the manner of death. We don't believe she lived in Oakmont or anywhere near there. We believe whoever is responsible for her death dumped her body in the cemetery. I'm sorry that I can't tell you more. Will you tell us about her, anything that might help us move in the right direction to find who did this to her?"

Although the iced tea was meant to be an ice breaker, it did little to improve the tense silence in the room. Ramona expected more than lip service. Ashlee Roberts was her foster daughter. She and her deceased husband treated her as their flesh and blood. As her wandering eyes bounced back and forth at them, she wanted more from them.

"Mrs. Montgomery, may I call you Ramona?" She smiled and nodded. "Great, thank you. Why don't you call me Beth? It's just more personable, you know?"

"Of course, Beth. I would like to know more."

"Yeah. I would love to tell you more, but it may compromise our investigation. We don't want that, and I believe you don't either. You wouldn't want anything to get in our way of finding who killed your foster daughter, right?" She reluctantly nodded, meeting Beth's thoughtful expression of empathy. "Okay, when you are ready, will you please tell us about Ashlee? Just take your time."

"Thank you. I appreciate your sincerity. Ah, Ashlee, we weren't her original foster parents."

"Ramona, I don't mean to be disrespectful or cut you off, but we know about Ashlee's previous foster parents."

"I didn't know that. When they died in that accident, we were empty nesters and thought about being foster parents again."

"Again?"

"Yeah. After many attempts to have children, we gave up and became foster parents, hoping we could find the right child to adopt, you know, call our own. Paul was our first foster child whom we eventually adopted. That was over forty years ago. He became quite successful and is happily married."

"You must be very proud of him."

"Yes, of course. After he went off to college on a baseball scholarship, being an empty nester was difficult. We were missing something in our lives. She was our first foster daughter. However, something was different about her, so we didn't go the adoption route, and I don't believe she wanted that either. We were committed to raising her the best we could. We loved her as though she was our granddaughter. Paul and Shelley made it clear they didn't want children."

As tears began to surface on Ramona's cheeks, Beth smiled and interjected, "It's okay. Do you need a break?"

After wiping the tears away, Ramona shook her head and continued. "With us getting older and all, we decided the foster parent wasn't our thing any longer. We made that decision right after Ashlee left. Even though we didn't adopt her, we treated her like she was our flesh and blood. Her leaving broke our hearts."

"Ramona, we are so sorry, right, Bernie?" He nodded. "Where did she go?"

"That's the weird thing. She kind of disappeared for a while. Then we heard she returned to the area but she never visited me. Then she disappeared again, and now you tell me she's dead."

Tears surfaced once more, and Ramona wiped them away. After rising from her chair, she walked over to a bookcase. She pulled out a scrapbook and walked over to Beth and Bernie. They realized Ramona wanted to share the bittersweet memories in her hand with them. After scooting apart, she sat between them and began sharing Ashlee's life with them. After many tears and sniffles, they learned more about Ashlee. After setting the scrapbook on the coffee table, she rose and returned to the chair.

"Ramona, thank you so much for sharing this with us. Bernie and I would like to hear about your son, Paul. Isn't that him in that picture?"

"Yes, it is. I always liked that picture of him and Ashlee. He was thirty, and she was about ten. He and Shelley visited a lot since they weren't too far from us. Anyway, I always felt Ashlee and Paul had some strange connection. I could never understand it or explain it. Anyway, he and his wife, Shelley, live in Florida now. He works for some international business firm, but I'm not sure what he does. His wife works in the county attorney's office down there. She's a lawyer, and a damn good one he tells me."

"You must be proud of them both."

"We are. We don't see them much anymore, especially after my husband died from a heart attack. Guess that was the last time they were home."

"I'm sorry. That's too bad, right, Bernie?"

"Yeah, we're sorry for your loss."

"So, is there anything else I may help you with?"

"Not me. You've been a big help, Ramona. What

about you, Beth? Do you have anything else you want to ask her?"

"Yeah, if you don't mind?"

"What?"

Beth pulled up the picture of Jane Doe number one on her phone and handed it to her. She studied it long and hard.

"Do you know her?"

"Should I? Who is it?"

"It's just a picture of a young lady from a cold case I'm trying to solve. She looks a lot like Ashlee, doesn't she?"

Ramona continued to stare at the photo for a couple of minutes. Finally, she shook her head. After returning her phone, she deflected Beth's intense stare.

"Ramona, are you sure you don't recognize her?"

"Yes, I'm sure. Is there anything else?"

"No, that's it. We'll be on our way. Here's my card if you think of anything else. Again, we're sorry for your loss."

CHAPTER 12

Beth and Bernie had made progress on the case. Jane Doe number two had a real name—Ashlee Roberts. She had foster parents who once loved her and a foster mother who still did. After leaving Ramona's home, they started their three-hour trip back to Oakmont. However, Bernie liked to eat. Polish cuisine was his favorite, but he did enjoy Italian almost as much. When he did his food recon before traveling to Point Pleasant and found Hillbilly Hotdogs, he discovered an Italian restaurant in a town west of Huntington just before the Kentucky state line.

Upon reaching the outskirts of Huntington, a strange rumbling noise filled the car. Thus far, their ride had been relatively quiet as they thought about their visit with Ramona Montgomery. The rumbling noises disrupted Beth's train of thought, and she glared at Bernie rubbing his belly. His questioning eyes flashed back.

"What?"

"You hungry?"

"I guess by that rumbling in your belly, you are, right?"

"Of course. I'm hungry all the time."

"I can tell."

"Ouch, that hurt."

"Get over it. What do you have in mind?"

"When I did my recon and found the hotdog place, Rocco's Ristorante came up. It's in a small town before the Kentucky state line. Reviews are great. It's supposed to be authentic Italian food. How's that sound?"

"Great, I'm hungry, and I can use a glass of Pinot Grigio after everything we heard today."

"Okay, Rocco's it is. I can use a Yuengling."

"Uh, remember, you're driving?"

"One beer ain't going to hurt, so get over it. You know, I could make you drive, and then you couldn't have that glass of wine."

"Right, one beer, okay?"

They arrived in Ceredo, a quaint town on the Ohio River, thirty minutes later. Rocco's wasn't hard to find at all. Spotting the parking spot down the street, he quickly grabbed it. After getting out, they entered the small lounge and bar area. The restaurant was not very busy, and the hostess ushered them to a table in one of the smaller dining rooms. They were quickly waited on and ordered drinks. While waiting, each reviewed the menu. With lasagna being their specialty, they chose that with a side salad and bread.

"So, Beth, what do you think? Can I pick great restaurants or what?"

"Yeah, it's nice with an authentic Italian flare. Good choice."

While enjoying the atmosphere with soft Italian

music in the background, their drinks arrived. After a quick toast to today's victories, their drinks eased their anxiety.

"So, what's your take on what we discovered today. Assuming Ashlee Roberts is Jane Doe number two, finding that out was way too easy, or we just got lucky."

"Sometimes we need a little bit of luck. With the last case, it took everything we had to break it open. So, I'll take these victories when we can get them."

"Yeah, I guess so, but where do we go? The fact that Ramona identified her doesn't help much in finding who is responsible, and who is responsible for the first Jane Doe."

"Have faith, Bernie. When I showed her the picture of Jane Doe number one, it struck a chord. Although she told us she had never seen or known her, I'm not sure I believe her. Her eyes and body language said to me she was hiding something or knew more. I'm making a mental note to call her later this week, see if I can get anything else from her."

"Well, good luck. Here's our salads. Let's eat."

"They look yummy. I'm with you."

After devouring the salad, their entrées arrived with more fresh, hot Italian bread. Beth had to agree with Bernie; he knew how to pick restaurants. The food at Rocco's was comparable to Pascali's in Oakmont. The server returned and offered up the dessert menu. Bernie couldn't resist the Tiramisu with a cup of coffee and ordered it. Beth declined; she wasn't into sweets right after a filling dinner. While the server cleared the table, Beth pulled out her iPhone and quickly searched Ashlee Roberts. A scowl met Bernie's curious eyes.

"So, what's the scowl for?"

"Ah, just not much on Ashlee Roberts. Oh well, I'll have to dig deeper starting tomorrow. Wow, that Tiramisu looks yummy. Enjoy so that we can get on the road."

"Don't rush me. You want a bite?"

"Nah."

Fifteen minutes later, Bernie's dessert plate was clean as a whistle, and his coffee cup was empty. After ordering a coffee to go, he paid the bill, and they left. Ten minutes later, they were on the interstate, heading to Oakmont. Twilight began to settle in on a pleasant spring evening in May. Silence captivated the car after a long day. As the radio played in the background, Beth's eyes drooped, and she quickly rubbed them. She needed to stay awake and keep him focused on the drive home.

"So, today was a good day, right?" He nodded while keeping his eye on the road. "Although we don't have all the answers, we know more than we did a week ago. You know the weird thing we found out today was Gabriela, Janice Hardesty, and Shelley are all related."

"So, why is that weird?"

"I don't know, just strange. Then Shelley's husband is Ramona's adopted son. Throw Ashlee into the mix—just plain weird, don't you think?"

"Yeah, I guess so. Are you saying that everyone mentioned today is connected or involved in this case? Now that would be weird."

"Yeah, it would be, but you never know in this crazy, whacky world, right?"

"Yeah. Wonder how Carla and Chris are doing."

"Let's not go there. Just enjoy the quiet ride home and keep your eyes on the road."

CHAPTER 13

After a quiet and peaceful ride back to Oakmont, Beth and Bernie arrived at the station much later than anticipated. Although exhausted as they entered the station, they agreed the long day was worth it. The information discovered in Point Pleasant lifted their spirits about solving this case and possibly the cold case. At least they had a name for the current Jane Doe, which was better than nothing. Each agreed they would take their time coming to work tomorrow morning. Bernie fired off an email informing Chief Evans of their decision.

The following day, Beth entered the station around nine o'clock and checked her in-house mailbox before moving to her workstation. She dropped her purse on her desk and visited the coffee station. After returning with a cup of coffee, she was ready to research Ashlee Roberts. A blinking voicemail light caught her attention. Picking up the receiver, she pressed the voicemail button. Bernie's message said he had a doctor's appointment he forgot about and would be in around noon.

That meant she was on her own reviewing what they learned yesterday and researching Ashlee Roberts, whoever she was in real life. Ashlee's first foster parents gave her their last name even though they never legally adopted her. After the Roberts died in the auto accident, their last name stuck with her for the rest of her life. This information was more than Beth had yesterday, and that's where her research would begin.

After entering Ashlee Roberts in Safari, the results yielded very little information other than she graduated from Point Pleasant High School and nothing more. From her discussion with Ramona yesterday, she already knew that. Beth knew Ashlee was not involved in extracurricular activities of any kind. In many ways, Ashlee was a plain Jane as far as social activities were concerned. Harold and Ramona provided Ashlee with a safe and stable home until she broke ties with them after graduation.

After collecting all of her notes from yesterday's visit with Ramona, she gathered all the information from the cold case and headed to the conference room. Placing the information from Jane Doe number one out on the table to her right, she placed what little information she had about Jane Doe number two, aka Ashlee Roberts, next to it. As she stared at the photos, the empty and hollowed eyes hid their past secrets and maybe clues that could help solve each murder. Both sets of eyes spoke to her. Beth was sure they were somehow connected.

One piece of information from the cold case glared at her from the table. The DNA analysis from Jane Doe number one was trying its best to send vibes her way. It had been of no use in the cold case investigation, and unless something else turned up, it would be of no help now. Beth took it in her hand and studied the graphs, bars, and everything else, hoping it would speak to her. A knock on the door startled her. Standing in the doorway, Sherry held a file in her hand.

"So, what brings you my way?"

"This does. May I join you?"

"Yeah, of course. What do you have?"

"Autopsy and DNA results from the recent Jane Doe. Do you want to go over them now?"

"Come in and have a seat. As you can see, I have the table covered with the cold case and what little information I have on the most recent victim."

"I can see."

"By the way, Jane Doe number two has a name, and it stays here. I don't want it out in public."

"Really, who is she?"

"Ashlee, Ashlee Roberts, as far as we know. According to Courtney Marcinco, she called herself Zioneé."

"Hmm, interesting name."

"Means Heavenly One, supposedly. Anyway, what do you have?"

Sherry explained the autopsy findings for Ashlee, and they matched the cause of death for the first Jane Doe. Based on what Beth saw on Jane Doe number two the day the body was discovered; she knew they were the same. As for the DNA results, they were meaningless. Beth already knew who Jane Doe number two was.

"Sherry, what else do you have? I already told you we know who number two is. Bernie and I spoke to her foster mother yesterday."

As Sherry sat feeling unimportant, her eyes gravitated to the DNA report from Jane Doe number one lying on the table. She picked it up, studying it. After rubbing her eyes, her intense focus caught Beth's interest.

"What is it? Your eyes tell me you've seen these results before."

"Yeah." Placing the results from Jane Doe number one beside Jane Doe number two, the similarity stood out like a sore thumb.

"What do you see?"

"Shit. They're very similar, right?"

"Yeah, but not quite. There are a few small differences, but based on my experience and training, there is a high likelihood that these victims are related. I'd say I'm about ninety-five percent sure."

"Sherry, is that even possible? Almost twenty years have elapsed between the murders."

"I know, but everything on the reports says they are. I need to rerun these, at least for Jane Doe number one. I'll perform a DNA analysis from the blouse number one was wearing twenty years ago. I'll perform a second sample on Ashlee's blouse to make sure, okay?"

"Sherry, take a look at the photos. Don't they look eerily similar to you?"

Looking at the photos side by side, she studied the eyes and facial features before responding.

Sherry replied with a quirky grin on her face, "The eyes and nose don't lie. They're related somehow, and I'd bet money on it. I'm going out on a limb here."

"Okay, what?"

"The DNA results I see here tell me Jane Doe number two is the daughter of Jane Doe number one. I know that's far out, but the science in me and these reports validate it."

"You're serious, aren't you?"

"Yeah, yeah, I am. Hmm, that throws a monkey wrench into your cases, doesn't it?"

"No shit. I wonder who Ashlee's mother is and who the killer is…I mean…the killer of both of them. Why else would they be dumped at the same place and near the grave of Jane Doe number one? Shit, that's weird, don't you think?"

"Yeah, weird and sick. Good luck. As soon as I get the results, I'll let you know.

CHAPTER 14

While Sherry left the conference room to rerun the DNA analysis, Beth thought about her opinion regarding the victims' relationship. Beth had suspected a connection between them from the very beginning. However, if Sherry was correct, the investigation got more complicated, and another trip to Point Pleasant was on her agenda. After assessing all the information available to her, she knew her fishing expedition with Ace would not be a waste of time.

Although the bodies were discovered in Oakmont, their investigation would take them back to the Point Pleasant area. Beth had so many questions swirling in her mind. Where were these murders committed? Why were these two young women's lives cut short? Did Ramona Montgomery or Gabriela and Courtney know more? Did Natalie Shepperd know more? And what about law enforcement in the area, did they know more than they were saying?

With this new revelation, she had lost track of time.

In her peripheral vision, Bernie stood in the doorway, watching her massage her temples, then rubbing her eyes. After motioning him in, he sat across from her. A mess of papers on the table piqued his attention. Beth had gathered up everything except the photos and DNA reports. Turning them toward him, he studied both as his confused eyes met her smile.

"What are you so happy about?"

"Just look at the photos. What do you see?"

"I guess McBride has corrupted you. Anyway, two dead young women."

"Right. You know what I mean."

"Okay, what do you mean?"

"Don't they look alike?"

"Sort of. What're the other two reports?"

"DNA results. The one on your left is Jane Doe number one, and the other is Jane Doe number two. What do you see?"

"A bunch of graphs and bars."

"Come on, Bernie. Look closely. Don't they look similar?"

"Shit, yeah, they do. The photos look similar as well. No, way. So, the victims *are* related."

"It appears so, and according to Sherry's professional opinion, Jane Doe number two is the daughter of Jane Doe number one."

"No way. Do you believe her?"

"Yeah, I do. I've felt a connection existed between them, just didn't think they were mother and daughter."

"Wow, guess we are going back to Point Pleasant, aren't we?"

"Yeah, I'm hungry for another delicacy from Hillbilly Hotdog. How about you?"

"You don't have to ask me twice, and let's not forget about Rocco's, okay?"

"Not a problem. We better look for hotels in the Point Pleasant area. Our next trip will not be a day trip. However, we'll need to wait until Sherry verifies the results again. I asked her to put a rush on it."

"Okay, what do you want me to do until she gets back with you?"

"Umm, just hang tight. I'm going to call Ramona Montgomery. I believe she's holding out on us. I can feel it in my bones."

"Yeah, I got that, too."

"Great, so we both agree on that. After I talk with her, we'll decide what to look for on the internet."

He nodded and left the conference room while she planned her course of questioning Ramona. Although this case was moving quickly, and maybe a resolution to both cases was imminent, she knew that was unlikely and too easy. Based on the last two cases, she learned to expect the unexpected because it was lurking around the corner. After jotting down her strategy to get Ramona to open up more about everything, she placed her iPhone on speaker and keyed in the number. It rang several times before she answered.

"Mrs. Montgomery?"

"Yes, this is she."

"Hi, this is Beth Pendergast from Oakmont. I visited you yesterday, remember?"

"Of course, how may I help you? Didn't I answer all your questions yesterday?"

"May I call you Ramona?"

"Well, of course, honey."

"Thank you. Anyway, yeah, you answered all of our

questions. Thank you for being so open. However, after thinking about your answers, I wanted to know more about your son, Paul."

"What does he have to do with Ashlee's death?"

"Probably nothing, sorry to alarm you. Would you tell me more about him, you know, growing up? Since you adopted him, just start there, okay?"

"Yeah, okay. I guess that will be alright."

"Perfect. I'll try not to interrupt you too much, okay?"

"No problem. Well, Paul came to us sort of the same way Ashlee did. His parents died in an auto accident. As I recall, he was just, hmm, about five years old. We knew his parents through the church. I guess you could call us good friends. We had them over for dinner on numerous occasions, and they reciprocated. That's how we got to know Paul as a child. When the accident happened, I was pregnant. Unfortunately, I lost the baby due to a miscarriage. I'd had several before, so I guess we weren't meant to have children. That's when...umm..."

"I'm sorry, Ramona. Is this too painful for you?"

"No. Anyway, I was beginning to tell you that we started thinking about being foster parents. We knew Paul had no other family, and he would be placed in foster care. We couldn't let that happen and contacted social services about him. To make a long story short, it was a long process, but I guess it was meant to be. He was placed in our home, and about a year later, we adopted him, giving him our last name."

"Do you mind telling me who his parents were?"

"No, not at all. They were good people. Just ordinary people. Mona and Michael Albertson of Henderson, just across the Kanawha River."

"Good for you and your husband. Foster care can be difficult. You know, I was adopted myself, different situation, though. Anyway, sorry for the interruption. Please go on."

"Oh, no problem. What else do you want to know?"

"As much as you're willing to tell me, you know, his schooling, his friends, how he met his wife, Shelley, right?"

"That's right. I still don't know what good it will do. He didn't have anything to do with any of this."

"Yeah, I know. But knowing Ashlee was your foster daughter, he knew her. Maybe he understood her. He might know something that could help us."

"Okay, I suppose so. I'm still not sure how this will help, but he was a good kid, good student, and a terrific baseball player."

CHAPTER 15

With Ramona more relaxed and convinced this conversation might be helpful, she opened up more about Paul. Beth could quickly tell how proud she was of her son. She described Paul as almost the perfect son. He was well-mannered and obedient, never in any trouble as a young boy. As she reminded Beth, he was very caring. She talked about how he bonded with Ashlee. Paul knew what it was like, and when he could, he mentored Ashlee as she adapted to a new family in another foster home.

"Wow, you must be incredibly proud of him for taking an interest in Ashlee."

"Yeah, as I said, it was strange how they connected. They understood each other, and she looked up to him."

"So, once he was in high school, you said he started to take an interest in girls."

"Early on, he didn't have any steady girlfriends until he met Mitzi. I guess it was the end of his sophomore year. She was from Gallipolis and was his first steady girlfriend. I didn't care for her because she was, you know, not our kind. Plus, he always had to drive there to see her. I was afraid he might be getting in over his head. I didn't want him to get hurt or get in trouble. I heard she was, well, experienced, you know. He only brought her around here a few times. Their relationship only lasted through that summer, or should I say, until he finally met Shelley. That was the end of Mitzi, and as far as I know, they never talked or saw each other again. Of course, I was glad he'd met Shelley. He fell head over heels for her and never mentioned Mitzi again."

"Do you remember her last name?"

"Let me think…I believe it was Hardy. Yes, Hardy."

"I know last names are hard to remember sometimes, thank you. Do you remember what she looked like? Yeah, I know, it's been twenty years since you last saw her and all."

"Well, as I remember, she was petite, short dark hair, wore lots of makeup, and I remember every time she was here, she always wore the same jean jacket. Kind of funny, you know. Shelley wore the same one a lot, too. Paul told me they bought them at the same place in town. I believe it's called Gabriela's Boutique. I often wondered if Mitzi had any other jackets. Anyway, that's all I remember about her."

"Great. Oh, one other thing. Do you remember the photo I showed you on my phone yesterday?"

"Yes, I remember it."

"You seemed to study it for a long time. Did anything jog your mind?"

"No…as I said yesterday, I never saw that girl before."

"Got it. Tell me more about Shelley?"

"Now, she was our kind. Pretty, sweet, and polite

with a good upbringing. Cheerleader, smart, and sensible. She had never been in any trouble, either. She was perfect for Paul. The All-American girl you could call her. She was always prompt and dedicated to anything she did. Of course, she was here a lot until they headed off to college in Oakmont. I wish they could've gone to school a little closer, like in Huntington or Charleston. Anyway, neither could pass up the scholarship offer from the university in Oakmont. It all worked out, and they both graduated debt-free. What parents wouldn't want that, right?"

"Yeah, my mom was ecstatic when I received my scholarship, so I understand how you feel. So, you liked her, right?"

"I loved her, and she adored Paul. I can't say that Ashlee liked her all that much. Not sure why. Maybe she didn't like Shelley taking Paul away."

"I could understand that. Did Paul date anyone else?"

"No, as I said earlier, after the fling with Mitzi, it was all about Shelley. Anyway, I've got to run to the store. Is there anything else I can answer?"

"Yes, ma'am. Shelley was supposed to be my partner's bridesmaid. She canceled at the last moment, and I had to take her place. Do you know anything about that?"

"No, I don't. But that's not like her. Once she commits, she carries through with that commitment."

"She told my partner she canceled because of some big trial. Does that ring a bell?"

"Uh, no. I talked to Paul before he left the country on business, and he didn't mention it or the wedding. You know, he doesn't tell me much these days. Kids leave home, become successful, and parents get left out."

"Yeah, I guess. Anyway, thank you. Remember, you

have my number if you think of anything else regarding Ashlee, okay?"

After the call ended, Beth remained in the conference room, thinking about Ramona's answers, or the lack of them, especially about the photo of Jane Doe number one. Her description of Mitzi was similar to Jane Doe number one. However, without a picture to compare it to, it was of no help. Although this conversation was about Paul, Beth learned more about Ashlee's life.

It was not all peaches and cream, according to Ramona. When social services placed Ashlee in her home, she had already suffered much heartbreak and abuse in other foster homes. And then there was the fact that Ramona and Harold didn't initiate the adoption process. Her relationship with them wasn't particularly a walk in the park, while Ashlee's relationship with Paul was much better until he married Shelley and moved away. After that, her relationship with Ramona and Harold grew more strained. Maybe that's why when Ashlee turned eighteen, she left for good. Out on her own, she was searching for something better or something else more important.

CHAPTER 16

Beth left the conference room more confused than ever. She was hoping that Ramona would remember something about the photo of Jane Doe number one, but that never materialized. Mitzi Hardy's description was similar, and it was time to dig into her past. When Beth reached her workstation, Bernie was doodling on a notepad, doing nothing. She dropped off her purse and legal pad, then headed for the ladies' room. Upon returning, Bernie was mumbling under his breath and rubbing his tummy. After a glance at the big clock on the wall, she understood why.

"Well, Beth, what did you find out?"

"Lunch at McGruder's, and I'll tell you everything."

"Don't have to ask me twice. Let's go."

"You driving?" Bernie nodded. "Good, you're buying, too."

Arriving at McGruder's, their usual booth in the corner was available. Beth scooted in where Carla usually sat. Bernie slid in across from Beth and did his pre-lunch settling-in ritual. After a few movements, he smiled. Within minutes, Sam arrived in her usual cheery disposition. She was all smiles as she greeted them. After taking their orders, she left. A couple of minutes later, Sam placed iced tea with lemons in front of them.

"Guys, your lunch should be out in about ten minutes. Anything else I can get you?"

"Nah, I think we're good, right, Bernie?"

"Yeah."

"Great. Where's Carla?"

"Honeymoon, remember?"

"Oh yeah, I'd forgotten about that, Bernie. Have you heard from her?"

"Nah, and we haven't even tried to contact her either."

"Okay, then I'll be back as soon as your orders are ready."

"Sounds good, Sam. Okay, Beth, what did you find out to help us identify Jane Doe number one?"

"Well, not much. Ramona is adamant about not recognizing the photo of the first Jane Doe. I did find out that Paul dated a Mitzi Hardy before he met Shelley. I asked Ramona to describe her. Based on her description, it could be Jane Doe number one, but who knows unless I can find a picture of her. Mitzi lived in Gallipolis, Ohio, just downriver from Point Pleasant. That's where I'll start when we get back."

"Doesn't sound like much. Do you think Paul is involved somehow?"

"I don't know. I just feel in my bones that Ramona and even Gabriela recognized the photo of Jane Doe number one. If that is the case, then Paul is the connection. Anyway, I'll research Mitzi Hardy, and I want you to research Paul. I'll also research Shelley, although I don't think she's involved in either case. For that matter, Paul may not be involved, either, and if that's the case, we're back to square one."

"Well, I don't feel our visit and your conversation with Ramona was a waste of time. I believe we're heading in the right direction. We have a name for Jane Doe number two. Sherry's pretty sure she's the daughter of Jane Doe number one. That's more than we had a week ago."

"Yeah, I guess you're right."

"Hello...I'm always right. Here comes Sam with our food. Let's eat. No more talking about the case, okay?"

After much-deserved silence at lunch, they returned to the station refreshed and nourished to delve into Mitzi Hardy and Paul Montgomery. Shelley was just not as crucial to them at the moment. Based on what they discovered about Mitzi and Paul, Beth would scrutinize Shelley's life, if warranted.

Who was Mitzi Hardy, Beth wondered? Entering her name with the city of Gallipolis in the search window, she was hoping for a hit, for anything. For all Beth knew, she could be married, dead, or neither. She thought Mitzi was an uncommon name, and she was hoping for quick results; however, Mitzi was more common than she thought. Mitzi Hardy was an average person, and after several search pages, she closed her laptop, thoroughly disgusted. Mitzi was a nobody, and the internet proved that. Bernie caught her gaze and smiled. Beth smiled and let out a big sigh prompting a mumbled response from him.

"What did you say?"

"Nothing. Paul is the All-American boy. All-around good athlete, pretty much what Ramona told you. By the look on your face, you found diddly-squat on what's her name."

"Mitzi, and you're right, diddly-squat on her."

"What about Facebook? Did you try it?"

"Not yet, but if she's married or dead, it's not going to be much help."

"Yeah, I understand. More stuff is showing up on these sites as more people want to reconnect. What about the website Classmates? You'll need to know what high school she graduated from and what year. You never know what you might find."

"Yeah, I've heard of it before. It might be worth a shot."

Beth was not a big fan of Facebook, nor did she have an account. However, she knew Bernie did and talked him into searching for Mitzi while she visited classmates.com. After finding the name of the high school in Gallipolis, she entered it, and the high school loaded. There were many tabs to select from, and she clicked on 1994. While lots of information popped up, one piece of information piqued her interest—the yearbook for 1994. After clicking on it, the site denied her access because she wasn't a member. After joining, she clicked on the yearbook tab, and it loaded.

Quickly, she scrolled through the pages of photos until she came to Mitzi Hardy. As she focused on the innocent face of the teenager, another image seized her attention. Maxine Ashley Hardy's pretty face sent her pulse skyrocketing. After Beth opened the photos folder on her iPhone, she selected Jane Doe number one. As she compared the two pictures, beaming excitement exuded from her soul. Glancing at Bernie, she waved her arms to get his attention. Finally, he caught her wild gyrations, and she motioned him over. He rose, walked a few steps, and glared at her laptop.

"Is that Jane Doe number one?"

"I'd bet money on it. Who are you, Maxine Hardy? Why did someone viciously take your life? Why did someone take your daughter's life? I'm going to find out. You didn't deserve such a fate, and neither did your daughter."

CHAPTER 17

Speechless, Beth's heart pumped faster and faster. Bernie smiled and patted her on the shoulder. High-fives sealed the discovery. After exhaling a few times, she closed her laptop and then stared at Maxine Hardy's photo on her phone. Both victims were no longer called Jane Doe. She wondered how she discovered both victims' identities in a relatively short time when Ace gave up so quickly twenty years ago. Because no one in Oakmont identified her, maybe he just didn't care because she was a nobody to him.

Almost twenty years ago, for some reason, Maxine Hardy presumably left her daughter in front of the Mason County Social Services in Point Pleasant. She must have believed her daughter would have a better chance of a good life in the hands of social services rather than trying to raise her herself. These speculative thoughts were swirling around in Beth's mind as Bernie sat staring at her photo.

After Beth wiped the bittersweet tears streaming from

her eyes, she opened her laptop and entered Maxine's full name. Disappointment glared back. Based on the lack of information, she was a nobody, even in her hometown. Using the white pages on the internet, Beth found out quickly that there were numerous people in the area with the Hardy last name. She knew they were likely hunting for a needle in a haystack. There were many questions to be answered. Were Mitzi and Maxine related? Twin sisters were a possibility; they looked very similar. However, if they were twin sisters, why was she never reported missing? That could be said of cousins as well. Maybe they weren't related, she thought. She wondered if Ramona had heard of her. After picking up the phone, she called her. It rang and rang, and she hung up without leaving a message.

Bernie had returned to his desk, settled in, and opened up his laptop, while glancing at Beth and the frustration painted her face. She had made tremendous progress and was happy about that, but she knew solving this mystery was far from over. Once again, she knew the Gallipolis-Point Pleasant area likely held the secrets of Maxine's life, her daughter, Ashlee's father, and maybe even the murderer. It was becoming more apparent that there was only one killer.

"Beth, all of this is crazy. If everything you found out today is true, we may solve this before Carla returns."

"Yeah, maybe. Finding this information so quickly was way too easy, so let's not get our hopes up. Anyway, what did you find out about Mitzi Hardy on Facebook?"

"Nothing, because I haven't tried yet. Let's go to the conference room, and we'll spend time researching Facebook together."

"Sounds good, and we'll look for all the major players. We have a lot of names with connections. Gabriela is Shelley's cousin, while Courtney remembered Ashlee. Paul dated Mitzi, and based on classmates.com, Mitzi and Maxine may have known each other. And there's Ramona, who I think knows more. And let's not forget, Shelley and Paul are husband and wife."

After settling in the conference room, Bernie opened his laptop and pulled up his Facebook account. His account was in name only. No picture, no personal information, but it gave him easy access to search this social media behemoth for valuable information. After entering Mitzi Hardy, they waited for anything to load. Mitzi would be about Paul's age. She could be married, divorced, or even dead. Finally, names loaded, many more than they expected. While scrolling through the list of names, they hoped there was a reference to Gallipolis. Any of the listings could be her or none of them. They were simply looking for a needle in a haystack.

After about a half-hour of clicking on the individual listings, disappointment crushed their hopes. Down near the bottom of the list, one piqued their interest. Mitzi Hardy-Smith stood out for some reason. Although the woman had long blonde hair, they thought it could be possible. After clicking on her information, her current city was listed as Gallipolis, bringing a smile to Beth's face.

"Beth, that's good, right?"

"Yeah, but we still have to find more information on her. The information on any account is only as good as what the individual enters. You know, some people enter erroneous information to protect themselves. I'll research her through normal channels to get the most current contact information."

A gentle knock on the partially opened door caught their attention. Standing in the doorway, Sherry inquired if they needed any help. A lightbulb went off in Beth's investigative mind, and she motioned Sherry to join them. Standing behind Beth and Bernie, Sherry stared at Mitzi Hardy-Smith's Facebook page.

"Is this what you need help with?"

"Not really. Let me get my laptop, and I'll be right back."

Beth left while Sherry and Bernie chatted about meaningless stuff. After she returned, she opened up her laptop and clicked on the open tab for classmates.com. Sherry stood staring at pictures from the yearbook.

"Sherry, can you take this photo of Mitzi Hardy and create an image of what she would look like today, but with long blonde hair. We might have a significant break in our cases. We think the lady on Bernie's laptop is the young woman in the photo here."

"Piece of cake. I'll enter that information, copy that photo, and run it through my program. It will take me about ten minutes. Sit tight."

"Thanks, you're a lifesaver."

While Sherry was working her magic, Bernie entered Ashlee Roberts. Like Mitzi, a full page of individuals named Ashlee Roberts loaded. They didn't realize how many different spellings there were for that name. They had their work cut out for them and began viewing all the Ashlee Roberts. Ten minutes flew by, and Sherry returned with what Mitzi would look like with long blonde hair at forty or so. As Beth held it next to the most recent photo on Facebook of Mitzi Hardy-Smith, she

smiled. It had been a successful afternoon, and Beth felt
great about their progress. A glance at the big clock on
the wall told her a celebration with drinks at McGruder's
was in order. After Bernie made reservations for two
rooms at a hotel in Point Pleasant for Thursday night,
they arrived at McGruder's ready to relax and celebrate.

CHAPTER 18

Finding Mitzi Hardy-Smith was like finding gold. Of course, that's if she knew anything about Maxine Hardy. After Beth searched the internet for Mitzi, she found the correct information to contact her in person when she and Bernie made the return trip to the Point Pleasant area. A quick phone call verified that information. She owned an antique business in the historic downtown district. Beth wanted to visit Mitzi first, hoping to learn a lot about Maxine. They planned to revisit Ramona, Courtney, and Gabriela on Friday before returning to Oakmont. Beth was putting a lot of faith in Mitzi that she knew Maxine and her history.

The Ashlee Roberts they hoped to discover on Facebook netted zilch. Although they did find an account for her, there hadn't been any activity for a couple of years. According to Ramona, after she left home, she was probably homeless and possibly didn't have internet or social media access. As far as Ashlee's information, Beth wasn't disappointed with the lack of it. She put all her chips on Mitzi, hoping for a significant breakthrough in their investigations.

So engrossed were they in the direction of the cases, she and Bernie hadn't thought of Carla one bit. She and Chris were enjoying themselves in the Caribbean and would dock on Friday morning. Then they would spend a few days with Shelley and Paul in their condo. Beth was surprised that Carla hadn't checked in with them yet, but she was sure that would all change once they were off the cruise ship.

Beth and Bernie planned to arrive in Gallipolis around noon to find a local eatery for lunch before tracking down Mitzi Hardy-Smith. Although they preferred stopping at Hillbilly Hotdogs again, their quickest way to Gallipolis was crossing over the Ohio River in Huntington, then heading north on Route 7. Hillbilly Hotdogs would have to wait for another time. However, Bernie was good at finding the best places to eat, and he had a place in mind. Making good time, they entered the city limits of Gallipolis before noon. Bernie's food recon found Remo's Italian Weinery on Second Street. After an enjoyable lunch of Italian hotdogs and sodas, they left thoroughly satisfied and ready to speak with Mitzi Hardy-Smith.

She owned an antique shop in the historic downtown district. Finding her available wasn't going to be complicated. After getting information off the website, they knew she would be re-opening at one PM. Parking in front of the store, Bernie cut the engine. They were a few minutes early, and the sign "closed" was still on the door. A couple of minutes later, a lady approached the door. Unlocking it, she turned the sign to "open" and closed the door. From the image Sherry created, the lady had to be

Mitzi. After exiting the car, they entered her antique store. An old-fashion door chime rang out. Mitzi approached them hoping they were there to purchase antiques or collectibles.

"Good afternoon, folks. How may I help you?"

"Mitzi Hardy-Smith?"

"Yes, that's me. What may I interest you in?"

"Information. He's Detective Kowalski, and I'm Beth Pendergast. We're with the Oakmont Police Department in Kentucky."

Simultaneously flashing their ID badges, Beth pulled up the photo on her phone of Jane Doe number one and handed it to the woman.

"Do you recognize this young woman?"

As Mitzi held Beth's phone, her rosy cheeks quickly lost their vibrant radiance. "Maxine. I wondered what happened to her."

"So, this is Maxine Hardy, right?" While nodding, tears surfaced on her cheeks as she handed Beth her phone. "Okay, we're investigating her death from about twenty years ago."

"Are you serious? I…"

"Yeah, I know, this is hard to fathom. How well did you know her in high school?"

"Wow, I can't believe that's what happened to her. I thought she just moved away. How did she die?"

"Ma'am, we're not at liberty to discuss that."

"Bernie, we agreed I would handle this interview, remember?" Bernie nodded and pulled out his note-book. "How well did you know her from high school days?"

"Miss Pendergast, we were sort of friends, many people thought we were related, but we weren't as far as I know. She did come over to my parents' home a few times for parties, but that's about it."

"Do you remember any of her boyfriends?"

"She had so many. Guys liked her, a lot."

"Any particular one stand out that you remember?"

"Not really."

"Okay. Tell us about Paul Montgomery. According to his mother, you dated him for a while before your senior year."

"You talked to his mother? What about?"

"Another matter. What about Paul?"

"Yeah, Paul Montgomery…wow, I haven't heard that name, well, since we stopped seeing each other that summer before my senior year. Does he have something to do with this?"

"Probably not. We're just gathering information on people who might have known Maxine. Did Paul know her?"

"Funny you asked that. He met her at one of my parties. The next thing I knew, he ended it with me and dated her for a short time before our senior year. My guess is she gave him what I wouldn't."

"So, he had sex with her?"

"From what I understand, she got around."

"As far as you know, did she ever end up pregnant?"

"I'd heard that back then, but I don't know for sure."

"Okay, what about her family? Do they still live around here?"

"From what I remember, her mother died when she was a teenager, and her dad raised her."

"Does he still live in the area?"

"No, he was killed in an auto accident soon after she graduated from high school. I remember, after he died,

she had to move out of the house they rented. I don't
know what happened after that. As I said, we weren't
close friends. You know, I'm thinking something is going
on that you're not telling me. You found me through
Paul's mother, then you asked me about Maxine, and
she's been dead for about twenty years. Come on, detectives, I'm no dummy. What's going on?"

"Yeah, okay." Beth thought it couldn't hurt and
pulled up the photo of Ashlee Roberts on her phone and
handed it to her. "Have you ever seen this person
before?"

"No, but she looks a lot like Maxine."

"Yeah, she does. Ashlee Roberts is her name, and
now she's dead. Several weeks ago, a cemetery worker
found her body in the city's cemetery. Initial DNA results
indicate she and Maxine are related, probably mother and
daughter."

CHAPTER 19

A s Mitzi's pulse rocked her soul, she searched for calmness. After taking a deep breath, she exhaled slowly and repeated the process as her anxiety began to subside. She didn't expect what she had just heard. Beth studied her facial expressions and her body language, hoping to learn more from her. She began to walk toward the back of her store, where a table and several chairs were set up. She motioned them to follow her. After everyone was seated, Beth glared deep into Mitzi's eyes, looking for more.

"Mitzi, I know this is a shock. Do you remember anything about a baby girl being abandoned at the Mason County Social Services over twenty years ago?" Her eyes wandered around the room as she tried to remember anything of that nature. "I'm sure as small as Gallipolis and Point Pleasant are, something of that nature would be a big deal, right?"

"Yeah, it would have. I do remember something vaguely, but that's about it. I assume the baby was put in foster care, right?"

"Right. After Paul Montgomery left for college, his parents became foster parents again. Paul was their first foster child, and they later adopted him. Ashlee was their first foster daughter, but they never adopted her. Ashlee's first foster family, the Roberts, were killed in an auto accident, and she kept their name. Do you recall anything else?"

"Not really. Wow."

"Do you know who Maxine ran around with back in high school, like best friends? Take your time. You've already been a big help."

"Will you excuse me for a moment?"

"Of course."

She rose and entered a small office down a narrow hallway. A few moments later, she returned with her high school yearbook. Returning to her seat, she began turning pages until she came to one particular page. As she massaged her temples, her eyes wandered back and forth between Beth and Bernie. Then it hit her, and she put her finger on one particular picture. She slid the yearbook toward Beth.

"Sharma Ann Harkness. So, she was one of Maxine's best friends in high school?"

"Yeah, they were like two peas in a pod, almost like sisters, always together."

"Does she still live around here?"

"She works at Remo's Italian Weinery."

"We had lunch there, great food. I remember the name tag. She waited on us, right, Bernie?"

"Yeah, sweet lady."

"Anyway, she might be able to help you. So, were Maxine and Ashlee found at the same place in the cemetery?"

"Yeah."

"That's creepy and sick."

"Yeah, it is. Thanks for your help."

Ten minutes later, they parked in front of Remo's and entered. The lunch crowd had left except for one older couple nestled in a booth by the main door. They took a booth near the hallway to the restrooms hoping for privacy. A couple of minutes later, Sharma approached them.

"I remember you two from earlier. Just can't get enough of those dogs and soda, right?"

"Sharma, I'm Detective Kowalski. She's Beth Pendergast and we're from Oakmont, Kentucky. We'll take a couple of those Italian crème sodas, and then we'd like to ask you some questions about an old high school friend, okay? Go ahead and get our sodas, and then have a seat across from us."

She nodded and left. Five minutes later, she returned with a tray containing three sodas. After putting them on the table, she sat across from them. They took a long sip, as did Sharma.

"Detective Kowalski, what is this all about?"

"It's about an old friend of yours, Maxine Hardy. We visited Mitzi Hardy-Smith, and she told us you and Maxine were best friends in high school."

"Geez, I haven't seen Maxine since we graduated. As I recall, her dad died in an auto accident. I guess that was the last time I saw her. I don't even know where she lives now or what happened to her."

Beth took out her phone and pulled up the photo of Maxine. Handing the phone to Sharma, tears began to roll down her cheeks. After wiping them away, she gave the phone back to Beth.

"I guess that explains why I never heard from her again."

"This photo is from about twenty years ago when a cemetery worker found her body at the back of the cemetery. We recently reopened that case because of new developments and leads. What can you tell us about her life when her dad died?"

"Miss Pendergast, after we graduated, our friendship began to fall apart. She got around with guys, and I didn't want to be part of that gang. I then went away to college, and never saw or heard from her again."

"Okay, I want to show you another photo. Here, take a look." As Sharma studied the photo, her eyes wandered as she returned it to Beth. "Do you know this person?"

"No, but it kind of looks like Maxine."

"This photo was taken a couple of weeks ago. A caretaker found her body in the same cemetery as Maxine. Preliminary DNA results indicate that Ashlee Roberts is related to Maxine, probably her daughter. We're rerunning the tests to make sure, but we're pretty sure she is Maxine's daughter."

"Wow, I'd heard a rumor she was pregnant, umm, guess she was after all. But with Maxine dead, how…?"

"We know someone dropped Ashlee off at the Mason County Social Services back then. Long story short, Ashlee ended up with Ramona and Harold Montgomery, Paul Montgomery's adopted parents Do you remember him?"

"Yeah, he dated Mitzi for a while, then gravitated to Maxine because Mitzi wouldn't give in to his hormonal desires. Maxine gave in to a lot of guys. So, I'm not surprised she ended up pregnant. Ashlee's father could be any of them."

"Did she ever confide in you about that kind of stuff?"

"No, not really. Hey, listen, I've got to get things ready for an early dinner crowd."

"Of course, thanks. This should cover our sodas and your time. Here's my business card. Call me if you can think of anything else, okay?"

"Of course. Miss Pendergast, thanks for coming in today."

Sharma picked up the twenty-dollar bill and stuffed it in the pocket of her apron. Silence and reflection consumed the booth for the next ten minutes. After finishing their sodas, they felt good about their progress on the cases. Carla would be proud of them.

CHAPTER 20

After a leisurely breakfast the following day, Bernie and Beth were ready to revisit Ramona. They also intended to revisit Courtney at the Pixey Stix Café, hoping for more information about Ashlee. Beth had informed Ramona they would be at her home around ten AM. They took a chance on Courtney working today; the café opened at eleven AM. Beth and Bernie planned their strategy by interviewing Ramona and Courtney before heading back to Oakmont. Although Bernie wanted to inflict his charm on Ramona, Beth convinced him she should control the conversation.

Arriving shortly after ten AM, Ramona answered her doorbell promptly. She showed them to the cozy living room. On the table, a carafe of coffee, three cups, cream, and sugar looked inviting.

"Ramona, thank you for seeing us again. We've had some recent developments in the case, and we want to touch base with you again about those. So, thank you again."

"You're welcome. Now, what about those recent developments?"

"I'll get to that a little later. You told us a few days ago Paul dated Mitzi Hardy. Did he ever date a Maxine Hardy, no relation to Mitzi?"

"Who is she?"

"Mitzi and Maxine went to high school together. Remember the photo on my phone I showed you the other day." As Ramona nodded, her eyes began to wander around the room. "Well, we're almost certain the woman in the photo is Maxine Hardy. So, did Paul ever date her or know her?"

"Uh…not…not as far as I know."

"Well, according to Mitzi, he did, and maybe their relationship was sexual. Mitzi told us Paul wanted sex from her, and she told him no. That was the end of their relationship. He had met Maxine at a party at Mitzi's parents' home and knew she was promiscuous. That's why he started dating her."

"Well, that's not something Paul ever discussed with me. Do you believe her?"

"We don't have any reason not to. Maybe that's why he never mentioned her to you. That way, he led you to believe it was always Mitzi he was dating."

"I guess anything's possible. So, what does all this mean."

"Ramona, DNA results from Ashlee and Maxine are almost identical. The science behind them suggests that Ashlee is Maxine's daughter. If Paul and Maxine engaged in sexual intercourse, Ashlee might be Paul's daughter."

Shock and awe quickly painted Ramona's complexion. As her respiration became labored, deep breaths followed as she searched for calmness in her soul. Her wandering eyes considered that possibility. When she returned her gaze to Beth, the possibility she had a grand-daughter crushed her heartstrings. Tears streamed down her cheeks as she began to sob quietly. Beth knew this new development was difficult for her to digest and accept—that her All-American son was not who she thought he was.

"Ramona, I know this is difficult, but would you be able to provide us with something of Paul's that might contain his DNA? When did he visit you last?"

"Maybe four weeks ago or so, it was unexpected."

"So, Shelley came with him?" Ramona nodded. "Would you let us look around in the bedroom they used while here?"

"Of course, follow me."

Ramona led them upstairs. There was a bedroom on the left and one on the right at the end of the hallway. Between them was what appeared to be a Jack-n-Jill bathroom. As Ramona opened the door, stale air hit them in the face. After putting on latex gloves, they entered. Ramona opened and entered the other bedroom.

Bernie began searching the bedroom while Beth took the bathroom. The bedroom looked spotless. The closet was empty, and a chest of drawers was also bare. In the bathroom, the trash can was empty. Opening the door to the vanity, two toothbrushes in a plastic cup brought a smile to Beth's face. Assuming they belonged to Shelley and Paul, she wrapped them in a Kleenex. Beth knew the toothbrushes might not reveal much, but it was the only thing they found. Beth and Bernie returned to the hallway and saw Ramona sitting on the bed in the other bedroom. From the décor, they assumed it was Ashlee's bedroom.

"Ramona, we're done. I found toothbrushes underneath the vanity. Do you know if they belong to Shelley and Paul?"

"I believe so, Beth."

"Okay, I'll have to take them." Ramona nodded. "Was this Ashlee's bedroom?" Again, she nodded. "May we come in?" After another nod, they entered. "I know you said it'd been about two years since she lived here, but may we look around?"

"Yes. I'll be downstairs. Take your time."

"Thank you."

Since Beth had already searched the bathroom, both quickly searched Ashlee's bedroom. After opening the closet doors, any clothes hung on the hangers were long gone. Other than dust, nothing was on the floor. Upon the shelf in the corner, a laptop caught Bernie's attention. He could only assume it belonged to Ashlee and retrieved it. After showing it to Beth, they left the bedroom. Joining Ramona downstairs in the living room, Bernie showed Ramona the computer.

"Yeah, it's Ashlee's. It doesn't work, and that's why she left it."

Bernie placed it on the coffee table and opened it up, pushing the power button. The screen flashed, and after the machine sputtered, it immediately powered off.

"Ramona, may we take it with us? Maybe our tech gurus can work their magic. Do you know if it's pass-word-protected?"

"Of course, Beth. *Heavenly One* is the password. I have no idea where she came up with that. You can take the laptop. Maybe something is on there that can help you."

"Thank you. We'll return it after we've finished examining its contents."

"If Ashlee is Paul's daughter and involved in these murders, let me know, okay?"

"Of course, and we appreciate your willingness to help find justice and closure for everyone. I'll be in touch. Thanks again."

CHAPTER 21

Entering the Pixey Stix Café around eleven AM, the aroma of fresh soup emanated from the kitchen. Although the smell was enticing, they planned to stop at Hillbilly Hotdogs on their way home. They wanted to be back in Oakmont before five PM. After gazing around the café, Beth spotted Courtney behind the bar. The lunch rush was still about forty-five minutes away, which should provide them enough time to question her. A few people were already seated at one of the tables, engaged in watercooler conversation.

Approaching the bar, they sat on stools at the far end, away from all the muted chatter bouncing around the café. Courtney had noticed them enter and take seats at the far end of the bar. Several minutes later, she placed glasses of water in front of them.

"Detective Kowalski and Miss Pendergast, correct?"

"Good memory, Courtney. May we have a few minutes of your time? I have just a few follow-up questions from the other day, and then we'll be gone, okay?"

"Sure, but make it quick, Miss Pendergast. The Friday lunch crowd is always huge."

"Of course. Have you ever heard of a Mitzi or Maxine Hardy?

"Neither name rings a bell with me. Who are they?"

"They both dated Paul Montgomery. Do you know him?"

"I've heard the name before, but I don't know him."

"You mentioned that Ashlee was here last winter most every day. Did she ever bring a laptop in here, use your Wi-Fi, that you recall?"

"Uh, no laptop, but she did have a phone."

"Did she ever mention Paul's name or Mitzi or Maxine's name?"

"You know, maybe that's where I heard Paul's name."

"Okay, what did she say about him?"

"I don't recall. She said she was just trying to find him and didn't say why. I don't pry into other people's affairs. It can't come back to haunt you. What else?"

"That should do it. Thanks."

Courtney left to wait on two individuals sitting at the other end of the bar. Beth dropped a five-dollar bill on the counter, and they left. Ten minutes later, they traveled south on Route 2 towards Huntington and a late lunch date at Hillbilly Hotdogs. Arriving around one PM, they placed their order and chose a picnic table viewing the Ohio River. Within ten minutes, the server delivered their gourmet hotdogs and sodas. While enjoying their lunch, Bernie could see Beth's wheels turning through her eyes.

"I guess your female intuition about Paul may be right. I wasn't sure where you were going regarding that line of questioning. There wasn't anything that connected him to anything in these cases."

"You know, sometimes you have to go look for the unexpected. Paul's connected somehow, and I believe that will eventually come out. Maybe Ashlee's laptop holds useful information."

"Yeah, let's hope so. Wow, look at the time. Carla and Chris should be off the cruise ship by now. I wouldn't be surprised to hear from her soon. I can't wait to tell her of our progress. I'm sure we've identified both victims, and if the DNA results confirm Ashlee is Maxine's daughter, that might be why whoever is responsible knew that and dumped the bodies in the same place. And who better than Paul Montgomery? He is the common denominator at this point."

"Whoa, we're a long way to proving that. It's an interesting theory, but it's just a wild hunch until we have more concrete evidence."

"My wild hunch came true in the last case, and Clarissa Morgan is behind bars. And let's not forget the Penny Miracle case. So, who knows, my hunch may pan out."

"Maybe."

"What do you think?"

"We need to get on the road to be in Oakmont by five PM. We need to get the toothbrushes and laptop checked in. Then on Monday, we'll see where these new developments lead us. Until then, we can enjoy the weekend and clear our minds."

"Yeah, sounds good to me. Let's go."

A few minutes before five PM, Bernie pulled into the police station. After they entered, Beth headed straight to forensics, hoping Sherry was there. Seeing her at her desk, Beth approached her.

"What have you got there?"

"This laptop belonged to Ashlee Roberts. Ramona, her last foster mother, let us take it. We tried to boot it up while we were there, but it just makes a few noises and then dies. I'm sure you guys can fix it."

"Let's see. It's a Hewlett-Packard, and we have a few of those. I'll put it on a charger first, and we'll see what happens. If that doesn't work, we can put the hard drive in one of ours and go from there."

"Great. I also have these toothbrushes. We need to see if we can get DNA off of them."

"Yeah, we can do that. Does the laptop have a password?"

"Heavenly One. I assume that's all one word."

"Okay, piece of cake. Enjoy your weekend."

"You, too. Thanks."

Beth returned to her workstation while Bernie had already left for the day. Suddenly, Beth's iPhone chimed. On her screen, a text from Carla lit up her face. After reading it, she smiled and responded. They were off the ship. Soon Carla would be visiting with her sorority sister and toasting a beautiful sunset on the Gulf of Mexico with Chris and Paul. Carla ended her text message with a question about the case.

Beth sighed and shook her head. Carla always had a difficult time staying away from work. At least the cruise prevented Carla from contacting her and Bernie. At first, she thought about calling her and spreading her good news. However, she replied with a simple message that, thus far, the case had few leads, still waiting on DNA results. Several happy emojis ended her reply.

CHAPTER 22

After Carla and Chris had cleared customs, they waited for a shuttle to take them to the rental car complex. Chris had rented a Corvette convertible to surprise Carla. They were on their honeymoon, and he felt the need to splurge. With all the papers signed, the convertible was theirs for the next five days. They boarded another shuttle to take them to the convertible. At this point, Carla still wasn't aware of what he rented. As the shuttle pulled to a stop, her face lit up.

"Seriously, a Corvette convertible, is that why you insisted I pack light?"

"Yeah, it was. I assume you approve, right?"

"You bet, and my favorite color, Competition Yellow…wow. I can't wait to feel the sun and wind through my hair."

After going over the final details and taking pictures and a video of the outside of the Corvette, they were all set. Chris opened the passenger door for Carla, and she slid in, positioning herself and adjusting the power seat to her liking. Chris moved around to the driver's side, slid in, and moved the driver's cockpit to the perfect position. After pushing the start button, the Corvette's distinctive growl pleased his ears. He turned toward Carla, whose smile ignited his hormones. Their lips met, and the passionate kiss kicked off the next chapter of their honeymoon journey.

"Are you ready?"

"Give me a minute. I need to enter Shelley's address into the navigation screen."

"Well, hurry. I can already taste that margarita on her balcony and kissing your sexy lips."

"You're such a romantic, you know that, right?" He nodded. "Here we go. We are now ready for liftoff, should be about a forty-minute drive. Let me call Shelley and let her know we are on our way. Earlier this morning, when I talked to her, she told me they both should be there by the time we arrive. However, if, for some reason, they are running late, she gave me instructions and the codes to get the key and enter the condo building."

"As I said, make it quick."

After rolling her eyes under her shades, Carla called Shelley's cell phone, going straight to voicemail. She left a short message, then sent her a text with their arrival time.

"Okay, honey, I'm starting the guidance system now."

"Hang on, you sexy lady."

Chris backed the Corvette out of the parking spot, put the gearshift in neutral, and revved it up. Before putting it in drive, he glanced at Carla; her large designer shades against her fiery red hair sent his pulse skyrocketing. The tires squealed, and Carla's head jerked backward against the headrest producing a wide sexy grin across her face.

Ten minutes later, they were traveling I-275 over

Tampa Bay. In another twenty minutes, they would be on Gulf Boulevard. While enjoying the breezes as the Corvette cruised across the Howard-Franklin bridge, she continuously glanced at her phone, looking for a reply from Shelley. Anxiety crept into her soul. She was excited to reconnect with Shelley and meet her husband, Paul.

Chris, enjoying the growl of the Corvette cruising at eighty miles an hour, rocked out to the Doobie Brothers as he took the exit heading to Redington Shores. He'd never been there before but heard good things about it. From his research before the cruise, he knew of several go-to restaurants within a few miles from Shelley's condo. While getting lost in the music, Carla focused on her iPhone, hoping for a text from Shelley.

"Honey, you've been staring at your phone ever since we got on the bridge. What's going on?"

"Oh, nothing. She would've responded by now. I hope nothing has happened to her or Paul."

"Hey, there's nothing to worry about. I'm ready for a margarita. How about you?"

"Yeah, you're probably right."

"Like always, right?"

Chris felt a slight jab on his arm, but he expected that because Carla repeatedly told him he was never right. The friendly bantering was working as a smile crossed her face. As she took a deep breath of the salty air, she exhaled. The next song got her singing. Tim McGraw's *Live Like You Were Dying* brought smiles across her face and memories in her soul. It reminded her of Bernie, and it was his anthem for living each day to its fullest.

"Hey, Chris."

"Yeah."

"Do you mind if I call Bernie? I miss that old dickhead."

"Really, according to the navigation, we're almost there. He's probably eating dinner about now. Can't it wait? You don't want to miss the sight of the ocean just on the other side of the bridge."

"Yeah, I guess you're right. That song got me thinking about him. Wow, there's the blue waters of the Gulf of Mexico just like you said."

"Yeah, and her condo is on the right about a half-mile ahead."

Chris turned into the parking lot and chose a visitor spot away from the other cars. Although the Corvette wasn't his, he treated it as if it was. Backing the Corvette into the spot, Shelley's condo was on the fourth floor on the south side of the building. Before turning the car off, he put up the power top. With the Corvette safe and silent, they exited the vehicle. Carla glanced at her phone again. Still no text from Shelley. She dialed her number, and it went straight to voicemail once more.

"Chris, she's not answering her phone. I'll get the key to her condo. Then we'll key in the security code, take the elevator, and surprise them. Hope they're not, you know, getting it on."

"Carla, I doubt it. Maybe they're just running late."

"Yeah, probably."

After retrieving the door key out of the lockbox, Carla keyed in the building's security code. The lone elevator was down the hallway, upon reaching she pushed the up button. After a couple of minutes, the elevator door opened. They entered and pushed the fourth-floor button. The door closed, and anticipation ran through her body while Chris remained calm. He had never met Shelley; however, Carla knew her well even though it had been several years since they last saw each other. Finally, the elevator stopped, and they exited. Carla knew her unit was on the right at the end of the hallway. The anticipation and excitement of reconnecting with Shelley ran wild in her mind. After reaching the door, their anticipation and excitement morphed into fear and uncertainty.

ried blood on the door handle stopped Carla and Chris in their tracks. With anxiety rocking her soul, her instincts told her to enter in hopes of saving Shelley's life if it came to that. However, her professionalism and experience changed the personal conflict raging in her mind. While on her honeymoon, she left her Glock at home. Then there was the love of her life; she didn't dare put his life in jeopardy. She had no idea whose blood was on the door or what might have occurred in the condo.

Carla motioned Chris to sit on the bench opposite the elevator while she approached the door. After placing her ear next to the door, dead silence flowed back. She backed off and joined Chris on the bench. Surveying the walls and ceiling of the hallway, she scoffed at the absence of security cameras. Obviously, no one had been in the hallway and saw the blood, or the condo would already be swarming with local law enforcement.

After pulling out her phone, she dialed Shelley's number once more, and like before, it went straight to voicemail. Although she had Paul's number, she didn't have a reason to call him until now. With her eyes glued to the elevator, the door opened. A woman and man got out and immediately turned left without acknowledging them. Paul's phone also went straight to voicemail. She immediately ended the call without leaving a message. After dialing 9-1-1, she reported her emergency.

"Carla, what do you think happened here?"

"I have no idea. When I talked with Shelley this morning, everything seemed fine. I sure didn't expect this. Now we just wait for law enforcement to arrive."

As Carla sat on the bench, she kept her eyes glued on Shelley's door. The smeared blood continued to rock her soul. She could hear the faint sound of sirens getting closer. A few minutes later, the sirens grew silent. Her focus moved from Shelley's door to the elevator. Carla wasn't sure whether it would be local police or the sheriff's department responding. Suddenly, the elevator door opened, and she rose to greet two deputy sheriffs who identified themselves.

"Deputy Ramirez, Deputy Garcia, I'm Carla McBride, a detective with the Oakmont Police Department in Kentucky. Here's my ID. My husband and I just got off our honeymoon cruise and were here to visit my sorority sister, Shelley Montgomery, and her husband, Paul. I talked to her this morning, and everything seemed fine. I called her phone a few minutes ago. It went straight to voicemail, and so did her husband's. There's blood on the door handle. I haven't touched anything. I put my ear to the door but didn't hear a thing. Here's the key. Let me know what you find out as soon as possible, okay?"

After nodding, Ramirez and Garcia put on latex

gloves and approached the door. Testing the door handle, it moved. After knocking on the door several times, only silence answered him. Pushing down on the door handle, each drew their weapons.

With Ramirez ready to proceed, Garcia positioned himself. Ramirez announced himself. After slowly opening the door, silence met them. The main living area was an open floor plan. After clearing it and the balcony area, they moved on to the two bedrooms off a short hallway. Ramirez chose the master to the right, while Garcia chose the bedroom to the left. Ramirez quickly cleared the master bedroom and bathroom. Garcia did the same with the other bedroom and bathroom. Ramirez assigned Garcia to begin searching the condo while he went out to interview Carla.

"Detective McBride, the condo is clear. It appears nothing is out of place. The inside is spotless. Garcia is currently searching the condo. Have we met before or maybe talked on the phone?"

"I worked with Detective Ramirez from Pensacola a while back. He helped me find my friend that had been kidnapped."

"Well, I'll be damned. You know you owe me the whole story about that kidnapping. I'm that Jimmy Ramirez. Nice to finally meet you. I retired from there and had the opportunity to move here. Wow, what a small world, right?"

"Yeah, nice to meet you as well. This is my husband, Chris. May I go inside, take a look around? I would not have expected this after talking to her this morning."

"I tell you what, I'll swab the door handle, and then you can go in as soon as Garcia is done. We don't even know whether a crime was committed here or not, so I think it would be okay. Here's a pair of gloves. He'll be out soon."

While waiting for Garcia to finish, Carla brought Ramirez up to speed on her relationship with Shelley. Carla knew very little about Shelley's husband, Paul, and she couldn't tell him much. Shelley and Paul had recently celebrated their eighteenth wedding anniversary a couple of months ago. They had never had any marital problems as far as she knew, but then again, Carla hadn't seen Shelley in many years. After about twenty minutes, Garcia reappeared, shaking his head.

"Ramirez, the condo is spotless. I don't see anything that would suggest it's a crime scene. There's no blood anywhere inside. It looks like someone tried to wipe it away. It even looks like it has been there for a while. Other than that, the condo is clean as a whistle. It almost looks like no one is living in it."

"Deputy Garcia, that's not possible. As far as I know, this condo is their primary residence."

"Detective McBride, that's just my opinion based on what I saw inside. The dishwasher was empty, nothing on any of the counters, and I noticed the bathroom didn't have toilet paper or tissues. It just looks like it's been vacant for a while."

"Okay, thanks. May I go in now, Deputy Ramirez?"

"Yeah. Garcia, let's get several swabs of the smeared blood on the door handle. We'll perform DNA analysis to determine whose blood it might be."

"Thank you, Deputy Ramirez. I'll be in touch with you. We don't leave until next Friday. Give me your contact information, I'll give you a call, and we'll touch base on what went down here. Maybe I'll have something that will prove whether this might be a crime scene or not."

"Here's my card and the condo key. Good luck. I hope your friends finally show up."

"Me, too. I'll let you know one way or the other. Sorry to have called you."

"Detective McBride, no bother. I'd have done the same thing."

CHAPTER 24

After Garcia and Ramirez left with nothing but blood swabs, Carla and Chris remained on the bench contemplating their situation. Chris knew finding a condo or hotel vacancy would not easy. All their plans were centered around staying at Shelley's condo. As they contemplated their options, it became evident that staying in her condo might be their best or only option.

While Carla inspected every aspect of the condo, Chris sat on the balcony, enjoying the view and searching for a place to stay. The first order was to perform swabs of the dried blood, then find something to remove it from both sides of the door. Leaving it on the door would alarm any tenants or vacationers staying in units near Shelley's. As far as she knew, no other individuals had seen the blood, or they would have notified law enforcement. Assuming this condo was Shelley and Paul's primary residence, she expected their DNA to be everywhere.

After taking a couple of photos of the smeared blood,

she swabbed it and put them in a plastic bag. She then wiped the door handle clean and secured both locks. Although small, the well-appointed kitchenette of high-end appliances exhibited their exquisite tastes. Marble countertops looked unblemished. A Cuisinart coffee maker looked unused, while a one-cup Keurig looked the same. Carla opened the top cabinets beside the refrigerator; everything was orderly. The other cabinets contained daily dinnerware and glasses, all neatly placed.

The gourmet electric range looked like it came straight off the showroom floor. A stainless-steel vent over the stove showed no remnants of use. To the right were cabinets with glass inlays; inside were all kinds of glassware for your drink of choice. The white farm-house-style sink was sparkling. Between the other cabinets, a custom wine rack fully stocked with premium wines exhibited their exquisite tastes. An under-the-counter built-in wine cooler purred softly. Four high-back stools, correctly placed, looked brand new. Place-mats perfectly positioned showed no evidence of food stains or anything else. As Carla stood glaring at the kitchen, whether they ever lived in this condo crept into her mind.

The living area was no different. The wood-grained porcelain tile was pristine, with no evidence of sand or anything else beach-related on the floor. The thought that Garcia was right rushed through her mind. The remotes for the television and soundbar were tucked away in the drawer of the coffee table. Walking out to the balcony, she saw Chris sprawled out on a chaise lounge, enjoying the sun and wind.

"Chris, did you find us a place to stay?"

"Not yet. There aren't many hotels close by, and a

condo search on all rental sites indicates no vacancies. What are you finding?"

"Nothing. This condo looks like it hasn't been lived in for some time. I have the bedrooms and bathrooms to check, but it's not looking good. Keep searching for a place to stay, okay?"

Chris nodded, and Carla returned to the living room, and then proceeded to the hallway. Eighty degrees, the thermostat read. After seeing the thermostat setting at eighty-two degrees, that didn't make sense considering it was in the mid-nineties outside. Maybe Garcia was right, and that's why the thermostat was set so high. The guest bedroom was spotless. Inside the closet, empty hangers hung on the rod. The chest of drawers was bare inside. She pulled back the bedspread and sniffed the bed linens; they smelled and appeared new. As Garcia noted, the bathroom was spotless, with no bath towels and no toilet tissue. Underneath the vanity, emptiness met her inspection.

A room off the hallway contained a washer-dryer combo. Lifting the washer lid, she observed the stainless-steel tub shined like brand new. She opened the door to the dryer and had the same result. Behind the washer-dryer combo, the water heater and the heating and cooling unit appeared new.

She moved on to the master bedroom; the king-size bed was well-appointed with high-end bedding. A picture on a rolltop desk drew her attention. After pulling the bedspread down, the bed linens smelled like those on the other bed. The master bath was high-end. Like the other bathroom, evidence of any use was absent. Men's and women's clothing hung in the walk-in closet off the master bath. This was the first evidence of life in the condo.

While examining the clothing, a jean jacket with sparkling rhinestones captivated her attention. She'd seen the jacket before. After peeling back, the collar, the Angel Hardesty label rocked her soul. After seeing the jacket and its connection to the Oakmont cases, she began to think that maybe Garcia was wrong. However, the lack of anything else tied to the blood on the door handle suggested this condo was not a crime scene. There just wasn't enough out of sync to think any different. Carla joined Chris on the balcony, where he was still relaxing on the chaise lounge.

"Well, honey, do we have a place to stay?"

"Uh, yeah, sort of."

"What does that mean?"

"What did you find?"

"I have to admit; this isn't a crime scene."

"Bingo. Then we should just stay here."

"Let's go inside, and we'll discuss it. Besides, it's scorching out here."

"I need to use the bathroom anyway."

While Chris was in the guest bathroom, Carla walked to the large bar facing the kitchen and sat on one of the high-back stools. Chris entered and sat beside her.

"Carla, staying here is our best option. If Shelley had contacted you, she would have insisted we stay here, right?"

"Well, yeah, but Chris, we can't—"

The click of the deadbolt startled them, and they quickly hid in the hallway. The turning of the door handle pushed their anxiety level up a few notches.

CHAPTER 25

Carla waited for the person to come into view, and if necessary, she was ready to use her physical skills and experience to subdue the intruder. As footsteps moved closer toward them, her moment of truth had arrived. Ready to strike, the individual entered the hallway, Carla sighed heavily, and the person turned around.

"Shelley, where the hell have you been?"

"Carla, why are you hiding in the hallway?"

"Why haven't you answered my calls or texts?"

"It's been one hell of a day. You knew how to get in, so I didn't feel it was necessary. Sorry to upset you. Let me get changed, and I'll open a bottle of wine and tell you all about my day. I assume that's Chris behind you."

"Chris, meet Shelley." He nodded. "Hurry and get changed. I need a drink, especially what we've been through since getting here. You scared the hell out of me."

"What are you talking about?"

"Get changed, open a damn bottle of wine, and we can trade stories, okay?"

Before Shelley entered the master bedroom, she set the thermostat to seventy. While waiting for her, Carla used the guest bathroom to cool her wheels. At the moment, she was super pissed at her. Once Carla was composed, she returned to the living room, where Chris sat comfortably on the sofa. He patted the space beside him, and she settled in next to him. Ten minutes later, Shelley appeared in a short skirt and tank top. As Carla glared at her, she noticed how Shelley had kept herself in shape over the years. Shelley put the modern ceiling fan on high, and the room began to cool quickly.

"I'm glad you guys are making yourselves comfortable. I'll open a bottle of red wine and pour it into a decanter to let it breathe. We can have some Prosecco until it's ready. Sound okay?"

Both nodded. While hearing a familiar popping sound, Carla's disposition began to change. After Shelley poured the Prosecco, she carried two champagne flutes over and handed one to Carla and Chris. She returned to the bar, picked up hers, and stood in front of the sofa table.

"How about a toast to old times?"

After holding her glass high, they stood and joined Shelley. As the champagne flutes clinked over the table, they sipped the refreshing prosecco and repeated the toast. They returned to the sofa while Shelley sat on a futon lounger nestled in the corner by the glass-siding doors leading to the balcony. As Carla savored the Prosecco, a strained silence floated around the room. Although Carla's outward disposition was relaxed, she was still fuming inside at Shelley's disrespectful attitude. After a long sip, her champagne flute was empty.

"So, Carla, you mentioned something about your shitty day. Tell me what could be so shitty about just coming off a cruise, then arriving at this little piece of paradise."

"Shelley, you could have returned my calls and texts. I was worried about you."

"Worried…that's funny."

"Seriously, when we got off the elevator, your door handle was smeared with blood. Here, take a look." Shelley viewed the photo and handed the phone back to her. "My instincts took over. I called 9-1-1."

"Now *that's* funny."

"Not funny, so don't laugh. Two deputy sheriffs arrived, swabbed the dried blood, inspected the condo, and found nothing. I felt like a fool."

"I'm sorry. I had a repairmen come in the other day. Maybe it's his."

"Don't you think you should have cleaned it off? You live here, don't you?"

"Well, sort of. Paul travels all the time, so I decided to rent an apartment closer to work. I use it on the weekends when Paul is usually here."

"By the way, where is Paul?"

"His flight was delayed. He'll be here by tomorrow afternoon. I see you approve of the Prosecco."

Carla nodded. Shelley rose and went to the bar, grabbed the Prosecco, and replenished their flutes, and returned to the futon lounger. Carla's demeanor continued to improve with each sip of the bubbly elixir. While becoming more relaxed, her anger began to subside.

"Yeah, I do. I'm looking forward to reconnecting with Paul and introducing him to Chris. It's been a while since I saw him."

"So, tell me everything about your wedding."

"It was everything I dreamed of growing up. Avondale Country Club was the perfect place for the ceremony and reception. Bernie, my partner, gave me away, and your stand-in, Beth, the department's forensic psychologist, did a fantastic job. I couldn't have asked for anything better."

"Sorry I couldn't be there. It was the most significant case of my career, and by the way, I won and earned a lot of brownie points should I ever run for county attorney."

"Wow, good for you. What does Paul do?"

"He works for an international company that's into biometrics, you know, DNA stuff, and who knows what else. It's cutting edge, and he makes a lot of money. The downside is he travels for weeks at a time."

"Sounds interesting."

"So, Chris, Carla says you are Avondale Country Club's general manager."

"Yeah, I love it and don't want to do anything else."

"Great, so, where do you want to eat tonight? Tomorrow night, I made reservations at the Salt Rock Grill, which you'll love. There's this place about a mile from here called the Seabreeze, with outdoor seating, usually a band, and the best margaritas on the beach. Grouper is their specialty. Sound good?"

"Sounds like a winner to me, Shelley. You okay with it, Carla?"

"Yeah, I'm empty and ready for some red wine. What kind is it?"

"It's a Spanish red blend called Jumilla by Juan Gil. I'll put out some champagne, cheese, and crackers."

"Perfect. I can't wait."

Shelley went to the kitchen, retrieved three wine glasses, and gave them a generous pour. After opening the refrigerator, she gathered several kinds of cheeses and put them on the bar. After another toast, they sampled cheeses and gourmet crackers from Bella Vino.

CHAPTER 26

After one glass of wine, Carla freshened up while Chris went to the Corvette and returned with their luggage. Chris quickly changed clothes and joined Carla and Shelley at the bar finishing their last taste of the Spanish red blend. Ten minutes later, they had their name in for a table at the Seabreeze. While waiting for the hostess to call their number, they sat outside at the bar enjoying the Seabreeze specialty. The twenty-ounce, four-dollar margarita lived up to its reputation, while the salsa Verde and chips satisfied their initial cravings.

Fifteen minutes later, the hostess escorted them to their table by the inlet. As Carla gazed at the shimmering waters, she had forgotten how mad she was at Shelley. While sipping on the margaritas, their conversation took them back to their college days. Shelley's jean jacket reminded her of their sorority days and, unfortunately, her current case back in Oakmont.

"I can't believe you still have that jean jacket."

"Well, you know, it's one of a kind. My cousin,

Gabriela, in Point Pleasant, had my cousin in Williamstown make it for me as a graduation gift."

"Angel Hardesty brand, right?"

"I can't believe you remembered the name. Wow."

"Well, I'd forgotten about it until one like it showed up in Oakmont a couple of weeks ago."

"Really? Who was wearing it?"

"A Jane Doe found in the city cemetery."

"Seriously?"

"Yeah, the victim's identity is unknown. However, I assume my team might have a real name after visiting the Point Pleasant area. They're pretty good at their job."

"So, you think the young woman is from there, right?

"You know, the funny thing is we have a cold case from about twenty years ago. The young woman found dead wore a similar jean jacket, Angel Hardesty brand. Weird, huh?"

"I'd say so. Hey, Chris, you're awful quiet."

"I'm a third wheel just letting two old sorority sisters catch up with each other. Anyway, I'm good, just enjoying the sun, water, and margaritas. I'm sure our server will be here soon. What do you recommend, Shelley?"

"Do you like a Reuben sandwich?"

"Yeah, do they have it on the menu?"

"Sort of. Believe it or not, the Grouper Rueben on their menu will surprise you. Order it fried and crispy. You won't be disappointed."

As Chris nodded, their waiter stood at their table. After considering Shelley's recommendation, he ordered the Grouper Reuben with authentic onion rings. Carla ordered red snapper with saffron rice, while Shelley went with a grilled shrimp salad.

"Let's see, Shelley, where were we before you changed the subject? Oh, yeah, the jean jacket."

"That was a long time ago. Many women from the Mid-Ohio Valley purchased them at my cousin's boutique. When my cousin bought the brand, her boutique was the only place in the area to purchase the jacket. It was a big hit, a fashion trend back in the day. Let's talk about something different, umm, more pleasant than your case, okay?"

For the remainder of the evening, the conversation centered on their college days. Occasionally, Chris got a few words in when he felt like it, but he knew this visit was about two sorority sisters and their long-awaited reunion. He wasn't about to get in their way. They were letting their hair down, reminiscing about the parties and their close friendship while in college. Unfortunately, time and distance have strained their relationship over the years. Although they communicated through emails, texts, and an occasional phone conversation, Chris could tell their reunion quickly became awkward.

After a filling dinner and too many margaritas, they returned to the condo. Chris retired early, giving them more opportunities to reconnect. It was a pleasant night, so Carla and Shelley sat on the balcony, enjoying the mild ocean breezes and the sound of waves crashing on the beach. While nursing on the red blend from earlier in the evening, Carla found it difficult not to pursue the jean jacket connection. And now that she knew Shelley's cousin owned the boutique where the victims likely bought them, her crime-solving instincts were in high gear.

"What a pleasant evening. Thank you for allowing us to stay with you."

"Hey, it's the least I could do for backing out on you. I'm truly sorry."

"You're forgiven, but what happened?"

"Okay, most of it was work-related. I was trying the biggest case of my career, and I needed to focus. Then there is our marriage. We are going through a rough patch."

"I'm sorry to hear that. I don't want to pry, but do you want to talk about it?"

"We're both career-driven. That's probably why we never had children. I spend many hours at work, and he spends a lot of time traveling. We've argued a lot lately. We both have accused each other of having affairs. My affair is with work. I'm not so sure about him. We haven't been intimate for quite some time. We've known each other for over twenty years, and at times I feel like we really don't know each other like we should. Sometimes, I think our past is coming back to haunt us. Hopefully, we'll find the magic we once had before it's too late. What about you and Chris?"

"Well, we've made it a week."

"Funny, ha-ha."

"No shit. I mentioned it in our last conversation. Our previous relationship was sibling-like. We were like best buddies, but I finally realized how much he loved me. I decided to give it a chance. I hope it works out for both of us."

"I see how he looks at you, so you'll be to blame if it doesn't work out."

"Funny, ha-ha. A few minutes ago, you mentioned the past. What did you mean?"

"Oh, that. Before we became a couple in high school, we dated other people. Some of the girls he dated, umm, let's just say, well, you know what I mean—especially a couple of girls from Gallipolis that had unbecoming reputations. Paul's mother was so glad when we started dating. She said I was a godsend. I wasn't sure what she meant, but she treated me like the daughter she never had. Yeah, I'll tell you more tomorrow while we wait on Paul to arrive. It will be sometime in the afternoon."

"Maybe we should call it a night. Tomorrow, we hit the beach, right?"

Shelley nodded, and they entered the living room. After placing their glasses on the bar, a sorority-sister-like hug ended the first chapter of this long-awaited reunion.

CHAPTER 27

Although the night went by quickly for Carla, it wasn't without interruptions. When she crawled into bed with Chris, sleep didn't come easy. Even though it appeared nothing occurred in the condo suggesting a crime was committed, she still couldn't get the blood on the door handle out of her mind. Things just weren't making any sense. Then learning Shelley and Paul were having trouble didn't help the situation. Also, the picture on the roll-top desk created even more questions than answers.

Chris had been up for an hour and had made himself at home. The fresh aroma of coffee made its way into the bedroom, awakening Carla. As she stretched and yawned, the power of the coffee made her smile. Scooting out of bed, she made a quick bathroom stop before walking into the living room. A slight movement on the curtains covering the sliding doors to the balcony caught her attention. Through the sheer curtains, Chris relaxed on the balcony with a cup of coffee. Walking out to greet him, the warm breezes and invigorating warmth of the sun eased her detective instincts.

"There you are, sleeping beauty. How did you sleep, honey?"

"It was a restless night, but you were dead to the world, lucky you."

"Coffee?"

"That would be nice, honey."

After Chris rose from the lounger, he gave her some needed love and attention. He carried his coffee cup into the kitchen and fixed him another K-cup. He retrieved a cup from the cabinet and placed it on the Keurig. He grabbed another K-cup, pushed the brew button, and within two minutes, Carla's morning joe was ready. Carrying both cups to the balcony, he handed the coffee to her. After tasting it, she smiled at him. They sat on the loveseat, enjoying the morning's quietness and each other.

"So, you and Shelley stayed up late."

"Yeah, catching up on each other's life. It was fun. I learned a few things I wouldn't have expected; all is not well in paradise. I always thought they had the perfect marriage. Anyway, I'm looking forward to some beach time and visiting with Paul this afternoon."

"Yeah, me, too."

Shelley appeared in the doorway to the balcony a little groggy. They exchanged good morning greetings, and she sat opposite them in one of the lounge chairs.

"Hey, did you both sleep well?"

"Chris was dead to the world, but not so much for me. I'm that way in a strange bed for the first night."

"Well, sorry. Maybe tonight you'll sleep better."

"I hope so."

"Shelley, we were just admiring the view. If you ever want to sell or…"

"Chris, we don't have time for this."

"Don't worry, guys, it's not for sale. I'm going to fix myself some coffee. You need a refill?"

"We're both good."

Chris nodded and Shelley left. She returned to the balcony five minutes later and sat in the chaise lounge. Except for minimal road-noise, silence encompassed them. Carla glared at Shelley. She looked tired, as though she had a restless night. Chris looked the most refreshed of them.

"Hey guys, Paul should be here by around three o'clock. I thought we'd head to the beach in an hour or so. I have a small room on the ground floor. We can gather the beach chairs and a canopy from there. We can take lunch with adult beverages, and we'll have a picnic. That way we can stay there until he arrives. I told him to change into his beach attire and join us as soon as he gets here. Sound good?"

"Perfect. I've been waiting for some beach time. On the cruise, we didn't have that option. I'm so ready to dip my toes in the gulf, aren't you, honey?"

"Yeah, can't wait."

About fifty minutes later, with the canopy up, beach chairs positioned, and champagne flutes filled, a toast kicked off their beach time. Although the temps were unusually high, the mild ocean breezes under the canopy made for a perfect day at the beach. After Chris finished his glass of champagne, he grabbed a local brew and settled in a beach chair for some people watching. While he enjoyed the view, Carla and Shelley enjoyed the ocean breezes on a walk. With a beverage in hand, they headed down to the breaking waves. After dipping their toes in the warm water, they were off on a two-mile walk. The various sounds of the beach activity took center stage as they began.

"Ah, this is paradise."

"Yeah, that's why we bought the condo. We spend the weekends trying to unwind after a stressful week."

"You know, yesterday when we arrived, I was worried that something had happened. Then when I went through the condo, it just didn't look lived in. I want you to know that I wasn't snooping when I went through everything."

"Don't worry about it. I know it was your detective instincts taking over. It's no big deal."

"Good. Hey, I noticed a picture on the roll-top desk. Is that Paul and his parents?"

"Yeah. Why do you ask?"

"No reason. Who is the young girl in the picture?"

"Oh, you probably don't know that Paul's parents became foster parents after he left for college. Her name is Ashlee. You probably don't know that Paul was adopted as well, do you?"

"No, I didn't."

"Yeah, and she was their last foster child. Ashlee and Paul had a strange connection. Anyway, Paul told me once she turned eighteen, she left home. He never heard from her again, and neither did his mom."

"That's interesting."

"How so?"

"Not sure how to tell you…"

"Tell me what?"

"The girl in the photo resembles the victim in our current case. Her eyes and nose resemble our Jane Doe."

"Can't be or we would know."

"Maybe I'm mistaken. Sorry to upset you."

"I'm not upset. Shocked is a better word if it is her."

"Has Paul mentioned anything to you about her?"

"No, but we can ask him when he gets here. If it's her, he'd want to know. They had a special bond. He can call his mother and see if she knows anything."

"Hey, let's just let it be. I don't want to upset him, and I'm looking forward to dinner tonight. I've heard the Salt Rock Grill is the best around. We can bring it up on Sunday if you want."

"Yeah, that makes better sense. The word is mum on it, okay."

"Yeah, I'm sorry I brought it up."

After returning from their walk, they joined Chris in the gulf's warm waters. While acting like teenagers, they enjoyed jumping in the waves and splashing each other like old times. After about thirty minutes, they retreated to the shade under the canopy. As the warm breezes cooled them off, they relaxed in their chairs. Chris grabbed the champagne and poured the ladies a glass. After giving them their flutes, he grabbed an ice-cold brew and settled in his chair. Time flew by quickly, and before they knew it, Paul arrived dressed in his business attire, a red flag to Shelley. After introducing Paul to Carla and Chris, she knew something had rocked his world.

"Is something wrong, honey? Why are—"

"My mom says she's dead."

"Who...who's—"

"Ashlee."

CHAPTER 28

As Paul strained to get those words out, Shelley's thoughtful embrace brought on his heartbreak. A quiet, almost synchronized sobbing took over the shade of the canopy. Carla wanted to offer sympathetic words of compassion, but her mind began to swirl. She had no clue who Paul was referring to. Was it the little girl in the picture or someone else named Ashlee, perhaps a close colleague of his? Paul, clearly bothered by Ashlee's death, clung to his wife, trying to regain his composure. As the tears and sobbing subsided, Carla and Chris offered their condolences.

"Honey, do you want to go up?" He nodded. "Hey guys, we are going up to the condo. Will you guys gather everything when you're ready to come up?"

"Sure. I'm sorry for your loss, Paul."

He nodded, and wiped his sadness away.

"Give us about thirty minutes before you come up, okay?"

"Of course. If you need more time, text me, okay?"

After Shelley nodded, she and Paul walked across the

white sands toward the pool area. While watching them disappear through the tall seagrass, Carla's thoughts kept returning to the cases in Oakmont. She knew there was only one way to find out. She grabbed her phone, pulled up her favorite list, and selected Beth. After two rings, she answered.

"Why are you calling me? It's Saturday afternoon. Aren't you supposed to be enjoying the beach?"

"Yeah, that was until Shelley's husband told us Ashlee was dead, whoever the hell she is."

"Uh…"

"What's going on, Beth?"

"We're pretty sure our Jane Doe number two is… Ashlee Roberts. Paul's mother identified her from the picture I showed her."

"Well, that explains everything. What else do you know?"

Over the next fifteen minutes, Beth filled Carla in on their findings from their visit to the Point Pleasant area. While Carla listened, her eyes wandered around, back and forth, absorbing all the information.

"Well, Beth, what's next?"

"After finding all of this out, I thought I didn't need to meet with Ace Hutchinson. However, now that I've given it more thought, I think it is necessary."

"Okay, why?"

"I have a hunch he knows more. Bernie and I found out the victims' names without too much trouble. It just doesn't make sense that he gave up so easily with the investigation of Jane Doe, aka, Maxine."

"Okay, but be careful about accusing one of our own. It can get messy and dangerous. Tread lightly, okay?"

"Of course. What are you going to do?"

"I'm not sure, because Shelley's my friend. I will have to tread lightly given what's happened here. Let's stay in touch about any new developments, okay?"

"Absolutely."

"Hey, Beth, great job. Give Bernie my best, and see you in about a week."

The call ended, and Carla sat in the beach chair, contemplating how to handle this situation. She had no choice but to question Paul because of his relationship with Ashlee. Furthermore, she knew she had to handle the situation delicately or she could destroy her relationship with Shelley. Based on her experience and detective intuition, Paul might be involved. However, he may have crucial information to help solve these cases.

"So, honey, this is now a working honeymoon, right?"

"Sorry, but Paul is now a person of interest. Furthermore, what information he can provide is crucial evidence in both cases. While I will work that angle here, Beth and Bernie will continue the case from there. They will be heading back to the Point Pleasant area on Tuesday to continue their investigation."

"Hey, I get it. I knew what I was getting into when I proposed to you."

"Yeah, I know, but you know how passionate I am about cold cases, so don't be mad, okay?"

"Hey, no problem. I'll research golf courses in the area. I'll rent clubs and try out some of the courses. Besides, when the time is right, you'll find a way to make it up to me."

"Yeah, you can bet on it. Now I know why I married you. Let's head to the condo. Hopefully, Paul will be ready to talk. I hope Shelley is up to, you know, finding out how many skeletons he may have hidden in the closet. I'm hoping they really know each other's past history, or it could cause an even greater rift between them."

Ten minutes later, Carla and Chris entered the condo where Shelley and Paul were relaxing on the sofa in the living room. Eerie quietness flowed between them while a tense thickness was in the room. Carla and Chris immediately went to the guest bedroom for a change of clothes. After returning to the living room, Carla sat on the futon lounger. Chris wanted no part of this conversation and grabbed a local craft brew out of the fridge. The balcony with its million-dollar view would be his sanctuary for researching his golfing options.

Stares and glares flew. Carla was unaware of their conversation, and breaking the tension between them was difficult. However, Carla now had a job to do and couldn't let emotions hinder her obligations.

"Paul, once again, I'm sorry for your loss."

"Thank you. I understand you had no way of knowing, given you're on your honeymoon. So, hey, no problem."

"Thanks. Anyway, until I called one of my partners in Oakmont a little while ago, I didn't know who Ashlee was and how you knew each other. My partners spent most of the week in the Point Pleasant area, and their investigation eventually led them to your mother. She identified Ashlee from the photo at the crime scene. What else did your mother tell you?"

"Your partners saw a picture of Ashlee and me, then started asking questions about me and my past."

"I see. What did your mother tell them about your past?"

Silence took hold as Carla studied Shelley's inquisitive expression. Carla already knew what Ramona divulged to Beth, but she wanted to hear it from Paul. She waited for either Paul or Shelley to break this emotional stalemate clouding the conversation. Paul turned toward Shelley, took her hand in his, and squeezed it. Carla breathed a sigh of relief. It appeared that Paul was going to open up about his past. Shelley's loving smile met his strained expression.

"Honey, everything that I'm going to tell Carla happened before you and I met. You know I love you dearly and would never hurt you. You know that, right?"

After Shelley nodded and sighed, a big smile eased Paul's reluctance. She leaned in and gave him a gentle kiss on the cheek.

"Yeah, honey, I know, and it's okay. Tell Carla everything so she can get justice for Ashlee."

"Carla, you can begin now. But don't ask me anything about whether I was involved in Ashlee's death because I wasn't. I'm not that kind of person."

"Okay. I want you both to know I'm in detective mode now, so anything I ask you is not personal or to cause you emotional pain. I want you to understand that. I'm just doing my job."

CHAPTER 29

Paul had already opened the door when he stated he had nothing to do with Ashlee's death. That sent up a red flag in Carla's mind. She would have eventually asked him that question, and depending on his answers, she still may have to. If his answers raised more red flags, she would press him to get to the truth. She continued to watch Shelley and Paul's expressions, demeanor, and body language toward each other, which would also help her decide what direction to take and what to pursue.

"So, Paul, are you ready?" After nodding, he glanced at Shelley and then squeezed her hand. "Okay, anytime you need a break or don't want to proceed any further, just let me know, and I will stop. Also, I will be recording our conversation. Are you okay with that?"

"Yeah, do I need a lawyer?"

"You tell me, do you?"

"No, because I've done nothing wrong."

"Great. Tell me what your mother told you, and we'll go from there, okay?"

"Sure, as I said earlier, she found out from your partners that Ashlee was dead."

"Any idea why her body ended up in Oakmont?" He shook his head. "Okay, could it be because you went to school there and lived there for a while?"

"I told you already that I didn't have anything to do with her death."

"Yeah, you did. What else did your mother tell you?"

Over the next twenty minutes, Paul told Carla about their conversation.

"Okay, Paul, there's more, right?"

"Like what?"

"Like, Mitzi Hardy. Do you remember her?"

As Paul massaged his temples, Carla could tell his pulse had moved into turbo mode. Beads of sweat dotted his forehead. He glanced at Shelley, who didn't seem alarmed about Mitzi. Maybe she knew, and it didn't bother her. However, it bothered Paul, and that was another red flag.

"Yeah, she lived in Gallipolis. I dated her before I met Shelley."

"Okay, and did your mother approve of Mitzi?"

"Well, not so much."

"Didn't your mother tell my partner that she was afraid you might, you know, get in trouble since Mitzi was older, more experienced?"

"Yeah, mom warned me about that, but I told her not to worry."

"Your mom was happy once you started dating Shelley, right?"

"Yeah, she was thrilled."

"Okay, does Maxine Hardy ring a bell?"

"Shit, that's enough for now. I need a break."

"Of course you do. I'll be with Chris. Let me know when you are ready to continue, okay? Shelley, do you have some white wine open? Beer just doesn't sound good to me."

"Yeah, there's a bottle in the fridge. You know where the glasses are. Help yourself, Carla."

Carla nodded and joined Chris on the balcony with a glass of Chardonnay. Chris seemed content in the chaise lounge researching golf courses in the area. As she sat across from him, she enjoyed the million-dollar view while her mind began plotting her strategy. Out of her peripheral vision, Shelley appeared.

"Carla, even with the news about Ashlee, Paul would still like to keep our reservation at the Salt Rock Grill. We all have to eat. Is that okay with you?"

"Yeah, of course. I'm not going anywhere until next Friday, and I understand that you and Paul are off until then. Is that still the case?" Shelley nodded. "Great, yeah, yeah, let's enjoy the evening as much as possible. I promise I'll leave my detective intuition here. What time is our reservation?"

"Six-thirty. It will take us about ten minutes to get there. They have valet parking, and we'll use that."

"That gives me about an hour. I've heard a lot about it. I'm looking forward to it. Shelley, I don't like what I have to do right now, but two young women are dead. My job is to find justice and closure for their loved ones. I'm sure Paul and his mother want that as well."

"Yeah, I get it."

"Great. We're good, then?"

Shelley nodded and left to join Paul in the master bedroom. Carla grabbed her wine and headed to the guest bedroom. Chris had freshened up earlier and stayed on the balcony planning his unexpected golfing week. Forty-five minutes later, Carla appeared on the balcony as radiant as ever. She motioned Chris inside for a toast before leaving. There was just enough of the Jumilla remaining for the toast. After a hearty toast to health and happiness, they were off to a night of fun and friendship at the Salt Rock Grill. Carla kept her promise of leaving her detective mode at the condo, and the evening was casual and enjoyable.

Upon returning home, they had just enough time to watch the sunset. After gathering champagne flutes and a bottle of Prosecco, they retreated to the beach. The sunset was gorgeous. With the sun setting, its reflection on the ocean was mesmerizing. The sound of the crashing waves on the shore put everyone at ease. Although Carla was itching to get back into her detective mode, the peaceful serenity on the beach gave her second thoughts. As she watched Shelley and Paul arm-in-arm, she knew her line of questioning could wait until tomorrow. Paul wasn't going anywhere, and he needed time to grieve the loss of someone special to him. Likewise, Carla needed to cleanse her mind and start fresh tomorrow when Paul was ready. Finding out how far Maxine and Paul's relationship had gone could wait until tomorrow.

"Chris, why don't we go for a stroll on the beach and give them some time alone?"

"Sounds good. Let's go."

"Shelley, I don't know how long we'll be. If you go up to the condo before we get back, just leave the door unlocked, okay?"

"Sure. Have a great walk."

"Yeah, we will. Good night."

CHAPTER 30

After a great evening Saturday, Sunday would be a day of leisure as long as Paul agreed to continue their discussion on Monday afternoon. Paul appreciated Carla's patience and concern. She wasn't a heartless bitch and wanted to show compassion while giving him time to grieve. Not answering Carla's barrage of probing questions would also allow him to inform Shelley about Mitzi and Maxine. Carla hoped he would do that, so Shelley wasn't surprised with his responses to her thorough, personal questions.

Monday morning came quickly. After enjoying the beach into mid-afternoon, everyone retreated to the condo. As Chris didn't want to be part of Carla's inquisition, he left to visit a few local golf courses. Fully relaxed with afternoon cocktails for everyone, Paul was ready to answer her questions. Carla and Paul did a quick review of Saturday's interview before starting.

"Okay, once again, I will be recording our conversation. Remember, anytime you want to stop for a break or need to inform Shelley, just let me know. Also, remember you declined to have an attorney present. Do you still feel that way?"

"I've...done...nothing...wrong, so I don't need an attorney present. Got that, Detective McBride?"

"Yeah. We ended the other day when I asked you if Maxine Hardy rang a bell. You do know that name, right, Paul?"

"Yeah, I heard of her."

"How, where?"

"Okay, I dated her after I stopped seeing Mitzi."

"Why did you start dating Maxine?"

Paul met Shelley's inquisitive stare. Carla wondered if he told Shelley about Maxine and why he decided to date her. Based on Shelley's fiery eyes, he had chosen not to inform her about his sexual relationship with Maxine. The reserved silence was tense.

"Paul, do you need a break?"

"No."

"Okay, tell me why you were so interested in Maxine?"

"I'd heard that she liked to have sex. I'd gone as far as I could with Mitzi. She wanted to remain a virgin, and I didn't."

"Shit, Paul, I can't believe you would dump a girl because she wouldn't give you sex."

"Honey, it wasn't like that."

"Really? What was it like then? Forget it, don't answer that."

Shelley's disgust met his glistening eyes. The intense silence echoed off the walls. She stood, walked to the bar, and poured herself a glass of wine. Instead of returning to the sofa supporting him, she sat at the bar throwing arrows of repulsion his way.

"I'm guessing you had sex with her, right?" He reluctantly nodded. "How many times?"

"You expect me to remember that?"

"Yeah, was it once, a few times, or every time you were with her?"

"Probably, umm, several. I wasn't counting."

"Right, and did you use a condom?"

"What kind of question is that? I don't remember."

"Okay, it's important to know that, so think hard whether you did or not."

As Shelley sent poison darts into his heart, he massaged his temples, straining his mind for the best way to answer the question.

"Well, Paul? How many times?"

"Look, I really don't remember. Why does it matter?"

"Okay, okay, do you know what happened to Maxine?"

"No, after I met Shelley, I never heard from her again. And I never... touched... another... woman. You have to believe me, honey."

"Paul, I want you to look at this photo on my phone. Is this Maxine?"

He nodded and deflected Carla's probing glare.

"Okay, about twenty years ago, her body was found in a drainage ditch at the back of Oakmont's cemetery."

"Screw you, Carla. I need a break."

"Paul, what hell is going on?"

"Nothing, honey. I said I needed a break, detective.

"In a minute, Paul. Take a look at the next photo. You know how to bring it up, just swipe it."

"Shit, that's Ashlee."

"Yeah, now swipe again."

"Damn, Maxine and Ashlee. Wow, they look alike. I can't..."

"Yeah, yeah, they do. You can have your damn break now. Refresh your drink. You're going to need it, big time."

Paul went straight for the bourbon. Woodford Reserve swirled in the bottom of his glass. After downing it, another shot found the glass. He downed it and went for more. After his third pour, he took it to the sofa and sat down. While rubbing his temples, he looked at his wife, hoping to see her loving smile. However, repulsive disgust met his glistening eyes, searing his soul.

"Okay, Paul. We're rerunning the tests to make sure, but science doesn't lie. Based on the DNA analysis, Maxine became pregnant and had a daughter. She named her Ashlee, after her middle name. For whatever reason, she or someone else left her at the Mason County Social Services. Now, do you remember whether you used a damned condom or not?"

"I'm telling you I don't remember."

"So, it's possible you didn't, right?" He reluctantly nodded. "Then it's possible Ashlee could be your daughter. Your mother said Ashlee and you had a special connection. If she were your daughter, maybe that would explain that bond."

The silence imploding in the room was eerie, deafening. Paul's bourbon glass was empty. With his face flushed, beads of sweat exploded on his forehead. As his pulse skyrocketed, his breathing grew heavier. The thought that he may have a daughter was too much for him to bear. Shelley was beyond herself as her complexion grew pale and clammy. It was apparent that Paul hadn't released every skeleton in his closet. Carla hoped their relationship was strong enough to survive his past demons erupting in his soul.

"I see where you are going with this. You think I dropped Maxine's daughter off at social services, then killed her, drove to Oakmont, and dumped her body."

"Yeah, Paul, did you? Did you kill Maxine Hardy?"

Paul stood staring at the glass sliding doors. He began to pace and turned toward his wife who looked away.

"Paul, sit your ass down and answer the damn question. Did you—"

"Hell, no. I…I told you that at the beginning. I… didn't…kill…Maxine. And I sure as hell, didn't kill Ashlee either. You got it…detective."

After another sip of the bourbon, he sat down and deflected Carla's intense glare. He glanced at his wife hoping for forgiveness. Her silent anger stung his soul like never before.

"Paul take a few deep breaths, okay." He nodded and sighed. "Anyway, we believe whoever killed Maxine also killed Ashlee. We don't know why, but we will find out. The only way to prove that you are not Ashlee's father is through DNA analysis. Will you submit to that?"

Shelley, exhausted by anger exploding in her soul, quickly left the living room. Paul's past history left her soul cold and empty. The slamming of the door shattered the intense silence smothering the room. Within minutes, uncontrollable sobbing flowed from the master bedroom. Although Paul had had enough bourbon, he made another trip to the bar. A generous pour of the amber elixir swirled around the bottom of his glass. Although he wanted to make amends with her, he knew this was not the time. Returning to the sofa, he silently contemplated the pros and cons of submitting his DNA. Although the bourbon tasted good, he knew it was compromising his judgment. He stood in defiance and left the condo with his bourbon.

CHAPTER 31

While back in Oakmont, Beth reviewed Charles "Ace" Hutchinson's notes once more before meeting with him at his cabin on Jackson Lake. Since retiring, he has spent most of his time there with his dog, Moocherrenie. She wasn't concerned for her safety and would meet with him without Bernie. She hoped Ace would be more open with her since his relationship with Bernie had gone south over the years. According to his personnel file and Chief Evans' comments, he was an exemplary member of the force. Plus, Bernie knew she was meeting at his cabin should something happen.

After following his directions, she arrived about ten minutes early. While sitting in her car, she observed her surroundings. What she saw was comforting to her. A welcoming porched spanned the front of the cabin. On this pleasant May afternoon, she hoped they would sit on the porch while having their conversation.

She gathered her file folder and exited her car. A short gravel walkway led up to the expansive porch.

After stepping up onto the porch, she took a deep breath and knocked on the door. Immediately, a couple of consecutive roars broke the pristine stillness encompassing the cabin. Within a minute or so, faint footsteps moved closer to the door. Seconds later, Ace stood tall facing her. He was a tall man, with short gray hair styled like a buzz cut. From Beth's observance, he took care of his body.

"Mr. Hutchinson, I'm Beth Pendergast. Here's my ID."

"You can put that away. I know who you are. I still have friends at the department, if you know what I mean. Why don't you call me Ace, and I'll call you Beth, if it's okay?"

"Yeah, works for me."

"Great, come on in. That's old Moocherrenie. Don't worry about him. His bark is bigger than his bite. Let him sniff you, and then he'll saunter off to his favorite spot."

Moocherrenie sniffed her shoes and hand, then found his favorite snoozing spot. As her eyes moved around the living room, she noticed the many photos on the wall. A lady in one of the pictures was probably his wife. Another picture appeared to be a family photo. Ace studied her as she began to move around the room.

"Beth, may I get you a beverage?"

"Water will be fine."

"You got it. Do you mind if I have a beer while we chat?"

"No, not at all."

He retreated to the kitchen for the water and his beer. While he was tending to that, she continued to look at the many pictures. Soft footsteps broke her gaze as he returned from the kitchen. After handing her the water, he offered a cheery toast.

"Ace, I assume the lady in the pictures was your wife."

"Yes. Suzy was a grand lady and a saint. She put up with me until a year ago. She lost her battle with ovarian cancer."

"I'm sorry for your loss."

"Thanks."

"So, the one picture looks like a family one. Is that your son?"

"Oh, that one. Uh, no, he's my nephew but like a son to me. I'd do anything for him when he was growing up. The other lady is Suzy's twin sister, Lucy. Suzy and I never had kids. Anyway, as I said, Jason was like a son to me. I guess, in many ways, I became the father he never had. His dad was in the Marines and lost his life overseas when Jason was about seven years old."

"Sorry to hear that."

"The kid turned out alright though. After his second year in college, the Cincinnati Reds drafted him. He was a pitcher and made it to the big time until he threw his arm out. Anyway, enough about him. What do you want to know about that cold case?"

"Yeah, the cold case. Can we go out on the porch to have this conversation?"

"Sure, but the back porch has a better view. Will that work?"

"Yeah, of course."

She followed him through the kitchen and onto the covered deck. The closing of the door woke Moocherrenie up, and he sauntered through the kitchen, stopping at the door. Ace heard him whimpering and glanced in his direction. After letting him out, he sauntered off to his favorite spot at the top of the steps and flopped down. Ace offered Beth one of the rockers while choosing the one across from her.

"Wow, you're right, a much better view."

"This was Suzy's favorite place in the world."

"I can see why. Anyway, thank you for seeing me and to respect your time, let's get started, okay?" He nodded. "I've read your report several times, but I'd like to hear it from you. And, if you don't mind, I'm going to record our conversation. That way, I won't have to bug you again should I forget something you told me. I'm pretty good at remembering most things, but this case is really important to me."

"Nah, I don't mind. I hope you catch the bastard that committed these heinous crimes."

"Great. Shall we begin?"

Ace nodded and nursed his beer. Over the next twenty minutes, he opened up about that day. It wasn't a whole lot different than what was in his report. She was hoping to hear something helpful. However, that wasn't the case, and disappointment grabbed her soul.

"So, who was first on the scene?"

"Me."

"Wasn't that kind of odd back then?"

"I was in the area when the call came. You know, Beth, I hadn't been a detective that long, and the sight of her body rocked my soul."

"Yeah, I'm sure it did. I felt the same way with this second victim found a few weeks ago in the same place. That's the creepy part of it."

"Well, I know nothing about that one."

"You know, what's weird is, like someone knew

about the previous victim in the cold case and placed the body there, and even weirder is that it's near the first victim's grave. Don't you find that odd?"

"Not really. We live in a demented, sick world. Maybe you got a serial killer on your hands. Have you considered that?"

"Not really. I guess anything is possible. I'll look into it. Now, getting back to the cold case you investigated. How long was it before it went cold?"

"Geez, I'm not sure, maybe a month or so. Back then, after her photo appeared in the newspaper, we thought someone would identify her. That never happened. As each day passed, no leads or tips made it to my desk. I sent information to other law enforcement agencies in the area, but I never heard anything back. I figured she might be a runaway, druggie, or who knows what else. I had other cases that needed my attention, so I ended the investigation."

"I understand. What about the jean jacket?"

"Yeah, I asked one of the female officers if she'd ever heard of it. She hadn't. I asked her to do research, said she found very little. That's when the internet was very young. After that, the case just died. Beth, you'll come to find out that some cases may never be solved, just like your current case."

"I beg to differ, Ace. We've identified both victims and where they're from."

CHAPTER 32

nxiety tortured Ace's face, and his heart and respiration pounded his soul. His beer had grown warm; its taste soured his mouth. He rose from his rocker, tossed the beer over the railing, and entered the kitchen. Beth heard the clinking of ice into a glass. Within a few minutes, he returned with a bourbon on the rocks. After taking a long sip, he returned to his rocker. He began to rock faster, wanting the bourbon to calm the anxiety ravaging his soul. She glared at him and the peaceful serenity around them disappeared. As his eyes wandered erratically, he deflected her probing stare.

"Ace... Ace, are you okay?"

"Uh, yeah. That caught me a little off-guard. So, you identified both victims. Wow, that's some fine detective work. How the hell..."

"The jean jacket, you know, the Angel Hardesty brand, I just followed it. Eventually, it led me to their identities."

"Shit, are these cases connected?"

"I'm glad you asked that. I was getting nowhere in

the cold case. Then when the other body showed up in the cemetery, the similarities were too much to ignore. Cuts to the body were similar; acid burns on the fingers were the same. The clothing on the bodies was eerily identical. The two young women look very similar even though almost twenty years separate them. Here, take a look at both photos side by side."

He stared at their likeness. After a minute of intense glare, he returned the phone to Beth. His forehead glistened under the bright sun. He wiped the sweat away and downed the bourbon. Rising, he went to the kitchen and returned with another one. After returning to his rocker, the bourbon burned as it went down. He coughed and sighed.

"So, what you are telling me is that these two women may be related?"

"Yeah, we believe they're mother and daughter. Our initial DNA results support that. We're rerunning them, but I don't think that will change our assumption. Science doesn't lie."

"Shit, how is that possible?"

"We're working on that."

Ace deflected her probing gaze, tasted the bourbon again, and sighed.

"I don't know what to say. Do you have names?"

"Yeah, nothing has been released to the public yet, so I expect confidentiality here, okay?"

"Yeah, of course. I know what it's like for stuff to get out."

"Yeah, especially if that Kiersten St. Clair somehow finds out."

"Oh, yeah, I've heard about that bitch. But you don't have to worry. What we talk about today stays here."

"Thanks. Maxine Hardy is the victim in your cold case. Does that name ring a bell?"

Ace quickly shook his head several times and took another sip of the bourbon. As he rocked faster and faster, he massaged his temples as embarrassment began to chill his soul.

"No, never heard of her. Where was she from?"

"Gallipolis, Ohio."

"Where's that?"

"It's on the Ohio River, just down from Point Pleasant, West Virginia. Do you know where that is?"

"I've heard of Point Pleasant before, never been there, though."

"Did you send information that far away?"

"As I said, we sent it out to law enforcement agencies, not sure about that area, too long ago."

"Ace, could I bother you to get me some more water?"

"Sure."

Five minutes later, he returned with a fresh glass of ice water and another bourbon for him.

"Thanks. Now, where were we?"

"Something about Maxine Hardy, you think she had a daughter."

"Right. We don't think, we know. DNA proves she had a baby girl."

"What's her name?"

"Ashlee Roberts."

"Never heard of that person either. Where's she from?"

"Point Pleasant. You ever hear of a man named Paul Montgomery?"

"Doesn't ring a bell."

"He's from Point Pleasant as well. He played baseball at the university here. Where did your nephew go to college?"

"He went to Marshall University, so I doubt they know each other. Why do you ask?"

"No reason. Paul's a person of interest in our cases."

"Really? Wow, you got this case on a fast track."

"Well, I wouldn't say that."

"So, why is he a person of interest?"

"Ashlee Roberts lived in his mother's home. Paul's parents were her foster parents. From everything we've learned, someone, maybe even Maxine, left Ashlee at social services in Point Pleasant. She was put in foster care and eventually ended up in the care of Paul's parents. Now, she's dead. Paul went to college here; she ends up dead here. He lives in Florida now; we are questioning him down as we speak. We don't think he's involved in her death, but we think he has valuable information that might lead us to the killer or killers."

"So, how is he involved in Maxine's death?"

"We don't know. They knew each other and even dated for a while. He might even be Ashlee's father and doesn't know it. Paul's mother told us Ashlee and him had this special bond."

"Okay, it doesn't make sense he killed her."

"Right, someone who knew Maxine is more likely."

"Yeah, that makes more sense."

"Anyway, where does your sister-in-law live?"

A puzzled expression lit up Ace's face. Another taste of bourbon eased his anxiety as he deflected Beth's probing eyes.

"That's an odd question."

"The more you get to know me, the more you'll realize I go everywhere with my questions."

"She lives in West Virginia, near Huntington, some small-town west of there."

"Okay, I don't recall you telling me Lucy's last name."

"Another odd question, right? She nodded. "It's Carbone."

"Thanks. I'll try to keep my odd questions to a minimum. By the way, did the cemetery have security cameras when you investigated the first case? I'm sorry that was another odd question."

"I don't remember, but it wouldn't matter. There are many ways to get into the cemetery without someone noticing you, especially at night."

"Interesting. I promise that's the last oddball question."

"So, you found out everything you've told me by following the jean jacket, right?"

"Yeah."

"That's damn good police work."

"Thanks, and the internet helped, too. So, as you mentioned earlier, your nephew played in the big leagues until his arm went out. What does he do now?"

"He's a lawyer in Cincinnati. A big law firm, making lots of money. He'll soon be up for partner. He's married now with a son, and set for life."

"Great. Does he come around much?"

"Not as much as I like, but enough."

"Well, Ace, I appreciate your time and information. I must be on my way. Thank you for everything."

"Well, Beth, I'm glad I could shed some light on the

cases. You know, I felt a little embarrassed today with how fast you found out as much as you did."

"Hey, don't beat yourself up. There's a lot of information available now, so it was easier to find what we did, and we just followed the jean jacket. And who knows, maybe Paul is our man, and then we can be done with the case and won't have to bother you again. If not, I can promise you that I'll find whoever killed those two young women. I'll find out why, and then we'll seek the death penalty."

"Well, good luck with that. You know, even though you feel you're on the right track, you might want to consider a serial killer scenario. I always say, keep all options open."

"Yeah, I'll give that some thought. Thanks again."

"Sure, and if I can be of any more help, just give me a holler, okay?"

She nodded, and he walked her out. While walking to her car, she kept glancing back at him. As she started her car and backed out of his driveway, she kept an eye on him in her rearview mirror. As she disappeared from his view, he entered his home. Several minutes later, he joined Moocherrenie on the back deck, enjoying the peacefulness of the lake. To calm his anxiety, he thought about tomorrow on the lake. He hoped the weather cooperated, and the fish were biting. One thing he didn't have to worry about was whether the beer was ice cold.

CHAPTER 33

After Beth left Ace's cabin, she stopped by the police station before heading home. Through group texts, Beth, Carla, and Bernie had agreed to have a conference call that evening at seven PM. Beth arrived home with enough time to pour a glass of wine and relax a few minutes before initiating the call. She briefly reviewed her notes, especially those not directly related to the case. With five minutes left until the call, she replenished her Pinot Grigio and sat at the kitchen bar. After putting her phone on speaker, she pulled up her favorite call list. Tapping Bernie's number, it rang and rang. Finally, his gruff voice bellowed over the speaker.

"Bernie, you ready?"

"You know me, and I'm always ready."

"Of course, hang on while I pull up Carla's number."

As muted silence filled Bernie's ears, the ringing on Beth's speaker finally stopped as Carla answered the call. After a brief moment, Beth merged them.

"Roll call, please. Bernie, you still on?"

"Why, of course."

"Carla, you still with us? Did you hear Bernie?"

"Yeah, I heard the dickhead."

"Watch it, McBride."

"Okay, you two, let's keep it clean."

"Hey, Bernie, good to hear your voice."

"You, too, McBride."

"Okay, that's much better. I'm going to summarize my findings from my interview with Ace. Then we'll let Carla bring us up to date with her conversations with Paul. Everyone okay with that?"

Carla and Bernie agreed, and the etiquette for this conference call was set. Beth kept her comments to about ten minutes, highlighting what she felt was most important.

"Wow, Beth, you really asked Ace some off-the-wall questions. Why don't you explain your thought process?"

"Carla, you know me. I have these strange hunches—some are right, some are wrong. What bugs me about Ace's investigation back then was how quickly he gave up. From his reports and evaluations, he worked hard to solve most of his cases. He said the sight of Maxine's body rocked his soul, yet he gave in too quickly, which didn't make sense. It didn't take us long to identify the victims; things just don't add up."

"Okay, so, do you think he is somehow involved?"

"I don't know. It's just a strange feeling. I think we should keep him on our radar. Bernie, after hearing all of this, what do you think? You were there that day."

"Yeah, I remember he was upset I showed up since it wasn't my beat. I do recall that everyone there were his good buddies, especially, Dannie Spencer, and Joe Ferguson. I don't know if that means anything. As far as I know, they were all good cops."

"Beth?"

"Yeah, Carla."

"Let's keep him on our radar. Let Chief Evans know about your conversation, should Ace contact him, okay? And remember, we have to be very careful when it might involve one of our own. Right, Bernie?"

"Damn straight, and it could be a hornet's nest if we were wrong."

"Got it, guys. Now, let's hear what Carla found out with Paul."

Over the next fifteen minutes, Carla informed them about her conversations with Paul. She explained how strained Shelley and Paul's relationship had grown. She also told them about the blood on the door handle embarrassment. Although Beth and Bernie agreed they would have done the same thing, they also had a hearty laugh at her expense.

"Carla?"

"Yeah, dickhead. That's right. I said I'd be nice, sorry."

"Right, so Paul had a sexual relationship with Maxine. Then Ashlee could be his daughter, right?"

"Yeah, Bernie, but he might not know that since Ashlee was dropped off at social services, which tells me whoever it was didn't want anyone to know about the baby or its father. Even if he knew, it makes no sense to commit murder. I don't think he is the father or the murderer, but I think he knows more that may help us."

"Carla, uh…"

"Yeah, Beth, spit it out."

"What do you think he knows?"

"Not sure. Maybe it's a hunch like you have. It may take some time to find out. Anyway, he hasn't said no to a DNA test. Knowing the current status of Shelley and Paul's relationship, it's kind of a no-win situation for him. I will press him on that tomorrow. Anything else?"

"Uh, yeah."

"What, Beth?"

"Ask him this off-the-wall question when he is not expecting it."

"An off-the-wall question...okay."

"Ask him if he's ever heard of Jason Carbone before. Based on his response, see if he will open up. I'd be interested in what he has to say."

"Okay, not sure what you're going after, but it couldn't hurt."

"Yeah, then ask him if he ever heard of Charles 'Ace' Hutchinson."

"Now that's far out, but okay. Anything else from either of you?"

Beth and Bernie simultaneously gave her a negative response. After some friendly banter, the call ended. Five minutes later, Bernie's phone rang. Recognizing the number, he quickly answered.

"What do you want now, McBride? I thought we all were done."

"Yeah, me, too. Where do you think Beth is going with this hunch that Ace might be involved?"

"I'm not sure. Maybe it's his condescending attitude toward the cold case or that he gave up too easily. I wasn't involved back then, so I don't know how true that might be. Chief Evans wasn't with us, and most of the officers on the case aren't with the police force any longer. I think most moved away..."

"Bernie?"

"Yeah, except his old female pal, Dannie Spencer. I'll look her up."

"Great. See what you come up with, and don't tell Beth you're doing it, okay?"

"You got it."

Back at Beth's apartment, she went for more Pinot Grigio. After a generous pour, she retreated to her bedroom. She placed the wine on the nightstand, grabbed her laptop, and entered Jason Carbone. Her search results loaded. Quickly scrolling through them, one on the third search page seized her attention. As she opened the story up, she grabbed her wine glass, taking a big taste. She finished the story and smiled. Retrieving her phone, she selected one of her recently called numbers and waited for an answer. It rang and rang and rang, eventually going to Ace's voicemail. She ended the call without leaving a message.

While nursing her Pinot Grigio, her thoughts drifted to Ace's reference to a serial-killer scenario. Although interesting, what she and Bernie discovered didn't support such an idea since the victims based on DNA are likely related. However, she'd check it out and, hopefully, enlist her fiancée's help. After all, he was an FBI agent.

CHAPTER 34

After the previous night's conference call, Beth and Bernie planned to continue their investigation in the Point Pleasant and Gallipolis area on Wednesday. They both believed there was much more to learn about Maxine Hardy. Although they had planned to leave in the afternoon, the morning flew by quickly. Furthermore, Sherry had left her a message about meeting with them before the day was over. Beth hoped Sherry had the DNA reports on Maxine Hardy and Ashlee Roberts confirming they were mother and daughter.

With Bernie nestled in his chair at his workstation, he glanced at Beth with questionable eyes. She caught his gaze, and he quickly looked away. She heard footsteps nearing her desk. Chief Evans' glare sent her pulse racing. The first thing that entered her mind was Ace. Had he contacted Chief Evans regarding her visit with him? She remembered Carla urging her to let him know about her meeting with Ace. She waited for the hammer to come down. However, he walked past her. She was relieved, but now seeing him jogged her memory. It was the perfect opportunity to follow through on Carla's request. She immediately rose from her desk and quickly caught up with him.

"Chief."

"Yeah, Beth, did you need something?"

"Do you have a few minutes? I need to discuss something with you regarding Ace Hutchinson."

"Ace, yeah. You were going to meet with him, right?"

"Yeah."

"How'd that go?"

Her pulse began to race. With her heart pumping, her eyes broke contact with the chief. After a deep breath, she met his questionable expression. He repeated his question and waited for her to respond. Bernie, observing them, wondered how she was going to handle it.

"Yeah, that's what I wanted to talk to you about. Do you have enough time to discuss it now? I only need about five minutes." He nodded. "Okay, can we go to the conference room? I want to keep this between us, okay?"

He nodded, and they walked to the conference room. After closing the door, they sat across from each other. At first, silence captivated the room. Beth took several deep breaths to calm her thumping heart.

"Well, Beth, what's this all about?"

"Right, uh, Ace is doing okay. He sent his regards. Anyway he seemed really agitated as we discussed the cold case, his case."

"So, I think it's natural for any detective that has a cold case reopened to be a little defensive."

"Yeah, I guess so. Did Carla inform you of what we've discovered?"

"Like what?"

"I guess not. Okay, we know the identity of both victims. I'm sorry this is a surprise. It's my fault for assuming Carla informed you."

"Let's hear the rest of it."

"The Jane Doe from the cold case is Maxine Hardy of Gallipolis, Ohio. The Jane Doe from the most recent case is Ashlee Roberts from Point Pleasant, West Virginia."

"Okay, that's good, right?"

"Yeah, but…"

"But what?"

"Chief, DNA results indicate that Ashlee is Maxine's daughter. Sherry—"

"Shit, are you kidding me?"

"No, chief. We are meeting with Sherry this afternoon to confirm this. She reran the tests just to make sure. We are keeping this information under wraps; we don't want it out in the public."

"Yeah, I get it. So, back to Ace. How does this discovery concern him?"

"Well, in talking with him, the names came out. I hope he can be trusted."

"He can, but what does that have to do with him?"

"When I told him that his Jane Doe was Maxine Hardy, his whole disposition changed immediately. I could tell it bothered him. He even switched from beer to bourbon, and he had several of them during our meeting."

"Okay, did you accuse him of anything?" Beth shook her head. "Is there anything else?"

"Yeah, he brought up the idea of a serial-killer scenario which I believe is a little far-fetched given the victims are likely mother and daughter. That doesn't make sense in a serial-killer profile, does it?"

"Not really, but anything's possible these days."

"Yeah, maybe. Chief, I think he might be involved or know something, and I wanted you to know."

"Involved, how?"

"I don't know, just a hunch or intuition. Anyway, if he comes to you…"

"Don't worry, I doubt he will. Thanks for letting me know, and good work on finding the identities. What's next for you and Bernie?"

"We are heading back to the Point Pleasant-Gallipolis area. There's more to learn up there about Maxine and who Ashlee's father is. I don't have time to tell you everything. When Carla returns from Florida, we'll meet and tell you where we are. She's talking with Paul Montgomery about Ashlee Roberts."

"Carla's working from Florida. What the…"

"It's complicated. We'll meet when she returns. Hopefully, we might have the case solved or well on our way to solving it."

After Chief Evans cooled down, Beth felt relieved. Although she likely got Carla in a little bit of hot water, she wouldn't care. She did things her way, which wasn't always by the book. They left the conference room together and chatted as they approached her workstation. They exchanged a few words; he continued walking to the common area.

She sat at her desk, put her hands to her face, and breathed a sigh of relief that he wasn't that upset with her. She glanced around the common area looking for Bernie. After not seeing him, she assumed he had left for lunch without her. At first, that bothered her, but she wasn't all that hungry after evading being in hot water with the chief.

While waiting for Bernie to return, she entered the criteria for serial-killer possibilities involving family members and waited for the results. Finally, the results loaded. As she scanned the results, disappointment flooded her soul. She grabbed her iPhone and pulled up her favorite list. Finding Scott's number, she pushed on the call icon. After three rings, he answered. She explained her hypothetical scenario to him. He told her he would comb the FBI databases for any possibilities and let her know when he arrived back from his conference tonight.

CHAPTER 35

Meanwhile, back in Redington Shores, Carla continued her conversation with Paul. Last night's questioning ended with him contemplating the pros and cons of agreeing to a DNA test. It was a long time ago since Paul lost his virginity to Maxine, and his faded memory couldn't validate whether he used a condom or not. But in the grand scheme of things, it didn't matter. As he thought about Ashlee and their special relationship, he had to know whether she was his daughter no matter how it affected his marriage. After a lengthy discussion with Shelley, they decided he would submit a DNA sample. With Shelley running some errands with Chris, Carla and Paul had the privacy they needed.

"Okay, Paul, I'll call Deputy Sheriff Jimmy Ramirez and arrange for us to meet with him for the sample. I want to make sure it won't be contaminated. Maybe we can get this done tomorrow morning. You okay with that?"

"I have a DNA sample on file at Gannon Biometrics,

my employer. Because we work in foreign countries, it's required, you know, if something were to happen. Sometimes we are in unstable countries conducting research. I'm sure you get the picture, right?"

"Yeah, I do. However, I prefer to have one done and shipped overnight to our forensic department. You can contact your employer and have them email your results, but we'll use the results of your sample."

"Sure, set it up. We can do it tomorrow. I'll contact our human resources department to email the file. Everything is confidential, so there should not be any concern with upper management."

"Great, thank you."

"Of course. I didn't have anything to do with Ashlee's death. If necessary, I'll even take a polygraph. We can do that tomorrow as well, if you want."

"Okay, maybe I can set that up, too. Perhaps that will ease the anxiety Shelley is experiencing. Now, let's talk about Maxine. You know, how long did you date her?"

"Not long, maybe just a month or so. We had some good times together, but I knew it wasn't real. Perhaps it was just a physical attraction. She was hot-looking and sexually active. You know, she's the one that initiated the relationship. After an American Legion game in Gallipolis, she and two other girls approached a few of us. Yeah, Sharma, uh…"

"Harkness?"

"Yeah, how'd you know?"

"It's not important. Who was the other girl?"

"Geez, that was a long time ago. Give me a minute or two. I'm going to fix myself a bourbon. You want one?"

"Do you have Jameson?"

"Should've known. McBride, an old Irish name. Yeah, coming right up. Neat or on the rocks?"

"On the rocks, please."

After retrieving two Waterford glasses, he placed a large crystal-clear ice cube in each. Seconds later, the amber liquid splashed across the ice into the bottom of the glass. Picking them up, he handed Carla her liquid lover. He sat across from her and massaged his temples, hoping to remember Maxine and Sharma's other sister-like girlfriend. After making eye contact with Carla, he held his glass toward her, and she reciprocated and mouthed "cheers."

"Ah, Jameson, smooth and silky. Thanks. Now, did you think of the other girl's name?"

"No, is it important?"

"Paul, everything's important in finding justice."

"Okay, I'll try harder. What else do you want to know?"

"I know this may be off the wall, but have you ever heard of Jason Carbone?"

"Seriously, what's he got to do with this."

"Let's just say his name came up and leave it at that."

"Yeah, major league baseball player until his arm went out."

"Did you ever play against him, you know, high school or college?"

"Both, well, sort of. He was a member of an American Legion team in Gallipolis. I can't remember if he lived there, maybe around there somewhere. Uh"

"What?"

"Mackenzie, that's her name. Mackenzie Adams, but everyone called her Mac. I remember her now. Yeah, she had it hot for Rob, one of our infielders. From what I remember, she was a real looker as well."

"Awesome, now what about Jason? Did he ever hook up with Maxine?"

"I'd heard after Maxine, and I broke up she went after him. Gosh, too long ago to remember. Hope that helps."

"It has. Moving on now, have you ever heard the name Charles 'Ace' Hutchinson?"

"Should I have?"

"He's a retired detective with the Oakmont Police Department and Jason's uncle."

"Nope, it doesn't ring a bell. What does this have to do with the case?"

"Ace was the detective who investigated Maxine's death. He didn't know that was her name back then; he thought she was a loner, druggie, and who knows what else. My partner thinks he quit on the case too early."

"Wow, small world. Is there anything else I may help you with?"

"Another Jameson?"

"Yeah, of course. How'd you get started on Irish whiskey?"

"My dad, he loved it."

"I don't remember my real dad, but Harold did his best to raise me. I always wondered what it would've been like, you know…"

"I always say, don't ever worry about what could've been, just cherish what you have."

Paul took her glass and replenished their drinks. After handing Carla hers, he took his out on the balcony and sat in the lounger. On the other hand, Carla retreated to the guest bedroom to call Deputy Sheriff Ramirez. After explaining everything in detail, they agreed to meet at the sheriff's department at nine o'clock in the morning. While talking to him, Shelley and Chris had returned and joined Paul on the balcony. After Carla finished her conversation with Deputy Ramirez, she sent Beth and Bernie a text about Mackenzie Adams. As Carla joined everyone outside, muted chatter and laughter greeted her.

"What's so funny, guys?"

Shelley quickly interjected, "Umm, nothing. Why don't we eat here tonight? While we were out, we bought a smoked fish dip Paul and I like so much. We also picked up some fresh shrimp."

"Sounds good. We are done for the day, right, Paul."

"Yeah, Carla. I've had enough for one day."

"Yeah, me, too."

"Okay then, let's head to the beach until dinner. Carla, why don't you and Chris stop and get the chairs?"

"You got it."

"Paul and I will grab a couple of bottles of Prosecco and four flutes and meet you there."

CHAPTER 36

With three o'clock fast approaching, Bernie was not back from lunch, and Beth wondered why. She hit his number; it rang and rang, eventually going to voicemail. She ended the call without leaving him a message. She didn't want to come across as a worrier. If he noticed her call, she would tell him it was a butt call. She was anxious to find out the DNA results from Sherry regarding Maxine and Ashlee before leaving for Point Pleasant and Gallipolis.

Out of her peripheral vision, Bernie stood in the common area shooting the bull with several other detectives. He felt her eyes on him and sauntered over to her. While glancing back and forth at the big clock on the wall and then at him, she just rolled her eyes.

"Where have you been?"

"Lunch and a secret mission."

"Secret mission, right."

"Uh, yeah, really, a secret mission."

"Okay, Mr. Spy-man, tell me all about it."

"Now, if I told you, it wouldn't be secret anymore, would it?"

"Forget it. Let's head to the conference room. Sherry should be joining us shortly."

After entering, they took their usual seats across from each other. Within a minute, Sherry joined them and closed the door. She sat at the head of the table, looking all queen-like even though Carla wasn't present. At first, silence stood still at the table as she glanced back and forth at them. She wanted them to know she was in charge, that was her style. As Bernie met her smirky expression, he cleared his throat and smiled.

"Okay, Bernie, I get it. You want to know about the DNA results and any other new information regarding the two victims."

"That's why we are here. So, let's not waste any time. What do you have to tell us?"

"Okay, guys, nothing has changed. Without a doubt, Jane Doe number two is the daughter of Jane Doe number one."

"That just confirms what we already suspected. Anything else that we should know before leaving tomorrow for Point Pleasant and Gallipolis?"

"Well, Beth, yeah, there is something else. The toxicology report for Jane Doe number two indicates a high concentration of a date-rape drug. Whoever is responsible for her death subdued her with it, then finished her off."

"In the autopsy report, was there any evidence of sexual assault?"

"None, Bernie. This murder had nothing to do with any sexual assault. Based on the autopsy, Jane Doe number two was still a virgin."

"Sherry, remember, her name is Ashlee."

"Oh, right. Sorry, Beth."

"I didn't expect that based on what we found out in Point Pleasant."

"Why's that, Bernie?"

"Leaving home, then probably homeless…just assumed she did about anything." While Sherry's angry eyes sent darts in his direction, Bernie felt a slight kick under the table. "Okay, ladies, I get it. I shouldn't assume, and I'm sorry. Now, anything else, Sherry?"

"No, that's it. What about you guys?"

"Sherry, concerning Jane Doe number one, did you look at the toxicology report from twenty years ago?"

"Beth, I reviewed it, and there was a high presence of a sedative. Not sure if it was a date-rape drug, but it was more than enough to subdue her."

"Okay, Jane Doe has a name, Maxine Hardy. We hope to discover more about our victims over the next couple of days."

"Well, good luck. By the way, McBride must still be on her honeymoon, right?"

"Uh, sort of."

"Either she is, or she's not. Which is it, Bernie?"

"Both. A situation occurred in Florida that needed her attention. She's been interviewing a person of interest in our case."

"What's the connection?"

"Ashlee Roberts. Paul Montgomery, the husband of her friend Shelley, knew her. Paul's mother raised Ashlee. He also knew and had a sexual relationship with Ashlee's mother, Maxine."

"Hmm, that's interesting, Beth. Could he be Ashlee's father?"

"Funny you should ask that. You will be receiving an overnight package on Thursday. It will contain a DNA swab from Paul; it will be from the Pinellas County Sheriff in Florida. You will also receive an email from Gannon Biometrics with a file of his DNA results. I guess Carla wouldn't trust the report. So, umm, we'll wait and see."

"So, is he a suspect in the death of Ashlee or Maxine?"

"That's the million-dollar question we're trying to answer. Paul is adamant that he didn't kill her or Maxine. Now, if he is the father, that changes things. Maybe we have a motive. It could be blackmail or something else. Right now, it's a big jigsaw puzzle, and unfortunately, we don't have the right pieces to solve it. It's one big enigma right now, but we'll get to the bottom of it."

"Wow, Beth, good luck again."

"Yeah. Hey, you worked here when Ace was here, right?"

"Yeah. Does he have anything to do with this?"

"Not really. I met with him about the cold case; he wasn't the most cooperative. Then, when I told him we'd discovered the identity of Jane Doe number one from his case, he kind of went off on me."

"Well, Ace can be a real asshole. We had our differences, but we managed to get along okay."

"Yeah, you could say that. Do you think Ace is a dirty cop?"

"Don't go there Beth, if you want a career here. Now, anything else?"

"No, thank you."

"You got it, Bernie. Soon as I get the samples and

report, I'll put it on the fast track and hopefully have the results when you return from your trip."

Sherry gathered up her files and left the conference room. Feeling like a whipped puppy, Beth sat silent as Bernie glared deep into her soul. Beth did her best to deflect his angry eyes.

"What?"

"Listen, Beth, what is it with Ace? You seem adamant that he could be involved when nothing gives us cause."

"I just have this burning in my soul that he knows more, hiding something, or he may be involved."

"You need to let this go before it destroys you. What motive could he have? Yeah, he let the case go cold way too early. I agree with you, but unless we have some definitive proof or evidence, we need to focus our efforts on what evidence we have, and none of it points to Ace."

"Yeah, I guess you're right. Where were you this afternoon?"

"Okay, if you must know. I ran into one of Ace's old buddies, Dannie Spencer. She was at the crime scene with him. They've stayed in touch over the years. I asked her about the case; she believed he let it go cold too soon. I remember Ace telling me he asked her about the Angel Hardesty clothing line, that she'd never heard of it. She told me she'd checked it out and told Ace all about it. Other than that, she had nothing else to say."

"See, I told you. He knows more, and I'll get it out of him."

"Beth, please leave it be for all of our sakes, okay?"

CHAPTER 37

After entering her apartment, Beth deadbolted the door. Although she didn't feel she was in any danger, it was a habit of hers and a demand of Scott's. She put her purse on the kitchen bar and headed straight for the refrigerator for the Pinot Grigio. It had called her name all the way home after being scolded by Bernie. His warning still burned in her soul. As the white wine swirled around the bottom of her glass, she sniffed it several times, wanting the aroma of fresh pears and lemons to ease her anxiety.

Her fiancé, Scott, would soon be home. She hoped he had some helpful information regarding serial killers when the victims were related. Even though she wanted to believe Ace wasn't involved, her nagging armchair-quarterback mentality wouldn't let her drop it. In the Penny Miracle case, she was right regarding a person of interest that Bernie overlooked in his investigation. Perhaps he was wrong again regarding Ace. She understood the ramifications of accusing a member of the law enforcement brotherhood, but that wasn't going to deter her inquiries into Ace.

While sitting at the kitchen bar, she savored the Pinot Grigio. The sound of keys in the deadbolt sent her pulse racing. The opening of the door brought a smile to her face. After tasting the fruitiness of the wine, she moistened her lips. Within a minute, she tasted Scott's sweetness as she melted into his arms. His burning desire swallowed her sexuality. As they both searched for more passion, a tear surfaced in the corner of her eye.

Although their hormones were heating up, she ended his passionate quest for more of her. At the moment, she was more interested in what information he had than a quickie. Later, there would be plenty of time to re-kindle their hormonal needs and wants. As their eyes locked on each other, she rolled her eyes and smiled.

"Which would you prefer, beer, bourbon, or wine?"

"How about you?"

"Later, you horny boy."

"Then a beer will do."

"A West Sixth Amber coming right up."

She opened the refrigerator, grabbed the only one left, and opened it. After reaching into the freezer, she pulled out a frosted mug pouring the amber liquid into it, forming a perfect head. She handed it to him, who immediately raised it toward her. She grabbed her wine glass, quickly replenished it, and joined him for a toast. Minutes later, they sat on the sofa. As soft music began to fill the room, they enjoyed the ambiance surrounding them.

"So, honey, what did you find out for me, you know, about serial killers involving family members as victims."

"Yeah, that. There's just not much information out there. I guess anything is possible, but it doesn't make any sense when almost twenty years separate them. If the victims weren't related, you might have a serial-killer scenario. However, unless another body surfaces, it's not something I'd recommend."

"You're no help...uh, forget I said that, okay?"

"I know you. Where are you going with that?"

"You remember me telling you about Ace, the retired detective, right?" He nodded. "Perhaps you can delve into his past, of course, discreetly."

"Beth, honey, we promised each other not to ask that kind of favor. You could get about everything you want to know by working with—"

"You mean Sherry, right?"

"Yeah, she should be able to dig into a lot of stuff."

"She could, however, I'm being told by her, by Bernie, even Carla to let it be. You know, going after one of your own creates big problems for everyone."

"Yeah, it can, especially if you're wrong. So, if you're extremely adamant about his possible involvement, you need to be careful."

"Yeah, that's why I'm asking for your help. If Carla and Bernie find out I'm still pursuing him as a person of interest, I'm positive they would take me off the case. I need to play it cool until I can convince them differently."

"Sell me on why you think he could be involved."

"He let that case go stone-cold way too early. I learned today that one of his colleagues told him she tracked down the jean jacket, but he never pursued it. I did, and it led us to the identities of both victims. He's the one who mentioned a serial-killer scenario was possible. He encouraged me to consider it. When I told him Maxine Hardy was the "Jane Doe" in his case, it disturbed him. He tossed almost a full glass of beer over the railing and stormed into his kitchen and returned with a bourbon."

"So…"

"I believe he's heard that name before. I admit it doesn't make sense right now. Call it a hunch, female intuition, or a wild, crazy assumption. I don't know…"

"Okay, I'll see what I can do."

"Great, thank you, honey. Umm, have you ever heard of Jason Carbone?"

"Who hasn't? Major league pitcher until he threw out his arm."

"Right, and Ace's nephew. You remember me telling you Carla is in Florida interviewing Paul Montgomery, a person of interest in the most recent case? Turns out Jason Carbone dated Maxine as well."

"Okay, that's interesting."

"Yeah, consider this crazy idea. Bear with me, and don't laugh. Ace told me he'd do anything for Jason, who grew up without a father. Jason, who had his whole major league future in front of him. Let's just say Jason gets Maxine pregnant, which could run his major league career. After the baby is born, she decides to blackmail Jason. In the heat of the moment, he kills her. Not knowing what to do, he calls his Uncle Ace to help him. The baby girl gets dropped off at social services, and the body ends up in Oakmont. It's Ace's case, and he lets it go stone-cold. What do you think?"

"You have one wild imagination, honey."

"Yeah, I certainly do."

She grabbed his hand and squeezed it softly, sending

a tingling up his arm. His eyes met hers; she leaned in toward him as she moistened her lips, rocking his hormones. Within seconds, their heat and passion exploded. Several minutes later, she led him to their bedroom.

CHAPTER 38

With Beth and Bernie traveling to Gallipolis, Carla continued her investigation in Redington Shores. Like the previous days, she and Chris would enjoy the beach until around three in the afternoon. Carla promised him that she would only put her detective hat on after they were done on the beach. Today Shelley and Paul decided to do their own thing. After Carla and Chris entered the condo, the master bedroom door was closed. Grunts and heavy breathing emanated from the room. Carla and Chris quietly entered the guest bedroom, hoping not to disturb them. After showering together, they returned to the living room refreshed.

Chris opened the refrigerator, grabbing a local craft beer and a frosty mug. He retrieved a bourbon glass, threw a few ice cubes in, and poured Carla a Jameson. Remaining seated at the kitchen bar, they enjoyed a toast. Moments later, a squeaky master bedroom door caught their attention. Shelley came into view with radiance spewing from her soul. She had learned things the past few days that rocked her world. However, maybe that's what she and Paul needed to rediscover their passion for each other.

"Hey guys, Paul will be out in a few minutes. We've been re-bonding if you know what I mean."

"Yeah, we all need to find that passion that brought us together in the first place. I'm happy for you."

"Thanks, Carla."

Paul's voice filled the room. He moved in behind the counter and hugged his wife—Carla, like what she saw. Paul grabbed a bottle of Chardonnay out of the refrigerator. After retrieving two wine glasses, a generous pour swirled around the bottom of each glass. After handing Shelley her wine, he held his glass toward her for a toast. As the glasses clinked, they took a sip and blessed it with a gentle kiss. While Paul motioned Carla to the sofa, Shelley and Chris moved to the balcony giving them privacy.

"Carla, where did we end up?"

"I believe I asked you if you knew Ace."

"Yeah, but as I said yesterday, I never heard of him."

"Right, well, I don't think he's involved because there's no plausible motive. Anyway, let's talk about Ashlee if you don't mind." Paul nodded and tasted the silkiness of the Chardonnay. "Please tell me about her; according to your mom, you two had a special bond. I believe your mom called it a connection."

"Umm, my mom said that on many occasions. If it turns out she's my daughter, that could explain the connection."

"We found a laptop in Ashlee's closet and your mom let us have it. We're trying to get it fixed to see what's on it. Did you know about it?"

"Yeah, I bought it for her."

"Hmm, do you know what's on it?"

"I think she mainly used it for internet stuff."

"Did she ever ask you if you knew who her father was?"

"Funny you asked that. You know we have similar characteristics, and out of the blue, one day, she asked me if I was her father. It shocked the hell out of me. I really didn't know how to answer her."

"Wow, what did you eventually tell her?"

"I told her I wasn't, but if she really wanted to know, she could submit a DNA sample to one of the online services that are out there now. We talked about it, and if she wanted to go through with it, I would help her. I don't know if she ever did or not."

"Well, whether she did or not doesn't matter. In a few days, we'll know."

"Yeah, funny how things work out."

"How's that?"

"If I'm Ashlee's father, it'll be the only child I'll ever have, and now she's dead."

"I'm sorry for your loss regardless of how it turns out. At least you have memories. And if she is your daughter, they'll be all the more special."

"I guess so."

"When was the last time you talked with her?"

"Probably about six months ago."

"Hmm, that's interesting. Your mom told my partner she hadn't had any communication from her for well over a year or more."

"Ashlee and my mom didn't have the best relation-ship. My mom disagreed with her life choices. Ashlee told me my mom blew her stack when she decided to leave. She was all my mom had after my dad died. She wanted that mother-daughter bond she never had."

"That's too bad. Given her death, maybe your mom was right. Maybe Ashlee's life choices are the reason she's dead."

"Maybe so, but one thing is for sure, I didn't have anything to do with her death."

"Okay, you've told me that so many times, I'm beginning to believe you. I see it in your eyes. I hear it in your soul."

"So, why are you giving me the third degree?"

"I need to consider everything. I've got two dead women, who are mother and daughter, back in Oakmont and no real definitive leads or motive. I could have a serial killer now resurfacing. However, that doesn't make sense because they are related. Maybe the killer didn't know that, so I have to consider all possibilities, including you as a suspect or a person of interest, perhaps both."

"Yeah, tell you what, I think we're done here."

"Yeah, of course. I appreciate you opening up about Ashlee. I hope you and Shelley will get through this regardless of what the DNA results show. Paul... Paul, look at me. I didn't want to be working on my honeymoon. Chris is a saint."

"From what I can tell, he's a keeper. As for Shelley and me, I think we will be okay. Let's join them on the balcony."

"Yeah, sounds great, but we both need our drinks refreshed."

"Yeah, I think we do. Give me your glass, and I'll join you on the balcony."

After handing him her glass, she joined Shelley and

Chris on the balcony. Minutes later, Paul arrived with a bottle of Prosecco and champagne flutes. After he filled the glasses, Carla offered up a toast to health, happiness, and friendship.

"Hey, guys. My investigation is over down here. Paul, no more questions, okay?"

"Yeah, of course, but if—"

"No, Paul, we're done. You have been a big help. Let's all enjoy the rest of our time here, okay? Cheers again."

CHAPTER 39

Beth and Bernie arrived in Gallipolis around two o'clock in the afternoon. Bernie was a little disappointed that Beth decided to start their third trip to the Mid-Ohio Valley in Gallipolis. It meant that Hillbilly Hotdogs would have to wait for another time. However, he knew that Remo's Italian Weinery would be their dinner destination. Speaking with Sharma again was their first priority of the day. They were hoping to learn the whereabouts of Mackenzie Adams, and maybe she had the answer to break their case open.

Remo's Italian Weinery greeted them in silence. Behind the bar area, Sharma prepped for the early dinner crowd. She glanced at them and smiled briefly before returning her focus to the task at hand. As they watched her from just inside the door, it reminded Beth of her days working at a local hamburger joint in her hometown.

They approached the bar area and sat watching her continue her methodical regimen. As the silence continued, Bernie cleared his throat, distracting her. She finally turned around, meeting their inquisitive demeanor. After promptly pouring them a glass of water with lemon, she placed them on the bar addressing them.

"You two were here last week, right?" As they nodded, she continued. "Detective Kowalski and Beth, right?"

"Great memory, Sharma. We want to ask you a few more questions. Is now a good time?"

"Yeah, I've got about an hour before the early crowd arrives. You know, factory workers stopping for a beer before going home. What kind of questions, detective?"

"Beth, she's all yours."

"Does the name Mackenzie Adams ring a bell?"

"Wow. Mac. I haven't thought of her in years. I heard she's divorced with three teenage daughters. They look just like her, which could be a problem for her, if you know what I mean."

"No, I don't know what you mean. Please, tell us about Mac."

"In high school, she was, hot, as hot as hot could be. Hmm, I can't believe I said that. Anyway, she was, let's just say, experienced in the love game. Every guy wanted her, even my boyfriend. That's why I ditched him."

"Okay, we get it. We understand Mac and Maxine were like sisters. What do you remember about that?"

"Of course, detective. Yeah, like two peas in a pod. You saw one. You saw the other. I even heard one time they shared a guy. Hmm, you know, a ménage à trois. They screwed all kinds of guys. Age didn't matter. Well, nothing older than, say, forty. So, what does Mac have to do with your investigation?"

"We don't know. Sorry for interrupting, Beth."

"No problem, Bernie. Where can we find her, Sharma?"

"Give me your business card, and I'll put her last known address on the back. Anyway, if you find her, please don't mention my name, okay?"

"Umm, of course. We'll be back later for dinner. Is there a special tonight?"

"Of course, detective. Even though we specialize in Italian sausage and hotdogs, we have authentic Italian dishes as well. Tonight's special is lasagna with zesty Italian sausage and marinara sauce. The sausage and pasta are homemade."

"Bernie, that's right up your alley. Make sure you wait on us, okay?"

"You got it, Beth."

Twenty minutes later, Bernie pulled in front of a white frame house on the outskirts of town. If it was Mac's home, it could use some tender loving care. On the front porch, old wooden rockers had seen their day. The door hadn't been painted in years. What was once bright red was now an ugly-faded variation needing attention. After seeing the absence of a doorbell, Bernie knocked several times. After a moment of silence, the door opened. By the description Sharma gave them, they had the right place. Mac still had everything a man wanted. With an abundance of perfect curves, Mac could still turn heads and capture any room she entered.

"Mackenzie Adams?"

"Who wants to know?"

"I'm Beth Pendergast, and he's Detective Kowalski. We're from Oakmont, Kentucky, and have a few questions about Maxine Hardy. May we come in?"

"Maxine… I haven't heard from her in like twenty years. Does she live in Oakmont?"

"Sort of."

"What does that mean? She either does or doesn't."

"Mrs. Adams."

"Yeah, Detective Kowalski. That's Polish, right?"

"Maxine's been dead for almost twenty years. May we come in? And yes, it's Polish."

As Mac's bright and radiant complexion faded away, she opened the door wider, inviting them into her home. She motioned them to sit on the sofa covered by a worn-out cover. Mac sat across from them in an equally worn recliner.

"So, detective, she's been dead for about twenty years. Wow, I thought she just moved away after her daughter was born."

"Mac, since you mentioned her daughter, I want to ask you about that. Did you know who the father was? We've heard she had many partners."

"Have you talked with that Sharma lady, that nosey bitch?"

"Mac, that's not important. Just tell us what you remember, okay?"

"Sure, Miss…"

"Pendergast, but you can call me Beth, okay?"

"Uh, sorry, Beth it is. I don't know. I'm not good at remembering names. Maxine kept that private to everyone, not even her father knew."

"Do you know why?"

"No. I'm sure she had her reasons. What else may I help you with?"

Up to this point, Bernie was happy to observe Beth's

relentless demeanor. However, he was itching to find out more and chimed in.

"We know she was involved with older men. Do you remember anyone in particular?"

"Detective, no, I don't. There were several, and they didn't last long. For that matter, none of her relationships lasted long. The father could be anyone. Sorry I couldn't be of more help. Do you know where her daughter lives?"

"She's dead."

"Damn, how, where?"

"A cemetery caretaker found her body in the same place that Maxine's body was found."

"Shit, that's creepy, detective."

"Yeah, it is. Are you sure you don't remember any of those older guys that dated her?'

"I really don't remember."

"We know Jason Carbone dated Maxine. Could he be the father?"

"Look, Beth. I don't know."

"Did you ever date Jason or Paul Montgomery?"

"Paul, no. Jason, yeah. We dated for a while. Jason, I remember his Uncle Charlie like it was yesterday. He was a strange dude, maybe even a pervert. Jason introduced me to him. I felt his eyes undress me several times that day. He gave me the creeps."

CHAPTER 40

eth remembered Ace saying he didn't know where Gallipolis was. Alarm bells went off as she stared into Mac's soul. Beth knew he was lying all along, but why? Mac's wandering eyes told Beth she knew more.

"Uncle Charlie…that's interesting. Was that here in Gallipolis?"

"Yeah, I ain't been anywhere else in my life. Well, maybe Point Pleasant. That's the big city for me."

"Did Jason's uncle ever meet Maxine?"

"Yeah, that same day. We ran into them downtown."

"Could Uncle Charlie have dated Maxine?"

"Not that I remember. I think he was married at the time, maybe just a couple of months or so. What a jerk, married for a few months and already looking at other ladies. You know, if he'd been married to me, I would have castrated him."

"Did you ever see Jason's uncle again?"

"Not that I recall."

"Okay, did Maxine ever mention his name to you?"

"Let's see, that was a long time ago. Sorry, I don't remember."

"That's okay. Bernie, do you have any questions for Mac?"

"No, I think that should do it. Thank you, you've been a big help."

"Of course. I'll show you out."

After leaving the house, intense silence flowed between them as they sat in Bernie's car. Beth knew Bernie was upset for questioning Mac about Ace. However, Beth didn't care since Mac opened the door when she mentioned his name. Beth took advantage of the opportunity regardless of the consequences. The next stop for them was Gabriela's Boutique in Point Pleasant. Bernie wasn't sure why Beth wanted to revisit the boutique, but this was her fishing expedition, and she would control the conversation. Before Bernie pulled away from Mac's house, he met Beth's gaze.

"What?"

"I told you, you need to let Ace go. So, he lied to you. Who knows why? It's no big deal. Just let it go, okay?"

"Listen, Mac brought his name up. I guess the armchair quarterback in me went wild, sorry. I'll let it go."

"Good. Why are we going to Gabriela's again?"

"Not sure. You never know what we might find out."

"Really."

"Don't be so pessimistic. Trust me. We'll find out something that will be helpful in our investigation. Remember, I'm the one asking the questions."

"No problem with me. She's all yours."

Bernie parked in front of the boutique. Gabriella glanced their way as they entered, then she turned her focus to the customer at the checkout counter. While waiting for the customer to leave, Beth wandered through the store looking for the jean jackets. As soon as Gabriella finished, Bernie waved at Beth, and she joined him at the counter.

"Detective Kowalski and Beth, right?"

"Yeah, good memory."

"It pays to have a good memory in my business. What brings you here again, Beth?"

"Did you sell out of the Angel Hardesty jean jackets? I didn't see any on any of the racks."

"Oh, yeah, we are out. I've placed another order with Janice. It should be in, umm, in about a week. Did you want to buy one? Shipping is free?"

"When did you sell out?"

"About a week ago I guess. You know, it was rather odd. A lady, fifty or so, stopped in. She had heard about them through her granddaughters and bought the last two."

"Do you know who she was?"

"No, but I could tell she wasn't a local. She said she was heading north, and we were on her way. I'm not the nosey type and didn't inquire about her trip. Let's see, she paid cash. I made out her receipt and turned around to give it to her, and she was gone."

"Did you get her name?"

"I wrote it on the receipt. Let me get it. Here you go."

"Mary Smith…interesting."

"Yeah, I thought so, too."

"What are the numbers for?"

"Oh, yeah. When I had Janice change the label to

Angel Hardesty by Gabriela, she started numbering them for some odd reason."

"Could you describe Mary Smith?"

"As I said, fifty, short dark hair, medium build, and wore glasses. Casual attire, how's that?"

"Okay, that describes a lot of women."

"Yeah, anything else?"

"How many do you usually have in stock?"

"Normally, around six, but this time I ordered more because we've had a run on them lately."

"That's unusual, isn't it?"

"Yeah, not sure what's driving the sales, but I like it. Normally, we might sell maybe two or three a month. Umm, come to think of it, about two weeks ago, I had another lady, maybe fifties, stop in and purchase two. I could tell she wasn't from around here as well. She paid cash and left. She wasn't very friendly either. It was like she wanted to buy them and get out of here. It was kind of weird. Because of that, her name stuck with me. Sharon Davis."

"Can you describe her?"

"As I said, fifty, auburn hair, medium build, dressed in jeans."

"Okay, thank you. Bernie, do you have any questions?

"Nah, thanks for your time."

They left the boutique with what Bernie thought was a useless visit and questions. He didn't think the questions about the jean jacket were helpful to their investigation and would address it with Beth at dinner.

"Hey, Beth, I'm kind of hungry. Maybe we should just eat over here and avoid the traffic back to Gallipolis."

"Now, Bernie Kowalski, I can't believe you would pass up lasagna with Italian sausage. Besides, we already told Sharma we'd be back, and our hotel is in Gallipolis as well."

"Yeah, I guess it makes sense. When you mentioned the lasagna, my mouth started watering. You win."

"It's not a contest. We'll be there in about thirty minutes. By then, I'll even be hungry."

Traveling back to Gallipolis, muted chatter from the radio filled the car. While Bernie was pondering Beth's questions regarding the jean jacket, she had her thoughts on Jason and Uncle Charlie. Although she told Bernie, she would let it go, that was just to shut him up. Arriving at Remo's Italian Weinery, they requested a table in Sharma's section. After being seated, she immediately approached them.

"What may I get you two to drink?"

"I'll have a Pinot Grigio. He will have a Yuengling, and to make it easy on you, we'll both have the lasagna and a salad with Italian dressing on the side."

"Great, I'll put in your order, get your drinks, and be back in a jiffy, okay?"

"Yeah, Sharma, sounds great."

"Well, Beth, that was pretty bold of you to order for me."

"I knew what you wanted. It's no big deal."

"Yeah, thanks. So, what were all of those questions about the jean jacket?"

"Oh, those. Hmm, just curious why they didn't have anymore. The last time we were there, she had several. I don't think it's something that sells out a lot, and she even confirmed it."

"Yeah, I get that, but what does it have to do with our case?"

"Hmm, just a wild hunch. I'll tell you about it sometime. Umm, here comes our drinks and salads. It shouldn't be long until the yummy lasagna arrives. What do you say, no talk about the cases, okay?"

"No problem."

CHAPTER 41

The remainder of the evening at Remo's was quiet and subdued. After enjoying the zesty lasagna, Beth and Bernie left for the historic hotel. Once checked in, they opted for a nightcap. They checked in with Carla on her progress. The following day, Beth and Bernie would revisit Courtney at the Pixey Stix Café. Beth believed there was more information to gain from her. Although it was a hunch of Beth's, Courtney may have been the last person to see her alive. Based on what she divulged to them on their previous visit, the café was Ashlee's respite from the harsh winter earlier in the year.

After a lazy morning and breakfast at the hotel, they arrived at the café just as it opened. Courtney was surprised when they entered. As they approached the counter and sat down, Courtney poured them a glass of water with lemon.

"Detective Kowalski and Beth, umm…"

"Pendergast."

"Right, what brings you two back here? I thought I answered all of your questions the last time."

"Yeah, you did, but we always have more as our investigation moves forward. If it's any consolation, we revisited your mom yesterday and other people in Gallipolis. We're just doing our due diligence, right Bernie?"

"Yeah. Previously, you told us Ashlee was here most days last winter. You told us she had a phone. Did she ever bring in a computer or tablet?"

"Umm, neither. She said her computer stopped working. Sometimes I'd let her use my tablet for internet stuff. I'm not nosey, so I didn't look at what she was actually using it for."

"When was the last time she was here?"

"I believe, maybe March."

"Is your tablet here?"

"Yeah. I bring it with me most days to use in my downtime."

"May I see it?"

She left the bar area and entered the kitchen. A few minutes later, she returned with her iPad. She placed it on the counter in front of Beth, pressed the home button, and keyed in her passcode.

"Here you go. I'm not sure what you will find."

"Thanks. I'll check the browsing history and see what I can come up with."

"You guys want something else to drink or anything to eat?"

"Nothing to eat, but some iced tea with lemon would be nice."

While Beth reviewed the search history, iced tea with lemon was placed on the counter. Beth went back as far as the search history would allow her. One search caught her eye.

"Courtney, are you using one of those genealogy sites like Ancestry or MyHeritage?"

"No, why?"

"There's a record of visiting one of those sites in late February, then mid-March."

"Well, I'm the only one that uses the iPad, so it must be when Ashlee used it. What would she be looking for?"

"Probably her biological parents."

Beth opened the site, and a sign-in page loaded. The username and password were blank. After showing it to Bernie, she let Courtney take a look.

"Any idea what the username and password are?"

"As I said, I'm not the nosey type."

"Yeah, go to settings and click on passwords."

After taking the iPad back, she hit the settings icon. She scrolled down to the password listing and tapped it. After entering her passcode, she handed the iPad to Beth. She scrolled through all the websites or apps on the iPad, looking for the DNA website. After finding it, she wrote down the username and password. She mumbled under her breath, then laughed.

"What so funny?"

"I should've known."

"Should've known what?"

"The username is *Zioneé*, and the password is *Heavenly One*. Here we go, let's see what she was looking for or who she found."

After entering the username and password, Ashlee's profile loaded. Poking around on her account only brought disappointment. If Ashlee submitted a DNA sample, the results were not on her account. After more snooping around, Beth closed out the website and handed Courtney her iPad.

"So, what did you find out?"

"Not much. She has an account, and that's it. Maybe she didn't go through with it or used one of the many companies offering DNA services. At least we know she was interested in finding out, I assume, her biological parents. If she did find anything out, maybe that's why she was murdered. I need to dig deeper and look at all the websites. Perhaps I'll get lucky. But that can wait until next week when Carla returns."

"Are we done here?"

"Courtney?"

"I guess that means no."

"Courtney, did Ashlee ever mention using one of those services?"

"Well, sort of, I guess so. Several times, she talked about finding her birth parents. All she knew was someone had dropped her off at social services. She knew nothing else. And if I were dropped off like she was, I'd be searching for my birth parents. I felt sorry for her at times. She told me Paul Montgomery was the only real friend she could trust. Maybe you should start with him."

"Is there a lunch special today?"

"Yeah. Reuben and homemade onion rings."

"Great, we'll both have the special, right, Bernie?"

"Yeah, but I'll have a Yuengling instead of the tea."

"Then I'll have a Pinot Grigio."

"You got it, guys."

Courtney left and placed the orders. A few minutes later, she put a Yuengling and a glass of Pinot Grigio on the counter.

"So, Beth, what's turning inside your head?"

"Oh, nothing, Bernie."

"Right, I don't believe you."

"Hmm, just enjoy your beer. We'll talk on the way home. But before we leave Point Pleasant, let's revisit Ramona Montgomery. I have a couple of questions for her."

After finishing lunch, Ramona's home was a ten-minute drive. Bernie parked in front of Ramona's house. She was relaxing on the porch with a glass of iced tea. Since Ramona was on the porch, Beth told him to wait in the car. As he watched the conversation taking place, he wondered what questions she asked her. Five minutes later, Beth returned to the car.

"What was that all about?"

"Ramona said Ashlee submitted a DNA sample."

"Okay, anything else?"

"Yeah, I have her phone number. We'll subpoena her records; maybe we'll get lucky. Now, let's head home. Carla won't be back to work until Monday, and I say we take tomorrow off. We need time away from the case."

"Sounds like a great idea. I'll notify the chief."

CHAPTER 42

A
s Carla entered the police station on Monday morning, Beth and Bernie were already at their workstations, catching up from being gone on Friday. While approaching her workstation, congratulatory well-wishes and welcome back comments met Carla's happy demeanor. After nodding and smiling at those making the comments, she settled in at her workstation. They smiled at Carla's refreshed expression. As she met their smiles, she was ready to throw herself back into the case.

While glancing in their direction, Carla caught a glimpse of Sherry in the hallway. Before Carla knew it, Sherry approached her, carrying a file folder. She tossed the folder on Carla's desk. As Carla read the label on the flap, her pulse began to increase. The names on the file meant she would soon learn if Ashlee was Paul's daughter. After opening up the file, she placed each report side-by-side and studied them. As Sherry looked on, Carla cheery disposition quickly soured.

"So, am I reading this right? Paul Montgomery is not Ashlee's father, correct?"

"Yeah, the report for Paul is from his company. I'd heard of Gannon Biometrics before and researched them. Based on that report which I believe is accurate, he's not Ashlee's father or a distant relative. We still don't have his DNA sample analysis back, but I don't think it will change anything."

"Okay, anything else?"

Sherry shook her head and left. Carla wasn't surprised at the results. Meeting Beth and Bernie's gaze, she grabbed the file and motioned them to the conference room.

"Okay, guys, Paul is not Ashlee's father. He's not our killer, either. After spending a week with him, I don't believe he had any plausible motive to kill her. And now, given he's not her father, there isn't any motive that he would be involved in Maxine's death either. Now, what did you two find out in Gallipolis?"

"Carla, Ace lied to me."

"So, Beth, how did you find that out in Gallipolis, and why is that important?"

"Carla, I told Beth to drop this Ace thing."

"Beth, please explain how this came about?"

"Okay, we found Mackenzie Adams to inquire more about Maxine's sexual escapades. She mentioned Maxine meeting Jason Carbone's Uncle Charlie or Ace in Gallipolis. Ace told me he didn't even know where Gallipolis was.

"Okay, so he lied about that. That doesn't mean he's involved in any way."

"Maybe not, but I feel it in my soul; he's hiding something."

"Unless you have proof, let's focus our efforts on what is possible, okay? What about Jason Carbone? Paul said Maxine left him to date Jason."

"Ace told me Jason is some bigshot lawyer in Cincinnati. That's where we go next."

"Beth, set it up as soon as possible. We'll travel to Cincinnati while Bernie continues the investigation from here."

"What else did you two find out?"

"Beth, this was your fishing expedition, so tell Carla everything while I visit the bathroom."

Bernie left the conference room while Beth told Carla everything they had discovered, including the increased sales of the Angel Hardesty jean jackets. When Bernie returned to the room, Beth got up and left.

"Where's she going, Carla? Are we done already?"

"She is contacting Jason Carbone and see if we can visit him this afternoon or tomorrow. The sooner we interview him and hopefully convince him to submit a DNA swab, the sooner we eliminate him as a person of interest."

"I know that look, Carla. What's going on inside your brain?"

"Bite me, Bernie. I want you to visit Ace and see if there's anything to Beth's adamant fixation that he somehow is involved."

"Seriously, you know what could happen."

"Yeah, but if Beth could be right, maybe the killer is right under our nose. You know, the unlikely one. It wouldn't be the first time. Let's not forget that she was right about Jackson Walker. He was responsible for abducting Penny Miracle."

Carla had pushed Bernie's anger switch and he

slammed his fist on the table. "That's a low blow. Screw you, McBride."

"Listen, Bernie, don't take it personally. We all make mistakes. Back then, you did what you thought was right. The important thing is not to make one again. Besides, you told me Dannie Spencer told Ace about the jean jacket. He dissed it, and it doesn't make any sense. Why would he do that?"

"You know, Ace and I didn't get along before he retired."

"Yeah, and before chief made us partners, we didn't have the best relationship either, did we?"

Bernie shook his head as Beth returned from her mission to set up an interview with Jason Carbone. Beth noticed a scowl on Bernie's face and knew he and Carla had had a little spat. She took her seat across from him as he massaged his temples. Carla's expression said it all, and Bernie was not a happy camper.

Breaking the silence, Beth said, "Okay, guys, what's going on?"

"Nothing. Bernie and I had a little disagreement, that's all, right, Bernie?"

"Yeah, we did. It's no big deal."

"What did you find out with Jason? Are we going to interview Jason today or tomorrow?"

"We caught him on a good day. He's in court all day tomorrow. He agreed to see us today if we could be there by one this afternoon. So, we're good to go."

"Great, that leaves us plenty of time to get there if we leave now."

"Bernie, you're on your own the rest of the day. See what information is out there on Jason Carbone. Tomorrow, we'll discuss your research."

"You got it, partner."

"Beth, why don't you find Sherry and give her Ashlee's mobile phone number. She can meet with Chief Evans to obtain her records. I assume you tried calling the number, right?"

Beth rolled her eyes, and nodded.

CHAPTER 43

Bernie dreaded his visit with Ace. But deep inside his soul he knew he had to do it regardless of their previous relationship. Beth had discovered too many red flags, and they couldn't be ignored. Ace lied to Beth about Gallipolis, and he dissed the information Dannie Spencer gave him twenty years ago. He knew Ace was a better detective than that. With Beth and Carla on the road to Cincinnati, he sat at his desk pondering the best way to handle Ace.

Bernie knew if Ace recognized his number or the police department's number, he might not answer it. After picking up his mobile phone, he opened the Settings icon and changed his caller designation to unknown. He keyed in Ace's number and hit the call button. After several rings, it was answered. He immediately hung up. With thunderstorms blowing outside, Ace was not fishing today.

Fifteen minutes later, he arrived at Ace's cabin. He parked behind Ace's vehicle and exited his car. After walking upon the porch, he knocked on the storm door several times. Silence met him. He knocked again. Silence again. While being the impatient person he was, he started to knock again when the cabin door opened. A defiant Ace glared at him.

"What the hell are you doing here, Kowalski?"

"I was in the area, and—"

"That's bullshit. What do you want?"

"Okay, I should've called. I want to ask you a few questions about the cold case we've reopened."

"I've already talked with Beth Pendergast. I'm sure she told you everything. I've got nothing else to say."

"Okay. I saw Dannie the other day. We talked about the case since she worked with you on it. She told me she gave you information on the Angel Hardesty jean jacket. What did you do with that information?"

"None of your damn business. Everything should be in the files in the evidence box."

"We didn't find any information on the jean jacket. Why?"

"Okay, I didn't find it essential. Obviously, I made a mistake. We all make them, right?"

"Yeah, I guess so. You know about our current case and its similarities to the cold case, right?"

"Of course. Beth told me. I told her you might be looking at a serial-killer scenario. Is she checking that out?"

"Yeah, we are. You know, it's highly unusual that victims of serial killers are related."

"So, it's not impossible in this crazy world, is it?"

"Right. Ace, do you have any other opinions?"

"Serial killer, that's what I think it is. Is there anything else?"

"Why did you lie to Beth about knowing where

Gallipolis was? We know you met Maxine Harvey there over twenty years ago."

Bernie felt the wrath of Ace's temper. The door slamming in his face echoed off the hills. Burning anger grabbed Bernie, and he thought about knocking on the storm door again. However, he knew this conversation was over. As he walked to his car, questions and red flags swirled in his mind. He began to consider that maybe Ace was hiding something, or he was possibly involved. However, the big question was why.

Over a hundred miles away, Carla and Beth crossed the bridge into Cincinnati. Once they found the building housing the law firm that employed Jason Carbone they used the underground parking garage. After finding a visitor spot, an elevator took them to the ninth floor. Beth spoke with the main desk regarding their appointment with Jason. The receptionist instructed them to wait in the visitors' lounge. Beth and Carla observed the modern motif on the walls.

About five minutes later, a tall, physically fit, and handsome gentleman stopped and chatted with the receptionist for a moment. Jason quickly approached them and introduced himself. After showing him their identification badges, he led them down a long hallway to a conference room. He opened the door and motioned them inside. Assuming he would sit at the head of the long table, they took the first chair on each side as he closed the door. Once seated, curious glances flowed around the table, followed by silence.

"Miss Pendergast, you wanted to meet with me regarding Maxine Hardy, correct?"

"Yes, Mr. Carbone."

"What a blast from the past. What do you want to know?"

"So, you do remember her."

"Yeah, we dated for a short while. Then she broke it off for another baseball player. She was good at that. She was a baseball groupie. From what I remember, we went out a few times. It was nothing serious, just enjoyed each other's company."

Up to now, Beth was in control, but Carla was ready to dig her claws into such a pompous asshole. She nodded at Beth and met his gaze.

"Right, Mr. Bigshot. When was the last time you saw her?"

"Umm, probably when she broke it off with me, hmm, probably nineteen, twenty years ago. What's this all about? Is she in any trouble?"

"No, she's dead."

"I'm sorry to hear that. How did she die?"

"She was murdered...almost twenty years ago. It's a cold case we've reopened. Her identity remained a mystery until just recently."

A reserved silence captured the room. His expression and body language told them he was surprised. As the silence continued, Beth peered deep into his soul, looking for red flags of guilt. However, a calm demeanor flowed from his soul. Beth could see Jason was a hard man to read.

"Detective McBride, where was—"

"We don't know where the crime occurred, who committed it, and why. Her body was discovered in a cemetery in Oakmont, Kentucky. Does Oakmont ring a bell?"

"Of course. My Uncle Charlie lives there, and I

played a few baseball games there while in college. So, what's all of this have to with me?"

"We'll get to that a little later. We're just having a conversation. You can ask us to leave anytime, or you can have one of your colleagues join us, if you like."

"I don't think that's necessary. I didn't have anything to do with her death. I'm sorry someone killed her. She was a sweet person."

"Great. Let's get back to your relationship with Maxine. How would you describe it? Just friends, you know to hang out with, or was a more than that, you know, a physical one?"

"By physical, do you mean sexual?"

"Yes. Did you have sex with Maxine?"

"Yeah, and so did about every baseball player she hooked up with. It was no big deal. Where's this going?"

"Did you know she ended up pregnant? She had a baby girl. Someone dropped off the baby girl at social services in Point Pleasant."

CHAPTER 44

Jason's calm demeanor quickly morphed into anxiety as he massaged his temples. Beth peered deep into his soul, looking for clues and answers. Up until now, he seemed unfazed by the questions. By the movement of his eyes, Beth assumed he was trying to remember his sexual escapades with Maxine. After several deep breaths, his calm demeanor resurfaced somewhat, and he met their gaze, ready to move on.

"When did she have the baby?"

"We're not sure. We didn't find out her identity until just a few weeks ago, so we have many unanswered questions. That's why we wanted to have this discussion with you."

"Do you know what happened to the baby after social services got involved?"

"Beth, tell Jason what you have discovered from your investigation in Gallipolis and Point Pleasant."

"Maxine presumably named the baby girl after her middle name, Ashlee. She was placed in foster homes, spending most of her life in Harold and Ramona Montgomery's home. Does Montgomery ring a bell with you?"

Jason's mind churned and churned, trying to remember how he knew that name before. It was apparent by his body language; that anxiety was invading his soul.

"Well, do you remember the name? How about Paul Montgomery?"

"Okay, yeah, that's how I know that name. He was a baseball player and dated Maxine just before I did. What does he have to do with this? Shit...I get it. He knew Maxine's daughter, Ashlee. Damn, what a small world. Is he the father?"

"According to his DNA results, no, he is not."

"That's why you wanted to meet with me. You want my DNA, right?"

"Yes. Will you give it to us?"

"I'm not the father of Ashlee."

"Then prove it."

"Listen, when I was young, I had a bad case of mumps. It rendered me sterile. I didn't find out until I got married, and we wanted to start a family. After many years of trying, my wife and I had tests performed. She's very fertile, and I wasn't. My sperm count was so low I had very little chance of getting my wife pregnant, much less Maxine. We eventually adopted."

"I see. Will you still submit a sample?"

"Where's Ashlee now?"

"She's dead. Her body was found in the same place as Maxine's. The cause and manner of death are identical, and they were dressed in the same clothing."

"When was she found?"

"About three weeks ago."

"Obviously, I didn't know her. I'm sorry."

"Okay. Now what about a DNA sample. Will you give us one, or will we need a court order? You know we can do it, right?"

"Of course, I know that. Before I decide, tell me more."

"We believe there is only one killer. Your Uncle Charlie thinks a serial killer is a possibility; however, we don't believe that. We believe whoever is Ashlee's father is responsible for both murders. Unfortunately, we don't know why."

"Okay, I'll provide my medical records regarding my sperm count. However, you will have to get a court order for a DNA sample."

"Have it your way. Mackenzie Adams told us she remembered meeting you and your Uncle Charlie. She remembered it because she said your uncle was creepy. She said he couldn't keep his eyes off her."

"That's an odd statement. Where's this going?"

"Do you remember that?"

"Vaguely, but which uncle?"

"Mac said your Uncle Charlie."

"Hmm, I have two uncles named Charlie."

"What?"

"Yeah, believe it or not, they are identical twins. Oras Charles, and Ezra Charles. Neither liked their first names, so they started using Charlie later in life. Yeah, I know it's crazy."

"What were they like growing up?"

"All I know, they had each other's back and would do anything for each other, but I imagine that's true of identical twins."

"How do you tell them apart?"

"Ezra Charles has a small birthmark below his left ear. Of course, now their hairstyles are different. Oras has a buzz cut, while Ezra's hair is much longer and covers the birthmark. I don't see why this is important."

"Where does Ezra live, and what does he do for a living?"

"He still lives in Gallipolis. He never left the valley. He's a high school principal, married into money. His wife is a doctor, and he has two teenage daughters."

"Hmm, interesting."

"I'm not sure where this line of questioning is going."

"We are just looking at every possibility."

"So, are you saying they might be involved?"

"Anything is possible these days."

"Yeah, I know, but—"

"That day Mac referred to; which uncle was with you?"

"Both, I remember it now. Yeah, it was the day of Ezra's bachelor party. That was a wild night. I'm not sure if anyone could remember what went on at that party."

"Were Mac and Maxine there?"

"As I said, it was a wild night; not sure who attended the party. It was a long time ago."

"Okay, you mentioned earlier that many baseball players likely had sex with Maxine. Can you think of anyone in particular that stands out?"

As silence captured the room, Beth watched Jason's wheels turning in his brain. His eyes moved around the room, and she wondered if he was trying to come up with another name to throw suspicion in a different direction. Finally, meeting Carla's probing expression, a smirky grin plastered his face.

"So, Jason, did you come up with a name?"

"Yeah I recall our catcher had a fling with her just after me. Umm, Johnny Masters, yeah. I remember he told me all about his time with her. Of course, she dumped him for another baseball conquest. As I said earlier, she had many partners. I don't have any contact with him, but I believe he still lives in Gallipolis."

"Great, we'll check him out. Now that you have heard anything, will you submit a DNA sample? You have already told us you are sterile, so your medical records and DNA sample will determine if you are telling us the truth. If so, we can rule you out as a suspect and person of interest. And we won't have to bother you again. What will it be?"

Twenty minutes later, they were on their way home. Jason agreed to submit a DNA sample to prove his innocence, and he even stated he would take a polygraph. They both decided that Jason was not Ashlee's father unless his results said otherwise. Carla was anxious to find out how Bernie's meeting with Ace went. They now had more questions than answers. This case was not making any sense at the moment. Based on today's discoveries, Jason's other Uncle Charlie, Ezra, was now a person of interest.

CHAPTER 45

The following morning, Beth, Carla, and Bernie would meet at ten o'clock to discuss their findings in either case. Up to now, they didn't have any clear suspects, just several people of interest. After catching up on mundane reports, each grabbed a coffee and settled in the conference room.

With the door shut, a thick, silent atmosphere flowed around the table. Carla sat at the head of the table while Beth and Bernie sat across from each other. After clearing her throat, Carla took charge. She was happy to be back in action and focusing on solving both murders.

To begin, Carla brought everyone up to speed on her conversations with Paul Montgomery. Beth and Bernie were aware that his preliminary DNA results provided by his company indicated he was not Ashlee's father. However, he likely had information helpful to the case. After finishing her comments, she inquired whether Beth or Bernie had any questions or concerns. However, they all agreed Paul was still a person of interest since he knew Ashlee the best.

Next up was Beth's turn. She had led the investigation in Gallipolis and Point Pleasant. After finishing all of her comments regarding everyone they spoke with, she opened up the floor for any questions or comments. As with Carla's comments about Paul, questions and comments were few. Up to this point, the purpose of this meeting was to review each other's findings. Unbeknownst to Beth, Carla saved Bernie's encounter with Ace till the end. Carla was unsure how Beth would react to hiding this from her or doubting her ability. The remainder of the meeting focused on their recent discoveries with Jason and Ace.

"So, there you have it, Bernie. Did you know Ace had a twin?"

"Nah, I didn't know that. I'm not sure anyone in the department knew that. Well, maybe Ace's sidekick, Dannie, might have known."

"Isn't she the police officer that helped Ace investigate the cold case?"

"Yeah, Beth, and—"

"And she's the one that told Ace she found information regarding the Angel Hardesty brand, correct?"

"Yeah, and anyway, if anyone knew he had a twin, she'd probably know it. I'll give her a call."

"Bernie, did anyone you and Beth interviewed mention Johnny Master's name?"

"Nah, I don't recall that name. Do you, Beth?"

"That name never came up. Maybe Jason is pulling our chain and wants to deter our investigation. Maybe Jason knows something about that bachelor party, or he's involved as well. We'll need to check him out."

"Yeah, we will check him out when Bernie and I are in Gallipolis interviewing the other Uncle Charlie."

"You and Bernie! Carla, what the hell is going on? Bernie and I have been handling that part of the investigation. Why the change?"

"No real reason, you've got us this far, and I appreciate that. I want you to stay here and learn everything you can about Ace and his brother. Is that okay?"

"I don't like it, but I could use a little change of pace."

"Great. Now, Beth, please don't get upset with me, but I sent Bernie to visit Ace while we interviewed Jason. I know you think Ace is involved somehow, but I wanted Bernie to speak with him and see if he felt the same way you do, that Ace knows something. You know we have to be careful with a member of the law enforcement brotherhood."

"Upset...huh... Don't you trust me? How much more do I have to do to prove myself. I was right with Penny Miracle and then again with Clarissa Morgan. Even after learning what we did yesterday, I still believe Ace is hiding something."

"Beth, it's not that I—"

"So, Bernie, what did you find out? Was Ace nice to you?"

"Beth, I'll just cut to the chase; Ace was a real asshole. He still thinks we have a serial killer on our hands. When I mentioned Maxine Hardy's name, he ended the conversation and slammed the door in my face. I thought about knocking on the door again, but I knew my conversation was over."

"See, Carla. Ace knows something about at least Maxine's death. I'm not saying he's our killer just yet, but after what we learned from Jason, I wouldn't put it past him."

"Please don't get bent out of shape, Beth. Given Bernie's cold reception and what you experienced, I'm beginning to jump on the Ace bandwagon. Hell, maybe after we get back from Gallipolis, I'll visit him. Maybe you are right that he's involved, but how and why?"

"Well, this is no serial-killer scenario he thinks it is. These deaths are about Maxine having a baby and how it would ruin someone's life. She evidently revealed that to the baby's father. When that happened, she threatened to expose him, which would destroy that person's world. Ashlee wanted to find her birth parents. The fact that she's dead means she at least found her birth father and maybe even her deceased mother. Exposing that probably got her killed, and until something else proves me different, that's my theory. And you can't deny it."

"Whoa, Beth. Calm down. I want you to dig deep into the Hutchinson twins and Johnny Masters. Your theory is interesting, but we need more than that to go after him. Maybe Scott can help you? Besides, Bernie wants me to have lunch at Remo's Italian Weinery, right, Bernie?"

Bernie nodded and deflected Beth's angry eyes.

"I also want you to get with Sherry on several things. Review the evidence from both crime scenes, clothing, autopsy reports, and hopefully, Ashlee's phone records. If we are going after Ace, we need all of our ducks in a row. If he becomes our man or involved, we need to be ready for all hell to break loose because it will be a damn war."

"So, are you saying Ace is now a person of interest?"

"Yeah, sort of. I need to bring Chief Evans up to speed. He's not going to like what I will tell him."

Although Beth was disappointed about not going with them, she was a team player. Her research broke open the last two cases, and she believed she was on the right track with Ace. Furthermore, to hear that Bernie felt the same made her happy. And that Carla was warming up too, it increased her confidence that she was right. And if all hell did break loose, which it will, lives would be in jeopardy, especially hers.

CHAPTER 46

With Scott's help, Beth began her dissection of Oras Charles "Ace" Hutchinson's life. She already knew Ace was a decorated veteran of the Oakmont Police Department. He retired after thirty-five years of exemplary service. When his wife died over a year ago, he inherited a sizeable amount of money from his wife's estate. Given that, he decided to smell the roses and live each day as though it was his last. He'd fought enough battles, taken fire, and survived.

Although he was still in the prime of his life, his wife's death rocked his soul like never before. Ace appeared to be a gentle soul. However, he could be a harsh and wild asshole when pushed hard or questioned about his tactics. Over the years, fellow law enforcement looked over his flaws because he solved cases, and he had many friends in the department who had his back.

Born in Gallipolis, he had a normal childhood with his sister and twin brother until their parents died in a home invasion when they were four years old. With no family to speak of, social services placed the three children in foster care with George Hutchinson, a Baptist minister, and his wife, Irene. They later adopted them and gave them a loving home with a normal childhood. George and Irene never told them what happened to their birth parents because of the grizzly nature of their deaths.

Ezra excelled in school, while Oras was an average student. Ezra was the nerd, while Oras was the athlete. While in high school, they both dated girls from wealthy families. Oras received a scholarship to play football at the university in Oakmont and his girlfriend Suzy followed him there. They were married while in college.

On the other hand, Ezra received an academic scholarship to attend Ohio University. His girlfriend, Macy, also received an academic scholarship from there as well. After graduating, she attended medical school there while Ezra pursued a master's degree in school administration. Because of Macy's medical commitments, they held off getting married until both completed their education. Once she completed her residency and fellowship, she returned to Gallipolis to begin her practice in Ophthalmology. Ezra had already completed his education in school administration and returned to Gallipolis to start his career. While madly in love with each other, they waited on each other until the time was right. Finally, after Macy established her practice, Ezra proposed, and they married later that summer.

After finishing her research at home, she headed to the police station. She obtained all the evidence from both cases and headed to a conference room. Now that Ace was a person of interest, everything about both cases would be heavily scrutinized. Given that, she turned on the cameras to record her activity reviewing transcripts and notes of Ace's investigation and the physical evidence.

Beth carefully removed the clothing from the cold case and spread it out at one end of the table. This was the second time she had examined the jean jacket, the black blouse, Levi jeans, bra, and panties Maxine was wearing. Because she was found in about eight inches of muddy water, any evidence on the clothing was likely compromised. The bra and panties were soaked with blood; however, the jean jacket was free of blood. Based on that, the killer put the jean jacket on her before dumping the body in the cemetery. Although it was soiled, she examined the buttons and buttonholes, which were not contaminated. Beth assumed the killer wore gloves, and finding any fingerprints was a long shot. She knew from the forensic analysis performed back then that fingerprints were non-existent.

After placing all physical evidence back into the box, she moved to the other end of the table, where the evidence box of the current case set was ready to be examined. Piece by piece, Beth removed Ashlee's clothing and spread it out on the table. The jean jacket, similar to the one found on Maxine, was not soiled by muddy water or anything else. It hadn't rained in Oakmont for weeks, and only the morning dew touched Ashlee's clothing. Likewise, the Levi jeans were not soiled. However, the black blouse, bra, and panties were soaked with blood.

Again, assuming the killer wore gloves, her examination did not yield any fingerprints. While examining the buttons and buttonholes one by one, she noticed a dried shiny substance around one of the buttonholes. Other than that, she found nothing out of the ordinary. She placed all of the clothing except the jean jacket in the evidence box. After reviewing the forensic report, she found nothing regarding a shiny substance on one of the buttonholes. She did not want to leave the room unattended and called Sherry. After a brief conversation, she ended the call. Within a few minutes, Sherry entered the conference room.

"Hi, Beth. What did you need?"

"I'm reviewing—"

"Is that the evidence box from your current case?"

"Yeah. Carla wanted me to review all the evidence again and a few other things."

"So, McBride doesn't trust our review. What's new."

"Oh, it's not that. She does, and so do I. Anyway, I've found a shiny substance around one of the buttonholes. I don't find any mention of that in the forensic report. Would you take a look at it?"

As Beth pointed out the spot, Sherry took the magnifying glass and studied it closely. She reviewed each button and buttonhole before placing the magnifying glass on the table. After picking up the report, she examined it and shook her head.

"What's wrong? Don't you see it?"

"Oh, yeah, I see it. I guess, uh, we missed it. I'll cut out the section, and I'll perform an analysis and see what I find. I'll get right on it and let you know when I get the results."

Sherry left and returned with an evidence bag. She cut out the section with the shiny substance and placed it in the evidence bag.

"Sherry, thanks. This discovery may be the break we're looking for."

"Where's McBride today?"

"She and Bernie are in Gallipolis interviewing Ace's twin brother."

"I didn't know he had a twin brother."

"It seems like no one did, except maybe Dannie Spencer. Do you remember her?"

"Yeah, she and Ace were pretty tight. Many of us thought maybe they were having a secret affair."

"Really?"

"Everybody thought he was a faithful saint, but I know different, and I'll leave it at that. I'll put a rush on this."

CHAPTER 47

Carla and Bernie arrived in Gallipolis around lunchtime, giving them plenty of time to eat before their appointment with Ezra Hutchinson. After entering Remo's Italian Weinery, a hostess escorted them to a table in Sharma's section. Carla's eyes began to wander around the restaurant. This was something she always did with any new place she visited. She believed that clues to cases were always around. Pictures of prominent locals hung proudly on the wall. One booth nearest to them had a picture of a baseball player. From a distance, she thought it might be Jason Carbone. She made a mental note of it and would inquire about it later.

Within a few minutes, Sharma arrived and greeted them, placing a glass of water in front of them. She remembered Bernie; his smile was unforgettable. While he was engaged in small talk with her, Carla cleared her throat, catching Bernie's gaze. He ignored her antics and continued his conversation with Sharma until he felt a thud on his leg. After feeling Carla's wrath, he introduced her to Sharma. She began her own little chit-chat with her as Bernie looked over the menu. After Bernie placed an order for two spicy Italian sausage dogs smothered with peppers and Marinara sauce, Sharma left.

"So, Bernie, you were right about having lunch here. It's a cool place. Thanks for ordering for me. I had my eye on the sausage dog as soon as I saw it on the menu."

"You are welcome. It's delicious, and you'll love it."

"I'll take your word for it. Now, see that picture above that booth? Doesn't that look like Jason Carbone?"

"Well, I've never met him in person. I've only seen his picture once, so I couldn't be sure whether it's him or not. I'll ask Sharma. She knows everything about everything if you know what I mean."

"Yeah, so let's talk about your visit with Ace."

"What's to talk about? He definitely didn't want to talk with me. He can be difficult for sure, but he was a real asshole that day, and he wanted me out of his hair."

"Okay, could he be involved?"

"Maybe, or at least he knows something about it."

"Okay, could he be the killer?"

"Possibly. Too many red flags. When I asked him about Maxine and Ashlee, he turned into a completely different person. It definitely ruffled his feathers big time. If he is involved, the biggest question we have to answer is why. Why Maxine, and the bigger question is why Ashlee?"

"It's looking like these deaths are one big enigma, you know, like trying to finish a jigsaw puzzle with several missing pieces."

"There you go using those big words on me."

"Bite me, dickhead."

As a discreet bird met her rolling eyes, Sharma arrived with their lunch and more water. The Italian sausage dog's aroma was enticing, and Carla grabbed it and took a big bite. After swallowing, she met Bernie's ear-to-ear grin. Silence took over their table as muted chatter and music played in the background. While eating, Carla's eyes continued roaming around. Sharma stopped by to inquire if they needed anything, and Carla beat Bernie to the punch.

"Sharma?"

"Yes? Do you need something else?"

"Food, no. Information, yes. That picture on the wall at that booth, is that Jason Carbone?"

"Sure is. He's a legend around here. He doesn't come in much anymore. Too bad he threw his arm out. He could have been a big star in the big leagues. Why do you ask?"

"Just wondering. Did you ever date him?"

"Me, no. I was not his type, and he was too wild for me."

"But he did date Maxine Hardy, right?"

"Yeah, they were an item for a short while. That Maxine, she used the boys and then spat them out like chewing gum."

"Is he suspect?"

"We're checking out as many people as possible that knew Maxine, that's all."

"Well, good luck with that. There were too many to count. Younger, older, she didn't care. So, good luck."

"Thanks. Did you know the Hutchinson twins?"

"No, never met them. I remember Jason told me they would do anything for him, and I mean anything."

"Okay, the sausage dog was great. Bring the check to Bernie. He dragged me here and said it was the best he had in a long time, and I agree."

"You got it."

"Bernie, what do you think about Jason? We have his DNA sample, we have his medical records regarding his sterility, and hopefully, soon will have his results. Could he be our killer?"

"Well, if he's a legend and had a promising professional baseball career, finding out he had a kid would certainly derail his future, wouldn't it?"

"Yeah. Maybe his name will come up in our interview with Ezra."

"If it doesn't come up, I'll bring it up."

"Yeah, and when we get back home, I'll visit Ace about him."

"Good luck with that, Carla."

Sharma returned with Bernie's check. He took out his wallet, pulled thirty dollars out, handed it to Sharma, and told her to keep the change. Five minutes later, they headed to the high school for their interview with Ezra Charles Hutchinson. A ten-minute drive from Remo's, silence grabbed their demeanor. Ezra Charles Hutchinson was another part of their enigma. They had no idea how this interview would go. Carla told Ezra that they wanted to talk to him about Maxine Hardy and nothing more. Although he inquired why she wanted to speak with him, Carla stonewalled him. After she promised everything discussed in their interview would remain confidential, he agreed to meet with her. After pulling into the school's parking lot, Bernie found the first spot available. Once entering, they checked in with the school's secretary. Since they had an appointment, they just gave her their names and signed a log-in sheet. At this moment, they were just ordinary citizens. There was no reason to alarm anyone that they were law enforcement. The secretary showed them to a lounge. A few minutes later, a man who could be Ace appeared in the hallway. Jason was right. Oras and Ezra were identical twins. If either or both were involved, that would spell trouble for their investigation.

CHAPTER 48

zra approached them with a confident swagger of a man at the helm of the largest high school in Gallia County. Dressed in a black suit and a red tie, he exuded power. Although Oras and Ezra were the same height, Ace was heavier. And, because of Ezra's hairstyle and thinner body frame, he looked much younger than Ace. After introductions and the indiscreet flashing of their badges, he escorted them to his office.

After entering, Carla glanced around, looking for anything to use as a starting point for their conversation. Carla and Bernie took well-appointed chairs in front of his massive wooden desk. After closing the door, he settled in his leather chair. As they studied each other, silence floated throughout his office until Ezra cleared his throat, demanding their attention.

"So, let's get started. Detective McBride, all I know is you want to talk with me about Maxine Hardy. I didn't know her that well. In fact, I only knew of her from Jason. So, I'm a little perplexed why you and Detective

Kowalski drove this far to speak with me about someone I barely knew."

"Right. That photo behind you, is that your family?"

"Yeah, me, my wife, Macey, and our two daughters, Lisa and Sara."

"Wow, that's a pretty family. So, I understand your wife is a successful ophthalmologist, probably makes a good living, right?"

"Of course, what's this line of questioning have to do with Maxine Hardy?"

"Nothing, I guess. I kind of use stuff I see like that as an ice breaker. It kind of makes it a less stressful conversation."

"I get it. So, let's get back to Maxine, okay?"

"Of course. How well did you know her?"

"As I said, I only knew of her through Jason."

"Right, tell me about your relationship with Jason."

"You know, when his dad died, he turned to me a lot since Ace lived in Oakmont. You see, he became a son to me. Every man wants a son, so I treated him like one, and he treated me like his father. I'll do anything for him, but so would Ace."

"Yeah, I understand. Ace told us the same thing."

"Let's get back to the reason you are here. What's this about?"

"Maxine Hardy is dead, murdered, about twenty years ago."

"Dead…I'm sorry. Who killed her?"

"More than likely the person that fathered her daughter."

"And that's why you are here. You think I had something to do with the death of someone I barely knew."

"Did you?"

"No, and I'm offended by that."

"Did Jason ever confide in you about his relationship with Maxine? He told us he had a sexual relationship with her. Just wondering if he ever said anything?"

"No, he never mentioned her, and I never inquired. Does Ace know you are here today?"

Silence grabbed the room momentarily as Carla's mind searched for the proper response. She hadn't expected that to come up and didn't have a reply ready if it did. Bernie cleared his throat, demanding Ezra's gaze.

"Yeah. I met with him the other day and told him we were going to meet with you. He wished me good luck, which I thought was a strange response. What kind of relationship do you and your brother have? How often do you guys talk?"

Bernie's line of questioning caught him off-guard as well.

"Maybe once a month. He has his life, and I have mine."

"So, you're not close anymore."

"Not as much as we used to be. Years ago, I wanted to learn more about our parents who were killed when we were both four years old. I wanted to pursue our heritage. He said he didn't have time for that kind of stuff. So, I pursued it myself. It's quite fascinating. What about either of you?"

"I'm sure it is. I understand about not being close to siblings. I'm not close to my sister as much as I used to be either. As for my heritage thing, my mom told me everything she knew, and that was good enough for me."

"Good for you. Anyway, I submitted my DNA and got my results back. It was a real eye-opener. I found relatives I never knew I had. Anyway, it's amazing what a simple DNA swab can do. It could change your life, it did mine."

"Yeah, we know all about that stuff. Now let's get back to Jason. He mentioned your bachelor party to me when I interviewed him. He said it got pretty wild."

"Is that right, Detective McBride? I don't remember much, and I don't think he does either. You know how those bachelor parties are, right, Detective Kowalski?"

"Of course, I forgot mine years ago. Do you recall if any girls crashed your party? That happened at my party."

"Well, as I said, it was a night to forget in many ways. What else may I help you with?"

"Did Jason have the mumps as a child?"

"I suppose so; most children had them back then, Detective McBride."

"Yeah, they did. Have you ever heard of Johnny Masters?"

"Yeah, odd that you bring up his name?"

"How's that?"

"He teaches here, and he's our baseball coach."

"Really, it must be our lucky day. Is there any possibility we could have a few moments with him? It would save us some time."

"Let me check his schedule." A moment of silence captured the room. "Yeah, he has study hall right now. I'll go relieve him."

"Great, we'll ask our questions, and then we'll be on our way. We appreciate your cooperation. Oh, one other thing, have you ever heard of the Angel Hardesty clothing brand, especially their jean jackets?"

"Funny, both my daughters have one of those jean

jackets. Before I relieve Johnny, you mentioned Maxine had a daughter. Where is she?"

"Dead, and we'll leave it that."

Ezra's reddish complexion faded as he left his office to relieve Johnny Masters. After a few probing questions, his answers left them puzzled and confused. He refused to submit a DNA sample. Although it had been a long day, Carla and Bernie had accomplished what they wanted today. Unfortunately, they added two other persons of interest to their ever-changing mystery.

CHAPTER 49

The next morning Beth, Carla, and Bernie gathered in the conference room, hoping to make sense of everything. With Chief Brock Evans in attendance, they had to be careful of accusing Ace's involvement. Beth brought everyone up to speed on her research of Ace, Ezra, and Jason's life. Anxious to hear Carla or Bernie's remarks from their interview with Ezra and Johnny Masters, Beth listened intently and made notes. Up to this point, Chief Evans remained silent and calm. With each finished with their respective remarks, Chief Evans took control of the meeting.

"Okay, let me get this straight. From what I'm hearing, you each believe that Ace is somehow involved in both deaths. Carla, you need to convince me before starting a war. You don't have any credible evidence that ties him to both murders, do you?"

"No, chief, but, uh—"

"But what, Carla?"

"We are working on it."

"Working on it just doesn't cut it. If we are going

after him, we need concrete evidence that ties him to both murders."

"Chief Evans?"

"Yeah, Beth."

"May I speak freely?"

"Of course."

"Thank you, and please keep an open mind, okay?"

"Of course. Let's hear what you have to say."

"First of all, I'm responsible for our investigation going in this direction. I may be wrong, but I don't think so. I know the risks, and I'm prepared to accept any consequences should I be wrong."

"Beth, you're not alone in this. At first, I didn't believe your hunch, but I do now."

"Listen, Carla, if I'm wrong, you and Bernie shouldn't suffer any consequences."

"We're a team, Beth, and I'm the lead investigator that let you run with your hunch."

"Hold on, everyone. So, going after Ace is nothing but a hunch. We've got to do better than that."

"Chief, hear her out. She might be on the right track. She was right about the Penny Miracle case and Clarissa Morgan causing Wilson Bortel's death. Besides, we have nothing else."

"I get it, Carla. Beth, let's hear it."

"You know I met with Ace to talk about the cold case. Well, I should have expected it. He took offense to my line of questioning. And when I told him we identified the first victim, he got agitated. When I asked him about the jean jacket, he left. He returned from the cabin with a glass of bourbon, hoping to ease the anxiety on his face. After I told him we identified the second victim, he downed the bourbon. He left and returned with another one. That's when he brought up the serial-killer scenario, which doesn't make sense. Although possible, serial killers don't normally go after people in the same family unless maybe they don't know they're related. Our cases are not a serial-killer scenario as Ace insists they are. It just doesn't make sense."

"Okay, if Ace is involved, what is the motive, Beth?"

"It has something to do with the second victim, Ashlee Roberts, Maxine's daughter. We hope to find out who Ashlee's father is through DNA analysis. We find that out, and we crack the case wide open."

"Carla, do you buy this scenario?"

"Chief, right now it's all we got. I know we need to tread carefully with Ace, but I believe his twin brother will contact him if he hasn't already."

"Motive?"

"Someone's life would be destroyed if Maxine spilled the beans about who the father was. Maybe it was Jason's professional baseball career. Perhaps it has to do with inheritance. Both Ace and Ezra married into money."

"Umm, okay, I'm still skeptical, but let's continue unless something else comes up."

As Chief Evans rose to leave, a knock on the door startled him. He opened the door, and the individual spoke to him briefly. He closed the door, grabbed the remote to the television, and turned it on. Everyone turned their attention to the breaking news on the screen. They knew this was not good. It was apparent that Ezra talked to Ace. A moment later, Kiersten St. Clair stood in front of city hall. In the background, Mayor Lester James and retired Detective Charles "Ace" Hutchinson stood waiting to be interviewed.

"Chief, what the hell is going on?"

"Well, Carla, I believe we are going to war. So much for treading lightly. Let's see what he has to say."

"Good morning. I'm Kiersten St. Clair reporting from city hall with an update on the young woman found in the cemetery. I'm here with the legendary Detective Ace Hutchinson and Mayor Lester James. Detective Carla McBride and her team have no viable suspects and are stumped as to who is responsible for the young woman found dead at the cemetery several weeks ago. According to Ace, her name is Ashlee Roberts from Gallipolis, Ohio."

Anger and frustration painted everyone's faces. Four-letter expletives exploded in the room. As Kiersten continued, silence captured the room once more.

"Let's hear what the legendary detective has to say about this case."

Ace, dressed in a black suit, white shirt, and red tie, appeared beside Kiersten, holding the mic toward him. Although anger painted his face, his voice remained calm.

"Miss St. Clair, thank you for your interest in this case. Today, I met with Mayor James to express my disgust in the current investigation. Because of a mistake I made about twenty years ago in a similar case, Detective McBride and her team are coming after me, my brother, Ezra, and my nephew, Jason Carbone. I admit my mistake, and I apologize. None of us have anything to do with Ashlee Roberts' death or the victim in the cold case."

"Well, Ace, what would you be looking at if you were on the case?"

"A serial-killer scenario. I told Beth Pendergast, their forensic psychologist, and Detective Kowalski what was going on and where they should be spending their time. My family members and I are not involved. We're all upstanding citizens in our respective communities. Oh, and one more thing, if they continue on this path, I'll be filing a defamation lawsuit on behalf of myself, my brother, and my nephew. If they want a war, they got one. That's all I have to say at this time."

The camera moved back to Kiersten St. Clair as she wrapped up her comments in front of city hall. The screen went blank, and the stagnant and stale atmosphere in the room exploded with fire, anger, and frustration. Chief Evans sat massaging his temples, contemplating what just blew up in front of city hall. As he glared around the table, they waited for him to explode, maybe even fire them all.

"Chief, what's next for us? It looks like your wheels are turning."

"Guys, after that display and what we've talked about today, I think Beth's got it right again. Let's go after the son-of-a-bitch. He wants a fucking war; then we'll give him one. Leave no stone unturned; now get to work. If you need more help, let me know. It's time to bring this dirty cop and anyone else in this cover-up down."

CHAPTER 50

C hief Evans left the room and immediately headed to city hall. His demeanor told everyone in his path to stay out of his way. Carla, Beth, and Bernie remained in the conference room to cool down and plan their strategy to take down Ace and anyone else involved. This case was moving in the direction of a massive cover-up. They also now had to consider any officers that worked on the case as persons of interest.

Obviously, those individuals who worked the original case had nothing to do with the current investigation of Ashlee's death. However, the motive was the same. Either Ace, Ezra, or Jason was willing to kill to keep their skeletons hidden. They were hoping the DNA analysis of the substance on the jean jacket would soon be ready. It could answer all of their questions, and their prime suspect or suspects would become more apparent. Until then, the war with Ace was on hold. They needed all the ammunition they could muster to bring him down and those involved.

As they left the conference room, colleagues threw expressions of disgust and acceptance their way. The tension was somewhat thick. Ace still had some old friends on the force. Others knew he was not always straight with them, and they were glad his distinguished record was being questioned. Carla, Beth, and Bernie now knew what happens when you accuse one of your own. Experiencing the tension around them, they headed for an early lunch at McGruder's.

After arriving, their favorite booth was available. Beth and Carla sat on their usual side. Bernie slid in across from them. Several minutes later, their favorite server approached them.

"Guys, having the usual?"

"Sam."

"Yeah, Carla."

"Bring us two Jameson on the rocks and a Yuengling for now."

"Wow, it must really be a bad day, right?"

"Did you happen to see the breaking news segment by Kiersten St. Clair?"

"Umm, okay. I get it, Carla. Yeah… yeah, I did. I guess that guy threw you a major-league curveball."

"Yeah, that son-of-a-bitch—"

"Carla."

"Sam."

"Look who just entered."

Ace was hard to miss, all slicked up in his photo-op suit. Both Carla and Bernie remembered he never wore anything like that while on the force. Catching Ace's gaze, a smirky grin sent Carla's pulse skyrocketing. Her dagger-like stare only made Ace's smirky grin more prominent. She stood up to go after him, but Beth's firm grip latched onto her arm.

With him was his lawyer, Burt Mercer. Burt was as sleazy as they come and would take on any client. He was not a friend of city hall and took every opportunity to raise hell with them. He played dirty and would do anything to win a case. Ace had stooped as low as he could go. Instead of taking a table on the other side, he and Burt walked toward them. With Carla's soul reaching the boiling point, Ace winked at her as they strolled past them and took a booth near them.

"Beth, why didn't you let me just cold-cock him right now?"

"He's playing you, and you were ready to take the bait. That can't happen, at least not here."

Carla's flushed complexion matched her hair. The warmth running through her body was sizzling as Sam delivered their drinks and glasses of water. Carla immediately grabbed her Jameson and downed it. She coughed a few times, took her water, and downed it. She then held up her glass toward Sam and nodded.

"Okay, Carla, I'll get you another one as soon as you guys place your order. Is the usual, okay?"

"Yeah, Sam, and get us some munchies right away, okay?"

"Of course, Bernie, coming right up."

"Thanks. Carla, what the hell is going on? If we are going to bring that asshole down, you need to play it cool."

"Bite me, Bernie."

"Carla...?"

"Yeah, Beth. Take some deep breaths, and please

calm down. We'll get him, he'll make a mistake, and then we'll nail his ass to the wall."

As muted chatter flowed in the background, silence captured their booth. While Beth and Bernie nursed their drinks, Sam delivered two bowls of beer nuts and an iced tea for Carla. Sam was serious about preventing Carla from moving past the point of no return. Moments later, Dannie Spencer and Joe Ferguson entered. After looking around, they spotted Ace and Bert. While walking past them, neither made eye contact with Carla, Beth, or Bernie.

"Ladies, I wonder what they are doing here. They were close with Ace. Umm, they worked with Ace on that cold case. I was there that morning, and so were they. I need to revisit Dannie; she may know more. Hmm, or maybe she's part of the cover-up."

"Bernie, you can do that while I visit Ace."

"Carla, if you go near that asshole, especially how you feel today, I'll shoot you."

As an in-your-face bird flew at Bernie, he chuckled. A shit-eating grin covered his face as Carla smiled back. Finally, Sam delivered their lunch orders.

"There you go, guys, enjoy."

"Sam, where's my Jameson?"

"Oh, I guess I forgot that, sorry."

"That's okay. I've changed my mind. Bring us a round of iced tea."

Sam left and returned with the iced tea as a replay of Kiersten St. Clair blared from several of the televisions above them. Moments later, Carla heard Ace's boisterous voice, and then he laughed heartedly. She then heard him mention her name in their conversation, knowing he was pushing Carla's trigger button. Although that was enough to send her over the edge, she took a few deep breaths and continued eating her Reuben. She knew she couldn't play his game if she wanted to bring him down and anyone else involved.

CHAPTER 51

Aweek later, the case was still on hiatus. It was part of Carla's game plan. She didn't want to give Ace any more information or stoke the fire. She wasn't giving up but wanted Ace to believe his threat was working. Carla wanted so badly to interview him but knew he wouldn't give her the time of day. She believed his threat of a lawsuit was real, and she needed to tread carefully. She also needed more evidence, which had to do with the DNA analysis they were waiting on. It was a game of cat and mouse for her, Beth, and Bernie. They spent their time reviewing all the evidence until those DNA reports were ready.

They had Paul's DNA, and although they were waiting for the sample he submitted, the one his company sent Sherry confirmed he was not Ashlee's father. Jason submitted his DNA without reservations because he was sterile. They were waiting for those results to come back as well. Ezra's DNA profile was on one of the online sites. They knew they would need a court order to get his results, and that could take a lot of time they didn't have.

Furthermore, unless Ace's DNA is already on file some-how, getting it was next to impossible.

They were reviewing every piece of information and evidence. Beth had just performed it a week ago and discovered a shiny substance. They were waiting for those results as well. As they looked at everything spread out on the conference room table, a knock on the door startled them. Beth went and opened the door. Sherry stood outside with a manila folder in her hand.

"Is that what I think it is?"

"If you mean DNA results, you would be correct."

"Come in and join us. We'll gather everything and put it back in its respective evidence box. Just give us a few minutes. I'll come and get you when we're ready."

"Sure, I'll be in my office. Why don't you all come to my office? See you in about five minutes."

Beth closed the door and informed Carla and Bernie what was going on. After returning all the evidence to the appropriate box, they returned it to the evidence room. Walking over to Sherry's office, she was ready to explain her findings. After they settled in front of her desk, Sherry met their gaze.

"Sherry, don't screw with us, just give us the results. Don't dick around with us, okay?"

"McBride, what's got your panties in a wad?"

"Just tell us what you got, okay."

"First of all, Paul Montgomery's sample matches the report submitted by Gannon Biometrics. He's not Ashlee Robert's father. We suspected that, so that's not earthshat-tering news, right, Carla?"

"Right."

"Okay, let's get to Jason Carbone's results. Based on his submitted sample, he is not Ashlee's father either."

"Shit."

"Yeah, Carla. You believed he was, right?"

"Sort of. What else do you have that might burst our bubble?"

"Funny you asked that."

"Let's get to it, and nothing's funny, you—"

"Carla, let me handle this, okay?"

"Have at it, Beth. Work your magic with her."

"Sherry, thank you for putting a rush on this. What else do you have?"

"Remember you found a shiny substance on Ashlee's jean jacket."

"Yeah, tell me we have good news?"

"Well, we have good news and bad news. You want the good news first?"

"Does it really matter?"

"Umm, I guess not. We ran it, and we got hit. That's the good news."

Before Sherry could continue, an indescribable silence smothered Sherry's office. Awe-and-shock morphed into ecstatic jubilation. It was the break they needed. High-fives met Beth; it was her discovery. As Beth, Carla, and Bernie refocused on Sherry; she was not joining their celebration.

"Guys, we got a hit, and that's it. The bad news, well…"

"Dammit, Sherry, who is it?"

"That's the bad news, Carla. I don't know."

"Why the hell not?"

"It's from a rape victim about nineteen years ago or so."

"Who's the victim?"

"You know that's confidential, besides, I don't know.

The police report says the young woman was at a party, drank too much, didn't remember anything, and maybe was given a date-rape-drug. She awoke the next morning in a field outside the city. That's when she realized someone raped her. She called a friend who drove her to the hospital, where she was examined, and samples of bodily fluid were collected. Once the results were in, the DNA was put in a national database."

"Where did the rape occur?"

"Gallipolis, Ohio.

"Shit. That is a huge fu—"

"Carla, that's not the half of it. Whoever that DNA belongs to is Ashlee Roberts' biological father and possibly the killer. Furthermore, that person managed to stay out of trouble. The individual's DNA has been hiding in the criminal database, waiting to be discovered. Now, it has. Guys, I guess you have your work cut out for you."

"Is there anything else, Sherry?"

"No, Carla."

After they expressed their sincere gratitude, they returned to the conference room. As they sat around the table, words could not describe the disappointment each was feeling. They were so close to breaking the case wide open. Now they had more questions than answers. The only sure thing they had on their agenda was another trip to Gallipolis.

Unfortunately, they were looking for a needle in a haystack. Gallipolis was a small town, and with the right people asking the right questions, those with pertinent information would eventually talk, even the victim. Typically, McGruder's would be their celebration venue after receiving such good news. However, any victorious celebration would be premature until they had the individual in custody.

Although they were happy with the good news, the bad news was another curveball. They pondered that maybe Ace was correct about a serial killer and perhaps even a rapist. Anything was possible in their whacky crime world. And even though Ace's threat of a defamation lawsuit lurked in the background, another visit with his brother was necessary. They were confident that their trip to Gallipolis would shed new light on their case.

CHAPTER 52

Beth, Carla, and Bernie arrived in Gallipolis around ten o'clock the following day. Carla had contacted the chief of police in advance to notify him of the reason for their visit. Police Chief Rodney Harris, a twenty-year veteran of the police force, had only been chief for a couple of years. He told Carla he vaguely remembered the case, but he was willing to meet with them. They also planned to visit the hospital where the victim was examined. The officer who took the victim's statement at the hospital was no longer employed or living in the area.

Entering the police department was like going back in time. With around four thousand in the community, the police force was small, employing a receptionist, nine patrolmen, and one detective. After asking for Chief Harris, the receptionist told them to sit in the chairs against the front wall. Chief Harris emerged from his office a few minutes later, carrying a small file folder. After greeting them, he took them to a conference room.

Once everyone was seated, he passed out a one-page

incident report. After reviewing the report's information, it wasn't different from what Sherry previously told them. Redactions covered the victim's name and personal information. They expected that.

"Again, thank you for seeing us today." Chief Harris nodded. "Is this everything? What about the police officer's notes used to type this report?"

"I'd say they got tossed. Anyway, as you can see from the victim's statement, there wasn't much she remembered. She admitted to being drunk when she got to the party. Then with more drinking, someone probably slipped her a pill. She only remembers waking up in a field several miles outside the city. She called a friend who convinced her to seek medical attention, which she did. The emergency room contacted us because they convinced her to file a report."

"Yeah, we get that. We understand the police officer who took her statement is no longer employed. Does that officer still live in the area?"

"No, Officer Leslie Graves got married and moved away. I don't remember where, sorry."

"No problem. I don't see anywhere on the report where the party took place."

"Detective McBride, I don't mean to be callous or give you the impression I don't care, because I do. But according to this report, she remembers nothing. And honestly, that's likely why there was no further investigation into this rape. That was a long time ago, and stories change."

"Hey, I get that. Our cold case was a long time ago, and now the DNA from that rape shows up on our most recent case. We don't think that's a coincidence. Have there been any other incidents like this one?"

"Nope, that's the only one. Gallipolis is a peaceful community. Is there anything else I can help you with?"

"What is the statute of limitations on rape in the state?"

"Twenty years, why?"

"Based on the date on the report, there's still time to go after the man."

"Seriously, based on what?"

"New evidence."

"Do you have any?"

"Not yet, but maybe after today, we might."

"Like what?"

"Maybe a name or witness. We've got DNA from our death investigation that turns out to be your rapist. We just have to find out who he is. It would be a huge feather in your cap to solve a forgotten rape case.

"Get me something I can work with, and hell yeah, we'll reopen the case."

"Thank you.

"Beth, Bernie, do you have any questions for Chief Harris?" They shook their heads. "Okay, then I guess we're done. Chief Harris, please be aware we have more people to see regarding our case. When we find what we need to bring this person down, I'll be in touch."

After leaving the police department, their next visit was with Sharma at Remo's Italian Weinery. They had no idea if she knew anything, but it was a small town, and someone knew something about it. They were hoping she was one of those people.

Arriving just as Remo's opened, Sharma was prepping behind the bar. After asking to be seated in her section, the hostess escorted them to a booth on the far wall. Once seated in the booth, Beth kept an eye on

Sharma as she continued her prep work. Finally, the hostess walked over to Sharma and told her they had requested her. Within a minute, Sharma placed three glasses of water on the table and gave them each a menu.

"Welcome back. Let me see if I can get this right, Detectives McBride, Kowalski, and Beth..."

"Beth Pendergast."

"Right, sorry Beth."

"Hey, no problem. I forget names and faces, too."

"What brings you back so soon, Beth?"

"We're checking out a lead in Maxine's daughter, Ashlee's death investigation."

"Hmm, well, good to see you again."

"Likewise. Is there a lunch special?"

"Yeah, spicy Italian sausage with sauerkraut and sautéed onions, your choice of fries or homemade onion rings. I'd go for the onion rings."

"Sounds great. We'll each have the special and iced tea, right, guys?"

Carla and Bernie nodded, and Sharma picked up the menus and placed their lunch order. Several minutes later, Sharma returned with a tray containing a pitcher of iced tea, three glasses, and a plate of lemons. After filling the glasses, she met Beth's curious gaze.

"Did I forget something, Beth?"

"Oh, no. While we are waiting for our lunch orders, do you have a few minutes to answer a few questions?"

"What kind of questions?"

"I mentioned a lead that just surfaced regarding Maxine. Can you talk with us right now?"

"Yeah, maybe."

"Great. We recently discovered DNA found on Ashlee's jean jacket that matches DNA from the rape of a young woman about twenty years ago in Gallipolis. According to the police report, the victim doesn't remember anything. The young woman woke up in a field and discovered she'd been raped. She called a friend who took her to the hospital. The rest is history, and nothing ever happened with the case. More than likely, whoever owns that DNA probably killed Maxine and Ashlee. Does any of this ring a bell?"

As she shook her head, her wandering eyes and body language screamed something different. She looked toward the bar area, hoping their lunch orders were ready. Returning her gaze to Beth, she took a deep breath and broke eye contact with her once more. After seeing their lunch in the window, she left without responding. A couple of minutes later, she returned, placed their lunch on the table, and walked away.

"Sharma?"

"Yeah, Beth."

"If you know something, we need to know. It might help us get justice for Maxine and her daughter. Don't you want that?"

"I'm sorry, I can't talk right now."

CHAPTER 53

Sharma quickly left and entered the kitchen area. A few moments later, Beth watched her enter the restroom in tears. While Carla and Bernie began eating the tasty sausage hoagie, Beth nibbled on a few onion rings waiting for Sharma to reappear. Beth knew she'd gotten lucky, but then, in small towns, everybody knows somebody who knows something. The longer Sharma remained in the restroom; the more Beth considered she might be the young woman raped. Or perhaps she took the young woman to the hospital.

"Beth, what's that all about?"

"Carla, I think I struck a nerve. I think she knows something."

"Let's hope so. You better eat the sausage dog before it gets cold. It's mighty good."

Although Beth kept her eye on the restroom door, the sausage dog was too tempting. Carla and Bernie were almost finished with their lunch when Sharma emerged from the restroom and entered the kitchen area. Beth knew

Sharma would eventually have to return to their booth. It was apparent she was upset, or maybe she was being put on the spot about ratting on a friend. Beth hoped she understood the ramifications of not saying anything. Finally, she returned to their booth with their check. At the top of the check, the name Mitzi was printed. She smiled and left. Moments later, she entered the restroom once more. Beth pulled out three twenty-dollar bills and put them under the check. Besides Mitzi's name, she wrote the word thanks. She then placed her glass on top of the money and check.

Fifteen minutes later, Bernie parked in front of Mitzi's antique shop. The sign on the door made Beth smile. Mitzi was likely inside. Beth wasn't sure what Sharma meant by printing Mitzi's name. Was she the victim, or was she the person who drove the victim to the hospital? After entering the store, a chime rang out. Within a couple of minutes, Mitzi approached them.

"Wow, detectives, you're going to wear out your welcome. What brings you back here so soon. Didn't I answer all your questions the last time you were here?"

"Mitzi, this is Detective Carla McBride. She's the lead detective in Maxine's death investigation."

"Nice to meet you, detective."

"Likewise, I'm not into antiques, but you have a nice store."

"Yeah, so, why are you all here?"

"Mitzi, we have a new lead in our cases, and need to ask you a few more questions."

"Okay, Beth. I'll help if I can."

"I discovered a substance on Ashlee's jean jacket. After a DNA analysis, it was run through a national database, we got a hit. The unidentified DNA on the jacket is the same DNA discovered from a rape victim around twenty years ago right here in Gallipolis."

"So…"

"Do you know anything about that rape? If you do, you need to tell us. We find that person, we get justice for Maxine and Ashlee. It's that simple."

"Okay, it wasn't me, and I didn't drive her to the hospital."

"Then who?"

"I don't know. Maybe you should ask Mackenzie Adams. Perhaps she knows."

"Mitzi, how do you know she knows something?"

"It's a small town. People know everything in this town, but those same people are afraid to talk. It's all about fear."

"Okay, we know where Mac lives."

"Good luck, and don't mention my name."

They pulled in front of Mackenzie Adams' white frame house twenty minutes later. Nothing had changed since their previous visit. As they walked up on the front porch, the rockers appeared in the same place. Bernie did the honors and knocked on the door. The door quickly opened as though Mackenzie was expecting them. She immediately recognized Beth and Bernie.

"What brings you all back, and who's the redhead?"

"I'm Detective Carla McBride. May we come in?"

"I thought I answered all your questions the last time you were here, Detective Kowalski."

"We have more. May we come in?"

After entering and sitting in the living room, Bernie continued his conversation.

"We have new evidence in the death investigation of Maxine and Ashlee. You may be able to help us. You see, a rape occurred in Gallipolis about twenty years ago. DNA from that rape is the same as we found on Ashlee's jean jacket. We find who committed that rape and we find who killed Maxine and Ashlee. Do you know anything about that rape?"

Mackenzie's complexion exploded with fear. As her eyes turned glassy, tears streamed down her cheeks. As she wiped them away, quiet sobs began to flow. She met Beth's caring expression.

"Mackenzie, take a deep breath and tell us what you know. Do you want us to find your best friend's killer?" She nodded. "Okay, we're ready when you are. Just take a few more breaths."

"It was me, Beth. I'm to blame. A bunch of us girls went to a party downtown. We'd been drinking quite a bit when we crashed the party. I believe someone slipped me a pill or two because I don't remember much after drinking that beer. The next thing I know, I'm in a field, lying face down. It was dark, and a man was on top of me. I could feel the cold ground underneath me as he forced himself inside me. I was incoherent, I thought it was a dream, and tried to wake up. It didn't take him long. I was so scared I thought I was going to die. I must have passed out. Eventually, the bright sun woke me up."

"I'm so sorry, Mackenzie. That had to be painful to relive that...that you've held that in all these years. You're a brave woman."

"Thank you."

"Do you know who it was?"

"No."

"Can you name people that were at the party?"

"A few. Paul Montgomery, Jason Carbone, and Johnny Masters are some of the other baseball players that played with them. I remember Jason's uncles. I made sure I steered clear of them."

"Who took you to the hospital?"

"Maxine. She was like a sister to me, always there for me. I still miss her."

"Again, I'm sorry it happened to you. When we find the asshole who did this to you, we'll add rape to his charges. We'll get justice for you."

"I'd like to help, but I don't remember much more, and besides, I'd rather not remember every little detail about that evening. I went on with my life."

CHAPTER 54

That emotional confession created a solemn silence in the room. Years of guilt flowed from Mackenzie. Carla, Beth, and Bernie felt her pain. Carla rose from the sofa and opened her arms to Mackenzie. Although they had never met before today, that emotional cleansing of the soul display bonded them forever. After seeing Carla's open arms, Mackenzie latched onto her as she whimpered uncontrollably. Up to this point, Carla had managed to keep her feelings at bay. However, her maternal instincts took over and comforted Mackenzie as though she was her child.

While watching this vulnerable moment, Beth's thoughts drifted to her mother, Judy, who she lost last year. Although this display of maternal love was different, the impact was the same. Beth wiped away a few tears on her cheeks as Carla and Mackenzie released their emotional bonding. Bernie felt the same pain as he watched. He'd lost his only daughter a long time ago. He was good at masking his emotions, however, his soul cried silently.

Silence once more crept in as they sat back down. Before this emotional episode, the atmosphere in the room was thick. Now that Mackenzie had released her demons from that night, a spring-like aura filled the room. As a smile crossed Mackenzie's face, she rose from her chair and excused herself. While she entered the kitchen, Beth discussed with Carla and Bernie what just happened and suggested hypnotherapy. With Mackenzie remembering different parts of that night, Beth wondered whether the other parts were tucked away in her subconscious and blocked forever.

After about five minutes, Mackenzie returned with a pitcher of sweet, iced tea and four glasses. She placed it on the coffee table, then filled each glass. A saucer of fresh lemons was available for those who liked them in their tea. Mackenzie held her glass up toward them for a toast; they followed her lead. With Mackenzie comfortably in her chair, Beth knew she was ready to move on.

"Mackenzie, you said you wanted to help more, but you didn't know how. I'd like to suggest hypnotherapy."

"What's that?"

"It's the use of hypnosis to help you face those demons in your past. I believe you remember more about that night than you think, but those thoughts are recessed in your subconscious. Your mind is blocking them. Have you ever been hypnotized before?"

Mackenzie shook her head. As her eyes moved around the room, Beth could tell uncovering those nightmares in her soul scared the hell out of her.

"I know you are scared, but would you consider it? I'm a psychologist and have performed it many times. It's safe, and you won't remember anything we talk about. We will only talk about that night and nothing else."

Carla smiled at Mackenzie and nodded. Mackenzie smiled back while remembering Carla's maternal love and comfort a few minutes ago. Mackenzie met Beth's caring expression and smiled. As Mackenzie took a deep breath, Beth saw the fear in her eyes.

"Mackenzie, I know you are scared but you may have information in your subconscious that can help us identify who raped you. And if we can do that, you will help us find who likely murdered Maxine, your best friend, and her daughter. Do it for her, and do it for your soul. If it ends up being too painful, I'll bring you back. You won't remember a thing, I promise you. Once it's over, we will not discuss it. Because Carla and Bernie will have my approval to witness it, they will be bound by the patient-client privilege. I will record it for legal purposes should we ever need it. We will step outside for a few minutes. Take your time."

While they walked out on the front porch, Mackenzie's considered the pros and cons of going under and reliving that night in her subconscious world. She'd had nightmares of that night but never sought help. The man's face was blank and his voice silent. As they enjoyed the fresh air, Mackenzie appeared in the doorway. Beth noticed Mackenzie smiling, then nodding. After they were back inside, Beth set up the room to make Mackenzie feel safe and comfortable to bare her soul and demons.

As Mackenzie lay on the sofa, Beth began talking to her in a comforting but authoritative tone. Beth asked her to close her eyes and take several deep cleansing breaths to relax. A surreal silence surrounded Mackenzie as she breathed deeply. Beth instructed her to open her eyes and follow the pendulum necklace moving back and forth in front of her.

"Mackenzie, continue watching the necklace as your eyelids grow heavy. Breathe deep, breathe deep. Your eyelids are now so heavy you can't keep them open. Close them, and breathe deep."

As Mackenzie's breathing became relaxed, it wouldn't be long until her subconscious would speak the truth. Beth put away her necklace and waited as controlled breathing flowed from Mackenzie's body.

"Mackenzie, where are you right now?"

"I'm at my mom's house waiting for Maxine to arrive."

"What time is it?"

"It's around nine PM."

"Where are you and Maxine going?"

"We're going to pick up Mitzi and Sharma. Then we're going out to the Pixey Stix in Point Pleasant. It's to be a girls' night out."

"You had fun there, right?"

"Yeah, we drank too many of those Pixey Stix Martinis. We danced a lot, just us girls."

"Where did you go after leaving the Pixey Stix?"

"Earlier that day, Jason invited us to a party in downtown Gallipolis at a bar called The Last Out. The party was in a private room."

"Who else was there?"

"Besides Jason, Paul Montgomery, Johnny Masters, and a few other of their baseball buddies. There were many others I didn't know. Oh, I remember Jason's uncles. At first, I thought my eyes were playing tricks on me because I saw two of them. I couldn't tell them apart.

I'd only met them one other time. I didn't like them because they both couldn't keep their eyes off me that day. That night, I could see them undress me with their wandering, lustful eyes. As they moistened their lips, they scared the hell out of me."

CHAPTER 55

As Mackenzie's breathing increased, Beth expressed comforting words making her feel safe. After comforting her, silence and relaxed breathing took over her body once more.

"Mackenzie, where are you now?"

"I'm still at the party. I'm having a good time with Maxine, Mitzi, and Sharma. We're dancing around, feeling good."

"Okay, what time is it now?"

"I believe it's midnight, and I heard someone yell out last call. The next thing I know, Jason's uncle gave us each a beer. I was already pretty drunk, but feeling like a free spirit, I chugged it. It tasted different."

"Which uncle?"

"I couldn't tell them apart. I don't know."

"What happened next?"

"I remember both uncles dancing with all of us girls. It was wild and crazy."

"While dancing around, did either uncle touch you?"

"They tried but I wouldn't let them."

"Okay, what time is it now?"

"I believe it's one AM. People are leaving. It's closing time."

"Where are the rest of your friends?"

"Gone, except Maxine and me. The next thing I see is Maxine leaving with one of Jason's uncles."

"Which one?"

"I can't tell them apart."

"Did he have a birthmark on the left side of his neck?"

"I couldn't tell."

"Okay, what happened next?"

"With Maxine gone, I had no way home. The other uncle offered me a ride. I could hardly walk, and said yes."

"Did he have a birthmark below his left ear?"

"I don't remember. I was always on his right side."

"Did he try to kiss you or touch you?"

"No."

"Where are you now?"

"In his car."

"Is he taking you home?"

"No, we are in the country now. I ask him where we are going. The music is so loud, and I couldn't hear him."

"What happened next?"

"My eyes are getting heavy. My vision is blurry, and the world is spinning around me. All of a sudden, it's pitch black. I hear the car door open and shut. Then another door opened. I feel a hand grab mine and pull me out of the car. I hear the door shut. We're walking in a field."

"Are you talking?"

"No, we just kept walking. I ask him where we are going. He didn't answer me. We're still walking."

"Why didn't you try to run?"

"I can't. He is holding my hand tight, and his grip is powerful. Suddenly, he forced me to the ground. I'm lying face down as my world spins around me. I felt his hands raise my dress above my waist. Then he pulls down my panties. Uh…"

"It's okay, Mackenzie. What happens next?"

"His hands all over me, under my bra, playing with my nipples. His hardness is between my legs. I feel it moving and moving. As he continues, he pulled my hips up toward him. Then I feel him inside me, thrusting, thrusting, and thrusting. I feel sick."

"Is he saying anything?"

"No. He moaned as his thrusts get faster and faster. As he emptied himself inside me. His cleansing moan made me sick. After a couple of more thrusts, he stopped and got off me."

"What happened next?"

"I hear him whisper, lay there and be quiet, don't look up, or I'll kill you. So, I just lie there with my face in the wet brush, trying to breathe. A moment later, I hear a car start and drive away. I'm shivering. I'm cold. That's all I remember."

"We're almost done. What's next, Mackenzie?"

"I feel the sun on my face, and I squint at the bright sunshine. I knew I was alive. I sit up, pull my panties up, and my dress down. My shoulder bag is still around my shoulder. I can see cars moving on the road about one hundred yards away. I walk toward the road. When I got there, I recognized where I was. I opened my purse and grabbed my phone."

"Who did you call?"

"Maxine. I described where I was and waited for her to come and get me. I guess it was twenty minutes or so before she got there."

"What happened next?"

"When Maxine arrived, I told her I thought I'd been raped. She asked me by whom. I told her I couldn't remember. She told me she would take me to the hospital."

"What happened at the hospital?"

"They examined me, swab me a lot. They asked me a lot of questions. Then a woman police officer arrived and took my statement. After she finished, she left. Then I was free to go."

"What happened next?"

"Maxine took me to get some coffee. I didn't feel like eating. We talked a lot."

"What about?"

"We talked about the party last night. I asked her why she had left without me. She told me that I told her I was having too much fun and I would get a ride home."

"What else?"

"I asked her what happened to Sharma and Mitzi. She said she took them home and then went back out."

"What else did you and Maxine talk about?"

"She told me she met Jason's uncle at a hotel."

"Which uncle, you said you saw two of them?"

"Yeah, I thought I had double vision. She even said she had trouble telling them apart except for the birthmark."

"So, she didn't know which one she met."

"No, I think she did."

"Then which one, Mackenzie. Was it the uncle that had the birthmark?"

"I told him no, but he kept thrusting and thrusting."

"Mackenzie, remember you are talking with Maxine about her night at the hotel with one of Jason's uncles?"

Mackenzie began to moan and shiver. Beth began her regimen of bringing her out of hypnosis, but Carla tapped Beth on the arm. Carla wanted her to keep Mac under a bit longer to find out which uncle Maxine was with. Beth nodded and began talking with Mackenzie again.

"Okay, Mackenzie, what did Maxine tell you? Who was she with?"

"Please don't hurt me I kept saying as he continued to thrust and penetrate me. I felt so dirty, so cheap, so ashamed."

"Mackenzie, Mackenzie, who was with Maxine?"

"Umm…umm…"

"Was it Uncle Charlie with the birthmark?"

"Yesssssss! I'm so sorry…"

"Okay, Mackenzie, I'm going to bring you out now. Focus on my voice. I'm going to count backward from ten."

"Okay."

"When I reach one, open your eyes, and take several deep breaths. You will not remember any of this, okay?"

When Beth said "one," Mackenzie's eyes flew open, and she breathed in and out several times. Her eyes wandered around the room and then focused on Beth's smile. After seeing Carla, she smiled and sat up on the sofa. Carla rose and walked over to Mackenzie with open arms. Mackenzie stood and hugged her as Carla whispered thank you.

CHAPTER 56

As Beth watched Carla and Mackenzie separate their emotional embrace, she couldn't help but think that Mackenzie knew more about what happened to Maxine after that night. She had just finished her account of the rape, which she would never remember again. Maxine and Mackenzie were like sisters, just by different mothers. It was a sure bet that Maxine and Mackenzie shared their deep and darkest secrets. So, Mackenzie might know why Maxine ended up dead but doesn't realize it.

The hypnotherapy had worked for the most part. Mackenzie's gut-wrenching and courageous account of that night didn't clearly identify her rapist; however, it shed more light on a likely suspect. Mackenzie also divulged that Maxine spent the night with Ezra Hutchinson. If the timing had been right, he would have been engaged to the daughter of a wealthy family in Gallipolis. According to Beth's internet searches, Macey Stewart was an only child. And although she was a successful ophthalmologist, she would inherit her family's successful construction business upon their death.

After Mackenzie returned to the sofa, the expression painting her face reflected relief. She appeared relaxed and free. Her eyes moved around the room as though she searched for the demons released from her subconscious world. As Beth continued observing Mackenzie's demeanor and body language, Mackenzie locked eyes with Beth.

"Beth, you look like you are trying to read my mind. What else would you like to know?"

"I believe you can help us more if you are up to it. If not, I understand. You've been through hell, and I don't want you to experience any more agonizing mental trauma. Would you tell us more about Maxine? You are the only one who knew her well. Maxine can't speak to us, but you can, and just maybe what you tell us could lead us to the person who killed her and her daughter. And just maybe, who raped you. Are you up to it?"

Mackenzie rose from the sofa and walked to the kitchen. After a couple of minutes, she returned with a bowl of ice cubes. Replenishing the glasses with ice, she poured everyone a fresh glass of tea. She returned to the sofa and met Beth's reassuring gaze.

"Okay, Beth. What else do you want to know?"

"Thank you, Mackenzie. You are one courageous woman. Even though I didn't know Maxine, I'm sure she would be proud of you."

After hearing that, a few tears surfaced on Mackenzie's cheeks. While taking several deep breaths, she met Beth's eyes and nodded. Beth pulled out her iPhone and pushed the record button. Carla and Bernie sat relaxed but focused on Mackenzie.

"Mackenzie, when did Maxine find out she was pregnant?"

"I guess it was later that summer. I remember she told me her periods were not regular. Although she was on the pill, she was not always religious about taking them. I fussed at her about that. I even remember saying to her one time that she would end up pregnant at the wrong time. She just laughed it off. That was carefree, Maxine."

"Okay. After she found out, what happened?"

"Although she wasn't thrilled about it, she was a devout Catholic and decided to keep it. Her dad was not happy about the pregnancy but respected her decision. As the baby grew inside her, she became a different person. She became more like an adult, you know, no more partying, no more running around. She told me several times she was looking forward to being a mother. She never mentioned giving up her baby."

"Did she ever tell you who the father was?"

Mackenzie broke eye contact with Beth. Her eyes moved around the room as though she was looking for those demons of her past. Beth knew it was best to let her have the time to keep calm. While taking a deep breath, she met Beth's waiting eyes.

"She suspected Ezra."

"Okay, did she ever confront him?"

"Yeah, but of course, he denied it. She asked him to take a paternity test, and he declined. She told me he told her to let it go, leave him alone, or things will get ugly."

"So, he threatened her."

"She didn't call it that; he offered up money to keep her quiet."

"What did she do next?"

"Maxine decided to take his advice. She talked about

taking the money and moving to Florida and starting a new life."

"Did she do that?"

"At the time, she was ready to go, but that's when her father died in an auto accident. That changed everything. She was devastated." Tears surfaced on her cheeks, and she wiped them away. After a big sigh, she continued. "I think that's when she decided Florida was not the place for her and her unborn baby."

"When did you find out she was having a girl?"

"I didn't. She told me she wanted it to be a surprise."

"After her dad died, where did she live?"

"She had to move out. She found a halfway house for unwed mothers somewhere in the state. I don't remember where."

"When did she go there?"

"After her dad's funeral, everything was settled. She took what little money her dad left her, loaded up her car, then she…" Tears began to surface once more. She rose from the sofa, walked over to the picture window, and looked at the Heavens. Carla rose from her chair, walked over beside her, and stood with her.

"Mackenzie, everything will be okay. Trust me, okay?"

After a brief hug with Carla, she returned to the sofa. Carla returned to her chair as Mackenzie continued.

"I remember that day like it was yesterday. Her car was packed, and she was wearing the Angel Hardesty jean jacket I bought her for her birthday. She loved it. Anyway, I guess that was the last time I saw her. You know, she told me she would name her baby after me."

"But wasn't Ashley her middle name?"

"Yeah, but so is mine. It's just spelled differently. If

she had a boy, she would name him Asher. She had it all planned. I watched her drive away, which was the last time I saw her. I never heard from her again. Now, I know why. I hope this helps."

"Mackenzie, it has. You just don't know how much. Is there anything else you can think of?"

"Before she left, she handed me a note."

"What was on it?"

"Three initials."

"What were the initials?"

"I've still got the note. It was the last thing she gave me. I'll go get it."

Mackenzie left the room and returned with a folded piece of paper and handed it to Carla. She unfolded it carefully, revealing the initials. After pulling out her iPhone, she took a picture of it, then returned it to her.

"Did Maxine say what it meant?"

"No. She didn't want me to look at it until after she left."

"What do you think it means?"

"I don't know."

"That's okay."

"Beth, you said earlier that everything we talked about would remain confidential, right?"

"Yeah, why?"

"If something got leaked, I know things like that happen. Would I be in any danger?"

"Mackenzie?"

"Yes, Detective McBride?"

"Listen to me. I promise you nothing will get leaked, okay? You have my word on that. I will not let anything happen to you."

CHAPTER 57

A s tears surfaced on Mackenzie's pale face, her account of the rape and the last time she saw Maxine had taken an emotional toll on her body and soul. After bidding farewell, Beth, Carla, and Bernie left her house. As they drove away, a reserved silence filled the car. Like Mackenzie, they were emotionally drained. From everything Mackenzie told them, their cases had a much clearer direction. However, it might be useless without Ace's or Ezra's DNA. Also, Carla promised Mackenzie it would never get out or used in a court of law, putting her life in danger. Carla originally wanted to revisit Ezra, but after Mackenzie's gut-wrenching story, she felt it would do more harm than good and nixed the idea.

This fishing trip was all Beth's idea. She wanted to revisit Gabriela's Boutique to ask a few more questions about the receipts she showed them on their last visit a week ago. After a twenty-five-minute drive, Bernie parked in front of the boutique and chose not to go in. Once inside, Carla milled around the store while Beth asked one of her employees for Gabriela. A few minutes later, she emerged from her office wearing the latest version of the Angel Hardesty brand. Beth motioned Carla to join her at the counter.

"Mrs. Marcinco, this is Detective McBride. Thank you for speaking with us. I have a few more questions to ask you. Do you have time? It won't take long."

"What else may I help you with? You know, ladies, we have the new shipment of Angel Hardesty jean jackets in stock. I'm wearing one. What do you think?"

"It looks nice on you."

"Thank you. Now, what did you want to ask me?"

"When I was here before, you mentioned two ladies from out of town bought two jackets each. They both paid cash, remember?"

"Of course."

"What else can you tell me? Also, I would like to get a copy of those receipts. Don't know if it will amount to anything or not."

"Yeah, of course. I'm not sure I can tell you anything more. I'll get the receipts."

While she entered her office, Beth asked Carla a couple of questions. Carla took out her iPhone and opened up Safari. Gabriela returned with copies of the two cash receipts and handed them to Beth. She reviewed the receipts paying close attention to a series of numbers printed on them.

"From what I remember, the numbers are like serial numbers, right?"

"Like I said before, Janice wanted to do this. I told her it wasn't necessary. Let me go get one off the rack."

While she retrieved one off the rack, Carla had finished her search on the internet and saved the search pages. Gabriela returned with the jean jacket showing them the numbers embroidered on the back of the collar.

"As I said, I thought it was a waste of time and effort, but she makes the jackets, and I sell them. Now, what else can I help you with?"

"Mrs. Marcinco?"

"Yes, Detective McBride."

"Have you ever seen this man before, or has he been in here?" Gabriela took a good look and shook her head. "What about this man?" Once again, she shook her head. "Okay, what about this lady?"

"Yeah, she looks a lot like the lady who bought the last two jackets a week before Beth was here."

"Great, thank you."

"You are welcome. Is there anything else?"

"Yeah, based on what you said, the second receipt was hers, correct?"

"Right, Beth."

"Thank you."

"You are welcome, anything else."

"No, you've been a big help."

"You know, Beth, you would look nice in one of those jean jackets. May I bag one up for you?"

"Yeah, why not. I've grown to like them."

"Great. What about you, Detective McBride?"

"You know, it's just not style."

"Doesn't hurt to ask, does it?"

Five minutes later, Carla and Beth were back in Bernie's car. Bernie gave Beth the strangest look, and she just smiled at him.

"Beth, did you buy one of those jackets?"

"Yeah. I've grown to like them. Do you have a problem with that?"

"Nope. Where to now?"

"Carla, are you up to a drink before hitting the road? We can celebrate and discuss how we move forward."

"Sounds like a good idea. Do you have a place in mind?"

"The Pixey Stix Café. Bernie knows where it is."

"Sounds good. Let's go."

Ten minutes later, they entered the Pixey Stix Café and were immediately escorted to a booth near the back of the café. Within a couple of minutes, Courtney arrived at their booth.

"I remember you guys, except her."

"Right. She's Detective McBride."

"I guess you are still trying to solve Ashlee's murder, or you wouldn't be here, right?"

"I believe we're close, probably won't be back after today. Bring Detective McBride a Jameson on the rocks, I'll have a Pinot Grigio, and he'll have a Yuengling. Oh, and bring us some munchies, too."

Courtney left, and silence surrounded them as they contemplated what they had discovered today. Bernie cleared his throat, breaking the silence.

"Ladies, what took you so long in Gabriela's?"

"We weren't in there that long, right, Carla?"

"No, but we got things figured out, didn't we, Beth?"

"Yeah, you should've gone in with us, Bernie?"

"Seriously…"

"Here you go, guys. Enjoy."

"Thanks, Courtney."

Courtney nodded and left. Beth held her glass to the center of the table, and Carla and Bernie joined her in a toast.

"So, Beth, why did you have me find a picture of Dannie Spencer?"

"Dannie Spencer, what the…"

"Bernie, it was a fishing trip. Gabriella identified her from that picture. I don't know why Dannie was here and bought two jackets. Anyway, let's enjoy our drinks and get on the road. I feel we've made great progress today, right, Carla?"

"Yeah, we're getting close, but we'll have to solve this case without the Hutchinson boys' DNA. We need to start thinking about that. Cheers!"

CHAPTER 58

B
ack in Oakmont the following afternoon, the
conference room was command central.
Although Beth, Carla, and Bernie were tired
from their trip, excitement ran through their souls. They
were close to solving their cases and the rape of
Mackenzie Adams. Her account of her ordeal, along with
her recollection of Maxine's last conversation with her,
gave them a more straightforward path to justice. The
initials on the note added another weapon to solving their
ever-changing jigsaw puzzle.

Everything they had was circumstantial except for the
DNA. With time running out on the statute of limitations
for rape in Ohio, time was paramount in finding the
DNA's owner. That will require a court order which
could take more time than they had. Their thought
process was coming down to forcing the hands of those
involved in the murders and subsequent cover-up. It
would also solve the rape of Mackenzie Adams. All the
pieces of the puzzle were in front of them. They just had

to find a legal way to put them together correctly and bring everyone down.

Chief Evans joined them in the conference room as they planned their strategy. The physical evidence was scattered on the table while reports dotted the wall. They all studied all the pieces that would solve each case. Beth played Mackenzie's testimony before their strategy session would begin. After it finished, Chief Evans opened up the discussion.

"Everything I see is still circumstantial evidence, and we have a lot of assumptions. These will not hold up in a court of law. So, Carla, explain to me where we are headed."

"Right, chief. We know that. I believe we are going to have to force their hands."

"You mean Ace and his brother, right?"

"Yeah, and maybe even Jason Carbone as well."

"Why him?"

"I believe he knows more. I don't think he had anything to do with Maxine and Ashlee's death. However, he may have been the one who slipped Mackenzie the date-rape pill."

"The piece of paper with the initials…what does that mean?"

"Maxine gave that to Mackenzie but didn't tell her what it meant. I believe the initials A.C.E. is Oras Charles Hutchinson. My assumption is that that's who raped Mackenzie. And if I'm right, he had something to do with at least Ashlee's body ending up at the cemetery. I'm not saying he killed her, although he may have. Furthermore, I believe he's responsible for Maxine ending up there knowing he would control the investigation. DNA is the key. The DNA found on Mackenzie matched the DNA found on Ashlee's jean jacket. Getting that from Ace and his brother will require a court order. That would take time, and with the statute of limitations expiring in a few months, I believe we will have to force their hands and let them make a crucial mistake."

"I see where this is going. Okay, what's your strategy?"

"First, we need to try and get a court order for Ezra's DNA. His DNA is on one of those online sites. Providing we can get a court order, we can either go after him or the online site. Neither will be easy. The online site may be the best option and won't alert him, but that won't be easy. We don't need Ace's DNA. Identical twins have the same exact profile. We get his brother's DNA then we get his."

"Okay, what next? We need to leak something to the press, mainly the television station. We need to get Kiersten to interview you about discovering DNA from a rape that matches the DNA found on the jean jacket. Ace will see this, and if he's the one, something will happen."

"Sounds reasonable. What do you think he'll do?"

"That's anyone's guess. I believe Ezra knows his brother raped Mackenzie Adams. At the same time, I'm trying to convince Police Chief Harris in Point Pleasant to reopen the rape case and hold a press conference. Ezra will likely see the report. Once he hears about it, he and Ace will act."

"Okay. We know the identity of the victim. Will she come forward?"

"Carla, you gave her your word…"

"Beth, we've got all the pieces to solving everything, and it's because of you. We somehow need to use her but not jeopardize her life. I think we can do that, and I'll leave it up to you to convince her it's right. She trusts you."

"Yeah, but she trusts you as well."

"I know, but I believe it's the only way. The court order is a long shot."

"I'll do my best."

"Carla, what else?"

"Chief, I want Bernie to press Jason. That's if he will even talk to us. I know that will get Ace moving on his defamation lawsuit, but we have to take that chance."

"Okay, now with what we know about everything, what's the motive?"

"What if Maxine changed her mind about pursuing Ezra for a paternity test. Maybe she used her knowledge about the rape as extortion. He goes berserk and kills her. Then drops the baby off at social services in Point Pleasant. He drives Maxine's body to Oakmont, and Ace takes care of the rest because he will control the investigation."

"Sounds plausible. Is Ezra capable of killing someone?"

"Maybe back then, but now I'm not sure. You know he doesn't fit the profile."

"Okay, how does Ashlee come into play."

"We know from Paul Montgomery that she wanted to find her parents and went online. Maybe she found both. Found out her mom was dead and who her father was. She confronts him, and then she ends up dead here."

"Interesting theory."

"Thanks, chief. You need to thank Beth. She's the one who jumped on the Ace bandwagon first."

"Great job, Beth. Is there anything else?"

"No, chief, that's it."

"What next, Carla?"

"Beth and I will be going back to Gallipolis to speak with Mackenzie and Chief Harris. That's the first move. We need to inform Mackenzie and convince Chief Harris of our plans. Once we do that, then we can put everything else into action. While we are there, Bernie will attempt to meet with Jason Carbone. When this all falls into place, I believe things will move fast. Unfortunately, I don't know how this might end."

CHAPTER 59

After hearing Carla's theory, and possible motives, Police Chief Rodney Harris didn't need convincing. Although he was on the force, he didn't participate in the investigation. However, after tracking down Officer Leslie Graves, he was on a mission to solve the rape case before the statute of limitations expired. His plans were in place, and he would hold a press conference simultaneously as Chief Evans and Carla held theirs in Oakmont.

On the other hand, Mackenzie was not entirely receptive to the idea. Even though her name would not be mentioned or released, she was concerned about her safety and that of her teenage daughters. The rapist would know who she is and that would put them in danger. After much discussion, Chief Harris created a plan to keep her and her daughters safe. Mackenzie wanted so much to find Maxine and Ashlee's killer, and by doing so, she would put her rapist away, sending a message that no woman should ever give up getting justice.

Both press conferences were to take place at eleven AM. As expected, Bernie's attempt to meet with Jason Carbone fell through. Furthermore, Bernie's attempt to meet with Jason put Ace's threat into motion. Ace's attorney filed his defamation lawsuit against the Oakmont Police Department. Mayor Lester James, Chief Evans, Carla, Beth, and Bernie were all named in the lawsuit.

Kiersten St. Clair arrived on time and had her crew ready to bring this breaking news to the community. Chief Harris, in Gallipolis, waited for Carla's call to go live as well. At the stroke of the hour, Kiersten appeared in front of the camera.

"Good morning. Several weeks ago, a cemetery care-taker discovered a body near the back of the cemetery. Well, we have breaking news regarding that death inves-tigation. The victim has been identified as Ashlee Roberts of Point Pleasant, West Virginia. Police Chief Brock Evans will have a press conference with details on new evidence in the case in a few moments. Okay, I see he is ready. Accompanying him is Detective Carla McBride. Let's listen to his comments."

Seconds later, Chief Evans stood in front of the police station. Carla was to his right. As the camera focused on him, he took a deep breath and began.

"Good morning. Thank you for being here. You have heard Miss St. Clair's opening comments about the case. So, let's get started. In Gallipolis, Ohio, Police Chief Rodney Harris is holding a press conference announcing the re-opening of a rape case there from approximately twenty years ago. The statute of limitations has yet to expire in Ohio. An individual has come forward with new evidence. That new evidence impacts our case. DNA evidence discovered in our case is the same collected from the victim in that rape case. We will be working together to find who committed the rape and who likely killed Ashlee Roberts. Also, Ashlee Roberts' DNA evidence helped identify that the body found about twenty years ago in the same cemetery is her mother, Maxine Hardy."

Silence filled the outside of the police station. Given the riveting news, all the media present wanted to ask questions.

"Let's hear from Detective Carla McBride."

"Thank you, chief. My team has been working diligently to solve this case. If there is anyone out there with information regarding it, we ask you to come forward. A former detective who worked that cold case is adamant that we have a serial killer on the loose. We have investigated that possibility. However, it's been several weeks, and there haven't been any other similar killings here. And now that our case is connected to that rape case in Gallipolis, we've ended any investigation regarding a serial killer and are focusing all of our efforts on the rape connection."

"Once again, if anyone has any information regarding this breaking news, I ask them to come forward. That's all we have. We will not be taking any questions at this time. Thank you."

The camera returned to Kiersten St. Clair for her final comments on this breaking news.

"Okay, there you have it. Detective Carla McBride and her team are close to cracking this bizarre case. The former detective who Detective McBride referenced is none other than the legendary Ace Hutchinson, who filed a defamation lawsuit this morning. This situation should get interesting; visit our website for updates. That should do it from here. I'm Kiersten St. Clair reporting from the Oakmont Police Station."

Chief Evans and Carla moved inside the police station and entered the conference room where Beth and Bernie watched the newscast. Carla called Chief Harris in Gallipolis inquiring about his press conference. He told Carla it went well and would send her the video link. Carla did the same for him. Now it was a waiting game for Ace and his brother to make a move.

It didn't take long as news traveled fast in Oakmont and even quicker in Gallipolis. Both breaking newscasts would be aired several times before the day was over. Everyone related to the case would know about it. Carla and her team weren't sure how Ace and his brother would react or if they would. If they didn't act, then all of this strategy would be for naught, and they would be no closer to solving either case.

While Mackenzie and her daughters were on their way to Florida for a vacation, compliments of the Oakmont and Gallipolis Police Departments, Carla and Bernie watched Ace's cabin for any activity. Likewise, Chief Harris had surveillance on his brother in Gallipolis. If either one made a move, they would know about it.

As nightfall descended on each surveillance team, activity at each home was non-existent. As Carla and Bernie were relieved, the same occurred in Gallipolis. By morning, they were still in the same boat. The Hutchinson brothers had not made a move. Nothing happened over the next several days, and Carla began to question her plan. She was sure that Ace and his brother were the guilty ones. Carla needed a breakthrough, and she hoped that would come when a judge in Ohio granted their request to obtain Ezra's DNA profile from the online site he used. Although they were sure the company would deny it, he would likely find out, which should set things into motion.

CHAPTER 60

Several days had passed since the press conferences. The Hutchinson brothers had not made a move. Beth, Carla, and Bernie were getting anxious since their strategy might fail. In a few days, Mackenzie and her daughters would return home. That heightened their concern. Also, as expected, the company owning Ezra's DNA refused to release his records. Carla knew that fight could remain in the courts for months, and they still might not get his DNA.

While sitting at their workstations, a middle-aged lady entered the police station, which caught Bernie's eye. Dannie Spencer was in the house. A minute later, the receptionist stood at Bernie's workstation. After a brief conversation, she left. Dannie sat in the waiting area for Bernie to meet her. Moments later, Bernie strolled over and greeted her. They exchanged a few words, and he glanced toward Carla and motioned her over. Moments later, they escorted Dannie to the conference room. Dannie and Bernie sat at the table while Carla went after

Beth. Moments later, Beth and Carla entered and sat across from them.

"Okay, Dannie, we can begin now. Meet Beth Pendergast, our forensic psychologist and profiler."

After cordial exchanges, Carla continued. "Bernie said you have important information regarding Ace. What is it?"

"I feel it's important even though nothing has happened."

"Carla, before she goes any further, I'd like to ask her a few questions, you know, about the jean jackets."

"Of course, Beth. We're pretty sure, you—"

"Miss Pendergast, that's why I'm here."

"So, you bought two Angel Hardesty jean jackets from Gabriela's Boutique in Point Pleasant, right?"

"Yeah, it was me."

"Why?"

"I'll get to that in a moment. I want to go back to the day the first Jane Doe was discovered. When I arrived, Ace was already there. I wondered how he got there so fast. Anyway, he seemed a little nervous and fidgety. He was acting a little strange. And when Bernie showed up unexpectedly, his anxiety level went up a few notches. I asked him what was wrong, and he bit my head off. That wasn't like him, either."

"Why did you buy two jean jackets?"

"Miss Pendergast, I said I'd get to it in a few moments, okay?"

"Beth?"

"Yeah, Carla."

"Let's let her finish. I know you're anxious to find out, but this may be the break we need. Go on, Dannie."

"At the time of the first murder, we were having an

affair. That was a no-no back then. So, for Ace to bite my head off meant something was bothering him. Anyway, fast forward to the jean jacket. A few weeks ago, after the second Jane Doe was found in the same jean jacket, I started to think about our case. Then Bernie ran into me and asked me about the Angel Hardesty brand. Remember, Bernie?"

After Bernie nodded, Dannie continued. "I had tracked that brand down and told Ace all about it. He told me he'd check it out. Weeks later, while we were together off the clock, you know, I asked about it. He told me to forget about it, that it had no bearing on the investigation. I told him I thought it could help us solve the case. He just laughed it off and told me not to mention it again."

"Then what happened.?"

"As the case got colder, I brought it up again. He got mad as hell and told me never to bring it up again or I'd be sorry. I thought it would come back to bite us in the butt. However, nothing about the young woman ever surfaced with each passing day. He said it was time to let it go, and I did. Soon after that, our affair ended. I believe it had something to do with the case. He also distanced himself from me at work, and then I was reassigned to a different beat."

"Why didn't you go to the chief with your concerns?"

"I mentioned that to Ace one time, and he went ballistic. He'd never done that to me before, and he scared me. He's no saint by any means."

"Do you need a break, Dannie? May I get you some water?"

She nodded, and Bernie left the room. He quickly returned with several bottles of water. He handed one to

Dannie. She immediately opened it, took several sips, and put it back down and continued.

"Over the years, we mended fences and got together for lunch. It wasn't an affair. I'd never do that again. Anyway, a couple of weeks ago, he called me and asked me to lunch. We met in Lexington, which I thought was strange. I guess he didn't want to be seen with me or something like that. After we finished our lunch, he asked if I would go with him to his hometown of Gallipolis. I didn't know what to think. Maybe he was lonely after his wife died. I thought it couldn't hurt. He was retired, and I wasn't with the police force any longer. After showing me around his hometown, we went to Point Pleasant and parked down the street from Gabriela's Boutique. He asked me to go in and buy two of the jean jackets. It was like he knew they had them. I asked him why he wanted them, and he said they were gifts, and it was none of my business. I asked him why he didn't want to go in, and he said he was a little embarrassed going into a women's store. He was like that sometimes. So, I did it for him, not knowing his motive."

"Okay, so why is this important?"

"I know this is far out there, but I believe he was going to use them for something else."

"Like what?" Beth asked.

"Miss Pendergast, he told me about your visit and how he suggested you had a serial-killer scenario on your hands. I think he was going to prove it to you by killing an unsuspecting young woman and dressing her in the jean jacket."

"Whoa, he would do that just to prove the serial-killer scenario?"

"Yeah, McBride, I believe that. Maybe even kill two

and divert you from going after him. It would give him time to flee the country. After your visit, Miss Pendergast, Ace became concerned he was becoming a suspect, and you embarrassed him. He didn't like that. He asked me what I thought about that scenario, and I told him it didn't fit the profile. He went off on me. When I saw the press conference and you asked if anyone had information to come forward, I knew I had to come in. I didn't want anyone else to die. If something doesn't happen soon, someone will. I believe it in my soul. You guys have backed him into a corner, and he's not going to give up easily. That's all I have."

"Okay, thank you. We've been watching his cabin for several days now. If he makes a move, we'll know. We'll get him."

"McBride, he's not there."

"But his car is in front of the cabin."

"Yeah, but he has a jeep he parks in the rear of the cabin."

"Yeah, I remember seeing it the day I was there," Beth interjected.

"Anyway, I have a key to the back door that he doesn't know about. I went there to stop him before I came here. He's not in the cabin at this moment."

"Where is he?"

"McBride, I wish I knew, probably stalking the next victim. I'd check out the homeless areas. Also, if you need my help, Bernie has my number. If it came down to a hostage situation, I might be able to help you. He trusts me more than any of you."

CHAPTER 61

Stunned by Dannie's revelation, silence swarmed around them. Bernie escorted Dannie out of the conference room while Carla and Beth collected their thoughts. While walking to the main door, Dannie expressed her concern and apologized for not acting years ago. She'd been carrying that guilt for years, and when Ashlee Roberts met the same fate as her mother, Maxine, she knew she had to do something but couldn't find the courage until now. Bernie thanked her for coming forward. He knew they had to act quickly, or another young woman would die to prove the serial-killer scenario to them.

As Bernie returned to the conference room, the silence pounded the walls. Dannie was pretty clear that Ace would strike soon, and some innocent young woman would die. Bernie joined them at the table as they pondered their next move.

"Okay, guys. We have to act soon. Dannie suggested the homeless areas. We need to check out each location, ask a few questions, and see if anyone has seen his jeep. Beth, you saw it. Give us a description."

"Let's see, Bernie. White with a black top..."

"Wow, that will really help us, right, Carla?"

"Oh, and the spare tire cover on the back. It says *gone fishing* over a picture of a fish."

In Oakmont, there were three distinctive locations where the homeless usually resided. After Carla made the assignments, she met with Chief Evans to involve other officers in those locations. Carla assigned Beth to the north end of town and Bernie to the south end. Carla took the city's east end. They were to hang out in their assigned areas and report back at four in the afternoon unless they encountered Ace. If Beth encountered Ace, Carla instructed her to call either of them. She was not to act alone. Although she had firearms training and owned a gun, she hadn't been put in this dangerous situation before.

Neither of them had seen Ace's Jeep by four in the afternoon, and they reconvened in the conference room. Carla called Chief Harris in Gallipolis regarding Ace's brother's activity. Nothing had changed there. His brother had left school and was on his way home. Chief Harris informed her they would continue the stakeout at his home. Carla radioed the surveillance team, still watching Ace's cabin. He had not returned. After agreeing to reconvene at seven in the evening, each left to decompress and prepare for the stakeouts to continue that evening.

At seven o'clock, Carla and Bernie had returned to the conference room. Beth had called Carla and informed her she was running a half-hour late. When seven-thirty rolled around, Beth called Carla again and suggested she and Bernie go on, and she would check out the city's north end again. While reluctant, Carla agreed as long as Beth checked in with her from time to time.

With their plan in place, each went out to their respective areas. At nine o'clock, Beth and Bernie checked in as planned. Neither had seen Ace. Carla radioed the surveillance team at Ace's cabin. No action there as well. Maybe Dannie was incorrect, that perhaps Ace had already fled. Ten o'clock rolled around with Beth and Bernie checking in with each other and Carla. Ace's jeep had yet to be spotted or seen by anyone. His cabin was dark and silent. It was starting to look like it would be a long night. Eleven o'clock came and passed, and no one had seen Ace. His cabin was still dark.

At eleven-thirty, Carla received a call from the surveillance team at Ace's cabin. The lights were on. Carla called Bernie to call Dannie to see if she was at his cabin. Bernie woke her up from a deep sleep. That likely meant that Ace was at his cabin. Carla called Beth, and her call went straight to voicemail. She immediately tried it again, and the same result. Carla instructed Bernie to go to the north end to look for Beth. Carla ran by Beth's apartment, and her car was not there.

After cruising the city's north end, Bernie finally spotted Beth's car. He pulled in behind it, got out, and approached the car. While looking inside, he saw her purse and phone in the passenger seat. He tried to open the door, but it was locked. A few homeless people were mulling around, and he asked a few questions. The responses he received sent his pulse racing. He then returned to his car, called Carla, and left. Fifteen minutes later, he arrived at Ace's cabin about the same time as Carla.

After conferring with the surveillance team, Carla and Bernie could only assume Ace had abducted Beth. They were unsure of his intentions. Maybe Ace couldn't find a suitable young woman resembling Maxine or Ashlee and took advantage of the opportunity when he saw Beth. With only one light on, a pitch-black backdrop surrounded the cabin. With no moon lighting up the area, the atmosphere was dark and gloomy. Beth was presumably a hostage, and it was a delicate situation. Carla was going to play everything by the book. She called in reinforcements, a SWAT team, and paramedics. After everything was in place, she pulled out the bullhorn.

"Ace, this is Detective McBride. We know you have Beth. Is she, okay?"

Carla's voice echoed among the trees while his silence sent her anxiety level up a few notches. She repeated the question, and the response was the same, silence. It was now a waiting game. She tried one more time with the bullhorn, then her phone rang. She immediately placed it on speaker, and Ace's defiant but erratic voice filled the air.

"Ace, it's over. Release Beth and then come out with your hands up."

"McBride, you'll play this my way, or she dies."

"We've got you surrounded. You have no chance."

"I have cameras all around, so I'll know if you rush the cabin. You do, she dies. Now, do you want to play it my way?"

"You kill her, and we kill you. Do you want that?"

"My days are numbered anyway. I have lung cancer, about a year or so is all I have left. So, it doesn't matter to me. You play it my way and she will live to see another day. I promise you that. What's it going to be?"

"I don't play that way, and you know that. Let's talk everything out without anyone else dying, okay?"

Immediately, the call ended. An annoying dial filled the air, as did four-letter expletives. A few minutes later, the only light in the cabin faded into total darkness and despair. Carla met Bernie's fearful expression. A terrorizing silence flowed between them. Beth's life was on the line and her whole future was in the hands of her teammates. Suddenly, a light illuminated the cabin, and Carla's phone rang, shattering the surreal tension among them.

CHAPTER 62

After two rings, Carla ended the call and whispered her favorite four-letter expletives under her breath. Although she didn't recognize the number immediately, she'd seen the number before. Then it hit her; the number belonged to Kiersten St. Clair. She thought possibly a butt call; however, they didn't call each other much, which meant Kiersten knew about this situation. Given the circumstances, she didn't need her here. Carla's phone rang again; four-letter expletives broke the tension in the air. She ignored her ringing phone and instructed two officers to secure the driveway leading to Ace's cabin. Again, her phone rang. After glancing at the screen, she answered.

"Ace, I'm not going to play your game, so give up or—"

Her phone screen went blank, and the light inside the house faded away once more. After picking up the bullhorn, she again directed Ace to give up. Her phone rang once more, and she answered.

"Listen, asshole—"

"Carla, it's me, Beth."

"Are you okay?"

"Yeah, for now. He's crazy—"

"Listen, McBride, we play this my way and now."

"Okay, Ace, your way. What do you want?"

"I want a helicopter, and when it gets here, you and I are going for a ride. That way I know they won't shoot the chopper down. You've got an hour. Screw up and she's dead. I have nothing to lose, so make it happen, got it?"

"Ace, you know I'll need more time."

"One hour, got it?"

"But Ace…"

The call ended. More four-letter expletives rang out. Up to this point, Bernie remained silent but felt the tension in Carla's voice.

"Carla, we need to talk about this. Giving in to him is something we don't do. His demand puts you in danger. Don't get me wrong; I want to save Beth's life just as you do. She's become like a daughter to me. We need to come up with something to make him believe we are meeting his demands and wait him out, okay?"

"What do you have in mind?"

"Hear me out. Dannie offered her help. She knows him better than we do, and he trusts her. We need to get her here. Maybe she can talk him down. She also has a key to the back door; she knows her way around here and can avoid his security cameras."

"Bernie, I don't know. Bringing a civilian here is risky. What if something happened? We both might get crucified."

"I think we have to take that chance."

"Okay, give her a call. I'm calling Chief Evans. I have an idea."

While Carla called Chief Evans and explained her idea, Bernie called Dannie, who agreed to help regardless of the risks. Carla explained the game plan. It would take Dannie fifteen minutes to arrive at the cabin, which meant Carla had to stall for more time. She picked up the bullhorn, and her voice filled the air once more. Her phone rang, and she immediately answered, putting it on speaker.

"Okay, Ace, I spoke with Chief Evans. He's working on the helicopter. Why don't we make the trade now? Send out Beth, and I'll come in."

"Not happening. When the helicopter arrives, I'll bring her out. You try anything, she dies."

"Okay, now that I have secured you a helicopter, I want something from you. How did a decorated veteran like you get put in this situation? While waiting on the chopper, tell me everything, and I'll guarantee your safety. Why did Maxine have to die? Who dropped off her baby at social services? Then why did her daughter have to die?"

"Fuck you, McBride."

"Listen, Ace. If you want to kill Beth, go ahead. We'll get you, get your brother, then your nephew, Jason."

"Leave them out of it. They had nothing to do with it."

"That's not what we found out."

"Right...what did you find out?"

"Jason got Maxine pregnant which would ruin his professional baseball career. She confronted him, and he killed her, dropped the baby off, then called you for help.

You placed the body in the cemetery and then did a massive cover-up."

"So, you think you got it all figured out. You're full of shit, McBride."

"Really, if that's not right, what is it?"

The call ended. Bernie glared at Carla, questioning her motives. Bernie's phone rang. He answered and hung up.

"Carla, that was Dannie. She's with the officers securing the driveway. I'll get her."

"Wait a minute."

She called Ace's phone, putting it on speaker. He immediately answered.

"McBride, where's the chopper?"

"It's in the air. Now, let's finish our conversation. So, if Jason didn't kill Maxine, then your brother did. She confronts him about the baby, kills her, and drops the baby off. You help him dispose of the body and cover up the investigation. Twenty years later, Maxine's daughter finds her father on one of those online sites. It turns out to be your brother, and you help him again. He kills her, and you dispose of the body. Isn't that how it happened?"

"McBride, you're full of shit."

Carla ended the call and waited. Immediately, her phone rang. She answered and placed it on speaker.

"Don't hang up on me, you bitch."

"Ace, tell me the truth, or I'll hang up and call off the chopper, then we will storm the cabin. I'm running out of patience. What will it be?"

"Okay. You've got part of it right." At this point, she began recording his confession. "My brother got Maxine pregnant. She confronted him, and he denied it. He thought everything was fine. After the baby was born, she confronted him again. He denied it. Then she told him I had raped her best friend and would go to the police. I'd be done, and so would he. He panicked and killed her. He then called me for help. I disposed of the body in the cemetery, knowing I'd control the investigation. Everything worked, and it went away, all of it. Of course, that was until Maxine's daughter grew up and started searching for her parents. I told Ezra not to submit his DNA, it would come back to bite him in the butt, and it did. The daughter, Ashlee, found him, confronted him, and he panicked again. He killed her the same way as Maxine. I disposed of the body and made it look like a serial killer on the loose. Unfortunately, Beth here didn't believe me, and now she's going to die."

CHAPTER 63

The call ended. Carla got what she wanted—a confession. Now she had to find a way to save Beth. She walked up the driveway to meet Bernie and Dannie. Bernie explained their plan. Although Carla didn't quite like Dannie putting herself in danger, it might be their only option to save Beth. Carla was pretty sure Ace was also out for revenge. After returning to the cabin, she called Ace's number and put it on speaker. After one ring, he answered.

"Ace, the chopper is ten minutes out. It will land in the open field to the left of your cabin. Everything you requested is on the chopper. I can hear it, can you?"

"Not yet."

"It's near, trust me. Is Beth okay?"

"For now. Where's the chopper? I can't hear anything."

"The chopper is getting louder and louder. You should be able to hear it now."

"Yeah, I do now. I'm surprised you would not follow

the protocol of giving in to a hostage situation. A while ago, you said you don't do that."

"Yeah, I did say that. However, I do things my way. Sometimes they're not by the book. You should know about that. So, you raped that innocent young woman almost twenty years ago."

"She called it rape. She was so out of it that night, she wouldn't remember what she did."

"Who slipped her date rape-pill? Jason?"

The call abruptly ended. Carla called him back. He answered immediately, and Carla placed the call on speaker.

"What now, McBride?"

"So, Jason slipped her a pill, right?"

"He gave every one of them a pill in their beer. I ended up with that Mackenzie bitch. She was hot looking that night. She was ripe, and for the taking. She wanted it."

"You son-of-a-bitch."

Ace abruptly stopped speaking as he heard noises on the back porch. Carla remained on the line. By this point, the SWAT team was in place, and paramedics were ready if needed.

On her phone, she heard voices.

"Dannie, what the hell are you doing here?"

"I came here to stop you, something I should have done twenty years ago."

"Does McBride know you're here?"

"No. When that second body was found, I knew you had something to do with it. It's over."

Carla could hear footsteps over the phone.

"Dannie, stay where you are. The chopper is almost

here. Why don't you go with me? It would be like old times. We had fun, right?"

"Yeah, Ace. But that was then. After what I've seen you turn into, that's never going to happen. It's over. Give up, or I'll kill you."

Carla heard something fall in the cabin.

"Dannie, someone's with you. I can sense it."

"Ace, it's over."

"Kowalski...you shouldn't have come in here. Either leave, or she dies."

At that moment, Beth rocked the chair onto the floor. Ace fired at her. At the sound of that first shot, Dannie fired several rounds, hitting Ace in the chest. Unfazed by the bullets, he began emptying his magazine. While Bernie rolled onto the floor, firing his weapon, Dannie went down. Bernie, realizing Ace had Kevlar on, went for his knees. As he went down on his knees, he fired his last round. With one round left, Bernie aimed and fired. Ace fell to the floor. Blood flowed from his head.

Turning his attention to Dannie, she lay motionless. Although she had Kevlar on, one of Ace's rounds struck her forehead. As the door crashed open, Beth lay silently in a pool of blood. Paramedics rushed to aid her as Carla and Bernie looked on. Within a minute, Beth was on a gurney being whisked out of the cabin and into an ambulance. Carla and Bernie rushed out of the cabin to see the ambulance doors close. With the sirens on and lights flashing, Beth was on her way to the hospital. Chief Evans arrived and met Carla and Bernie at his car. Bernie immediately handed him his weapon, and Carla and Bernie were on their way to the hospital.

When they arrived, Beth was already in surgery. After being directed to a private waiting room, Scott greeted them. Beth and Bernie apologized for putting Beth in harm's way. However, Scott told them she always wanted to be in law enforcement and knew the risks. As he spoke to them, Carla scanned the tension-filled waiting room. Immediately, emotions grabbed Carla's soul.

The surroundings looked all too familiar; the big clock on the wall took her breath away. It read 1:30 AM. Less than a year ago, she comforted Beth in a similar waiting room in a Cincinnati hospital as her mother's fate hung in the balance. Now, Beth's fate hung in the balance, and the waiting would be hell.

While waiting for news about Beth, Carla called Police Chief Rodney Harris about Ace's confession. He immediately put his plans in motion taking Ezra Charles Hutchinson into custody. She was unsure whether they could arrest Jason for slipping four unsuspecting young women a date-rape pill about twenty years ago; however, she would deal with his participation in this ordeal later.

Two hours later, Doctor Walt Lewis entered the waiting room. His stoic expression struck fear in Carla's soul. She'd seen that look before. They gathered around him as he explained Beth's condition. Although the bullets missed her vital organs, she still had lost a lot of blood. Even though he described Beth's condition as critical, he was optimistic about her chances. Although they wanted to see her, he advised against it. Beth needed rest if she was going to pull through. He told them he would update them in an hour or so. A long and agonizing night was in store for them. Carla prayed the outcome would be dramatically different this time around.

CHAPTER 64

The big clock on the wall was relentless. Two AM glared back. Although only thirty minutes had passed, it seemed like an eternity. The waiting was hell. As Carla glanced at the big clock, she caught a glimpse of Doctor Lewis passing by the door. False alarm. She knew them all too well from waiting with Beth as her mother's fate hung in the balance.

————

3:00 AM

Doctor Lewis stood outside the door. Carla watched him take a deep breath and then enter the waiting room. Immediately, Bernie and Scott stood up and joined her. His stoic expression sent Carla's pulse racing. She remembered the same expression on the doctor's face who treated Beth's mom. As he began his update, his mouth moved in slow motion. Finally, after a few brief comments, he left. Beth's condition remained unchanged. He assured them she was getting the best care possible. However, he explained Beth's fate was in her own hands. Carla remembered Dr. Charles saying that to Beth before her mom passed.

———

4:00 AM

The big clock on the wall continued punishing their patience. While Bernie and Scott returned to their chairs, Carla paced back and forth, glancing at the clock, then at the door repeatedly. Beth, in many ways, had become her surrogate daughter. The thought of losing her was taking its toll on her. Finally, Carla walked over to the door assessing the flurry of activity around the nursing station. In the distance, Doctor Lewis stood reviewing a chart with a nurse. She wondered whether it belonged to Beth. After reading his lips, she walked over to Bernie and Scott.

As eyes of sheer concern met each other, Carla held out her hands. Bernie and Scott rose from their chairs and latched on to her cold and clammy grip. As they held hands, a coldness bolted throughout Carla's soul. She apologized to Scott once more. He gave her hand a gentle squeeze. Without warning, Carla began to speak.

"Dear Lord, thank you for the many blessings you have bestowed on us. We ask you to hear our special prayer. We ask you to cast your spirit, love, determination, and will upon Beth. She is fighting for her life. We need you to help her see the light of life. She has so much to give to this world. Please pray for her. Thank you for hearing our prayer; in the name of Jesus Christ, our Lord and Savior, amen."

"Carla, what a beautiful prayer."

"Thank you, Bernie. Hopefully, God will intervene and give Beth the will to pull through."

"Guys, I know he will. We have to believe that. We must continue to have faith. Let's each take another moment of silence to add your special prayer."

After about twenty seconds of solemn silence, the door to the waiting room suddenly swung open. After turning around, they faced Doctor Lewis. His expression remained unchanged. He walked over to them and explained nothing had changed in Beth's condition. She was still in an unconscious state but breathing on her own. He suggested they go to the canteen and wait there with a cup of coffee. He reassured them she was getting the best medical care, and left the room. The tension in the room remained the same as the big clock on the wall continued its assault on their patience and sanity.

————

5:00 AM

Bernie and Scott returned to their chairs and sat with their hands on their knees in silent prayer. Carla continued her vigil of impatience and uncertainty. Staring at the clock and then at the door took over her psyche. She was punishing herself as an unbearable guiltiness zapped the life out of her soul. She continued to pray as she paced back and forth, hoping for a miracle. The activity outside the waiting room remained active and frantic. She kept looking for Doctor Lewis to come into view, to give them some good news.

Carla walked over to Bernie and Scott; their eyes were tired and red. They rose to hug Carla, struggling to keep her heartstrings from imploding in her soul. As she met Bernie's weathered face, her emotions exploded. He wrapped her in his arms, reassuring Carla everything would turn out just okay. Scott, watching this unfold, reassured them Beth would pull through. He suggested maybe coffee in the canteen was a good idea, and a change of scenery couldn't hurt as well. As Carla's eyes met Scott's, she lashed out.

"No offense, Scott. If you want to, go ahead. I'm staying here. When Beth and I were waiting as her mother's fate hung in the balance, we did just that. We no sooner got our coffees when Beth got the call, and her world was shattered forever."

"Carla, I get it—"

"No, Scott—"

Suddenly, the door to the waiting room swung open. Carla, Bernie, and Scott turned, expecting the worst as Doctor Lewis entered. However, hope covered his face as he approached them.

"I have some promising news. Beth opened her eyes briefly."

The thick atmosphere around them began to wither. Although his news was promising, he reminded them Beth was still not out of the woods.

"May I see her?"

"Mr. Carlson, not just yet. She is resting comfortably and breathing on her own. Although her vitals are stable, we shouldn't get our hopes up until she regains consciousness. Medically, a full recovery is possible, but something is holding her back."

"Maybe for just a moment? It couldn't hurt, could it?"

"Mr. Carlson, let me check in on her again and then I'll be back, okay? Keep those thoughts and prayers going."

As he left the room, the thick tension returned to punish their souls. The big clock on the wall was now pushing 6:00 AM. After another prayer, they watched the morning news recap of last night's tragic event. Two individuals had died in the shoot-out, and Beth's condition was updated. Doctor Lewis stood outside the waiting room with the head nurse. Carla, Bernie, and Scott stood up as he entered. His disposition was unchanged.

"Mr. Carlson, I will give you one minute with her. Something is controlling her will to survive; maybe hearing your voice will bring her back to reality."

"Thank you. May Carla and Bernie go with me? They're family just as I am. Maybe our collective spirit will touch her soul. She needs to feel our presence."

"Of course, but remember, one minute, and don't get your hopes up. Follow me."

CHAPTER 65

While walking down a long corridor, solemn silence surrounded them. After about a hundred feet, the last room on the right heightened their anxiety. Doctor Lewis stopped, then motioned them into Beth's room. She laid silently as numerous beeps broke the silence. Carla, Bernie, and Scott entered. Scott went to the right side of the bed while Carla and Bernie stood at the foot of the bed. Doctor Lewis remained in the doorway. To them, Beth looked as though she was sleeping peacefully. Scott caressed her right hand, touching her engagement ring. Her hand felt warm but lifeless. It was difficult for him to find the right words to say, but finally he told her he loved her. Still no response. Scott glanced at Carla and Bernie; fear flowed from his eyes. He returned his gaze to her as Carla cleared her throat.

"Beth, this is Carla. I'm sorry, I'm responsible for this. Please forgive me."

"Honey, I'll be waiting for you, no matter how long it takes. I love you."

Beth's stillness was not promising. She lay peacefully, fighting the uncertainty controlling her will to live. Doctor Lewis entered the room informing them their time was up. He escorted them back to the waiting room. After a few encouraging comments, he left. 7:00 AM glared from the big clock on the wall. The morning news on the television continued in the background. A flurry of activity moved in the direction of Beth's room. The waiting was hell.

In her room, she lay silently. As her eyes opened, the white blurriness burned them. She blinked; the searing white aura continued. She closed them, allowing the darkness of death into her soul. Although she couldn't hear anything, alarms rang in the room. Doctor Lewis rushed in with a host of nurses attempting to save her. As they began Beth's resuscitation, numerous people dressed in white glared at her. One person stepped forward as though she was real. She could not feel the efforts to save her life; she could only hear the voices from the other side. Her mom smiled at her.

"Honey, I love you, but your time on earth is not up yet. Your father and I would love to have you here where pain and suffering do not exist. However, after seeing the love in Scott's eyes, you cannot leave him. He needs you. And the lady, I assume, that's Carla. Her love for you covered her face, and her soul cried out to me. And the black man, I believe that's Bernie. His love for you is undeniable. He lost his only daughter a long time ago; his eyes told me he didn't want to lose you."

"Yeah, mom, I know that. Where's daddy?"

"I'm right here, honey. You know, your mom is right. You are not ready to join us. You have your whole life ahead of you. So, grasp it and don't let go. I love you."

"Love you, too, daddy."

"Beth?"

"Yeah, mom?"

"How's Aliyah?"

"Spry as ever. She misses you."

"Yeah, but she'll miss you more if you don't go back to the other side. Don't abandon her like this. We're leaving now. Don't follow us. I love you."

As Doctor Lewis continued to save her, she felt his strength pumping life back into her body. Her mother's spirit and parting words resonated in her soul as she felt the warming sensation of life return to her soul.

"Doctor Lewis, we've got a pulse, normal sinus rhythm. She's improving. Blood pressure, one-ten over seventy. I think we've got her back, Doctor Lewis. Nice work."

"Thanks, you guys are the greatest. Let's keep an eye on her, okay?"

As Beth opened her eyes, the many smiles of life hovered over her and brought a smile to her face. Doctor Lewis smiled back, and sincere applause filled the room.

"Beth, can you hear me? I'm Doctor Lewis. Do you know where you are?"

"Hospital."

"The regional medical center. Do you know why you are here?" She shook her head. "You suffered gunshot wounds, and you lost a lot of blood. Do you remember what happened?" She shook her head once more. "That's okay. Get your rest. I'll let your loved ones know what's going on, okay?" She nodded and closed her eyes. "You're going to be okay, Beth."

While pacing the floor in the waiting room, Carla focused on what was happening outside the room. The big clock on the wall was pushing 8:00 AM. Doctor Lewis appeared at the nurses' station for a moment, then quickly approached the waiting room. As he entered, Bernie and Scott joined Carla waiting for their moment of truth. His expression hadn't changed, and they were expecting the worst. After facing them, his lips seem to move in slow motion. He cleared his throat and sighed.

"We got her back."

"What do you mean?"

"She coded, and we revived her. I think she's out of the woods. I expect a full recovery."

"May we see her?"

"Sorry, Mr. Carlson. She's sleeping and needs a lot of rest. I'll be back a little later, and then you can visit her. Don't worry, she's going to be fine now."

He left, and heartstrings exploded in the room. A group hug broke the anxiety and tension holding their souls hostage. While Carla called Chief Brock, Bernie and Scott went to the café. They all needed a jolt of caffeine now that the wait was over. When Bernie and Scott returned, tears of relief and happiness rolled off Carla's cheeks.

"Carla, please don't tell me—"

"No, Bernie, Beth's fine. Doctor Lewis said we could see her now. She asked for us."

"Scott, are you ready?"

Tears of happiness flowed from his eyes. He could no longer hide the relief leaving his soul. After leaving the waiting room, they met Doctor Lewis at the nurses' station. He spoke to them for a few moments, explaining that she remembered very little about last night. He accompanied them to her room but remained in the hallway. Beth's glowing smile was too much for Scott to handle, and he rushed to her side, hugging her gingerly. Carla and Bernie stood at the foot of the bed, hiding their heartstrings.

CHAPTER 66

As Carla and Bernie watched Scott tenderly kiss his bride-to-be, they had dodged a bullet with Beth's life. Although their relationship with her was supposed to be professional, she quickly became like a family member, like a daughter. Going forward, if they ever lost her, neither would forgive themselves. They allowed Beth to put her life in danger, which wouldn't happen again regardless of the circumstances. Almost losing Beth was a defining moment in their career. Scott turned to face them, and they caught a glimpse of Beth's smile. That smile ignited their heart-strings as they moved beside her bed.

"Guys, she wants to ask you something."

"What is it, Beth?"

"Carla, tell me about last night. I don't remember much. I'm sure it's recessed in my mind somewhere, but I need to know what went down."

"Are you sure?"

"Yeah, Carla, I'm sure."

"I'll make it brief. You need to get your rest, okay?"

"Yeah, I—"

"Bernie and Dannie had a way into Ace's cabin. Once inside, they startled him. Somehow you had the presence to rock the chair over. As you hit the floor, Ace fired, hitting you. After that, a firestorm erupted, and Dannie died in the process. Bernie is fine. We were all lucky last night."

"I'm sorry about Dannie, but I'm glad you are fine, Bernie. You saved my life."

"No, Dannie did. She's the hero in all of this. If it hadn't been for her, well…"

"I'm sorry I let you all down. I didn't mean to."

Heartstrings and guilt crashed Beth's soul as a thousand tears flowed from her soul. Scott latched onto her arms, easing her emotional pain.

"It's okay, Beth. Doctor Lewis expects you to make a full recovery, and that's all that matters. He told us you coded this morning, and while they were reviving you, you were mumbling incoherently. He wondered if maybe you went to the other side, you know, had an out-of-body experience. Did that happen?"

"Carla. I…I talked to my mom…and dad. They said my time wasn't up yet and not to follow them. I wanted to be with them, but she said you and Bernie were good people and loved me. She said you needed me."

"She's right. We want you back when you're fully recovered, okay?"

"Yeah, and I promise not to put myself in danger."

"Don't worry, we won't let you. We are going to leave and let you get your rest. We'll be back tomorrow to check in on you."

"Thanks, I'm so—"

"Don't worry about it."

"Thanks."

"Scott?"

"Yeah, Carla."

"Please take care of her and call me later, okay?"

He nodded, and Carla and Bernie left her room. The elevator ride down to the ground floor was deathly quiet. As they walked to Carla's car, a pang of numbing guilt grabbed their souls. Once inside, Carla started the car. *Live Like You Were Dying* flowed from the speaker. Even though this was their anthem to live by, and usually, they sang along with Tim McGraw, today was different. They listened to the lyrics, although they could recite them verbatim. However, today was all about reflection and thankfulness. Carla knew she could have lost Beth and Bernie last night. The events of last night grabbed her soul like never before.

Carla left the parking lot and headed to the police station as the song ended. Ten minutes later, they entered the police station to appreciative applause followed by an eeriness never experienced before in their career. As they walked to their workstation, silence followed them. Bernie sat at his workstation, feeling an emptiness in his soul, one he'd never felt before. Expecting Carla to sit across from him, she kept walking toward Chief Evan's office.

"Hey, McBride, where the hell are you going?"

"I need to take care of something with the chief. I'll be back in a few minutes; hold your pants on dickhead."

As Carla entered the chief's office, guilt continued to crush Bernie's soul. He needed someone to talk to and couldn't believe Carla abandoned him after all that happened. Within a minute, Lydia's caring voice eased his pain and emptiness. While talking with his wife, he kept an eye on the chief's door.

He glanced at the big clock on the wall, and ten minutes had elapsed. After returning his gaze down the hallway, the chief's door opened. He ended his call and walked toward Carla. As she approached Bernie, she smiled at him. Her demeanor left him perplexed.

"McBride, what the hell's going on?"

"Follow me."

"Where?"

"Just follow me, you loveable dickhead."

After they both entered the conference room, she shut the door. As they faced each other, he knew something was different. He'd never seen her like this before.

"Carla, uh…what…what…the hell is going with you?"

"You know, last night could have turned out totally different. We almost lost Beth, and I almost lost you. That's twice now, and I'm not sure I can handle a third time."

"What are you talking about? It comes with the territory, with the job. You know that."

"Yeah, I do, but it doesn't have to, does it?"

"You're not making sense. Maybe you are just tired, in a daze—"

"Yeah, I'm tired, alright, but I'm making perfect sense. Maybe it's time we really smell the roses. You know, live like you're dying. Bernie, the past two years have taken a toll on us. Things have changed. You took fire for the first time, and then prostate cancer grabbed your soul. I got married, and I need to think about Chris now."

"You're not serious, are you?"

"Dead serious. Now, who were you talking with when I came out of the chief's office?"

"I needed someone to talk with since you left me here all alone, so I called Lydia."

"Yeah, what did she have to say?"

"Uh…like always…she's glad I'm okay."

"Yeah, and how many times has that happened in your career?"

"Every damn day. Yeah, she prays that I'll return home safely…every damn day."

"Yeah, and that's what I'm talking about. Remember us discussing starting our own detective agency one day?"

"Yeah, and—"

"It's time. I'm serious about it, Bernie."

"Shit, I didn't see this coming."

"Yeah, I…I didn't either."

"And?"

"I turned in my shield and service weapon. I told Chief Evans I was taking all my paid time off, which should give us the time we need to get it up and running. After that, I don't think I'll be coming back to get my shield and service weapon."

"Shit, McBride, are you fucking crazy?"

"Are you in, or not?"

Her serious eyes, her stern expression was all he needed to see. Bernie stomped out of the room. Several minutes later, he returned. His glaring eyes were hard to read.

"Well, what's it going to be, dickhead?"

A reserved silence met her scowl while an in-your-face emphatic bird soured her face. Then a quirky smile confused her wandering eyes.

"What the—"

"Gotcha!"

As Carla's wrath burned, Bernie rubbed his arm several times.

"What did you do that for, McBride?"

"That wasn't funny."

"It was to me, the look on your face was priceless. When do we start?"

"Do you think Lydia can whip us up a kielbasa and kraut hoagie this morning?"

"Yeah, I'm sure she will."

"Great, do you still have any Jameson left?

"Of course, why?"

"Then that's where we begin, okay?"

"Yeah, as I said, I'm all in."

"Then, let's smell those damn roses, partner."

After leaving the station, they both turned around facing the double-glass-doors of their storied career. Glistening eyes stared at the station while their heartstrings welled-up. After taking a deep breath and exhaling, they stood at attention and offered a final, solemn salute.

ACKNOWLEDGMENTS

First and foremost, I thank my wife, Bonnie, for her guidance, insight, and encouragement.

I want to thank a high school classmate of mine. After reading The Gold Fedora, she reached out to me offering to be a beta reader. I needed another set of eyes, and I also thank her for insight and recommendations in *Enigma*. Thank you, Nancy Szlemko Cowen.

I also want to thank those who have read the previous books in this series, and offered up reviews, and comments. Reader input is important and valuable going forward.

A LOOK AT: CATALYST

BY NIK MORTON

A fast-paced thriller with never-ending threats and sexy suspense...

A catalyst is a person who precipitates events. That's Catherine Vibrissae. Orphan, chemist, model, and crusading cat.

Seeking revenge against Loup Dante, the Head of Ananke—and the man responsible for the takeover of her father's company—Cat will stop at nothing to uncover his wicked agenda. A trained chemist and an accomplished climber, she is not averse to breaking and entering. So, when she crosses paths with an attorney for the bloodless organization and uncovers a mysterious product called Catananche, Cat risks injury and death to learn more.

Ranging from South England to Northeast, from Wales to Barcelona, Cat's quest for vengeance is implacable. But will she be able to escape the clutches of an unexpected and whip-wielding enemy?

The first in The Avenging Cat series, Catalyst follows a strong female character who has a thirst for action.

AVAILABLE MARCH 2023

ABOUT THE AUTHOR

Author Nick Lewis lives in Richmond, Kentucky, with his wife, Bonnie. He graduated from Marshall University in the fall of 1970. Upon graduating, he taught school and coached football for one year at Eidson Elementary. He then switched directions and began a forty-year newspaper career. He held circulation and marketing positions at four different newspapers in Ohio, West Virginia, and Kentucky. In 2004, he was appointed publisher of *The Richmond Register* in Richmond, Kentucky. He retired from that position in June 2013 and began his quest to become a full-time author.

In January 2014, Nick created The Detective Carla McBride Chronicles. The first book in the series, *The Gold Fedora*, debuted in October 2019. *The Black Rose, Chasing Truth and Redemption,* and *Quandary* completes the series to date. Book five in the series, *Enigma*, is forthcoming. He has another published novel, *When Eagles Soared*.

When Nick is not writing and revising manuscripts, he enjoys golf, gardening, and creating new adventures with his wife of fifty years. Bonnie plays an essential role in his journey of writing novels. He is an avid Marshall University football fan with three grown children, three grandchildren, and two cats named Zorro and Ziva.